Sign up for our newsletter to hear
about new and upcoming releases.

www.ylva-publishing.com

OTHER BOOKS BY GEORGETTE KAPLAN

CANDICE CUSHING
AND THE LOST TOMB OF
CLEOPATRA

GEORGETTE KAPLAN

Time laughs at all things, but the pyramids laugh at time.

—*Arab proverb*

PROLOGUE

DUBAI, UNITED ARAB EMIRATES
(back when music didn't suck)

THE BURJ AL ARAB WAS the third tallest hotel in the world, and too good for the mainland. A bridge curved off the beach to an artificial island where the mainmast of the building sloped up almost seven hundred feet to the world-famous helipad that had been converted into a tennis court for a recent match between two Grand Slam winners.

If Easy Nevada fell off the building now, it would take almost seventeen seconds for gravity to turn her into a pancake.

This far up, the ground stretched outwards as unreal as a mirage. Nevada wondered if this was how the rich always saw the world. Buildings were models, and the ocean was a painting with speedboats flittering through it like insects, just flecks of white on the endless blue vista of Jumeirah Beach. And people were less than nothing—specks, static, not even visible to the naked eye. Killing one wouldn't even be a conscious act. From here, it would be like swatting a gnat.

Nevada looked over her shoulder as a helicopter approached, its looping curves doing their best to turn the ungainly vehicle into something ergonomic. It mostly succeeded. The Sikorsky S-76C++ rode down to the helipad like a magic carpet. Holding the bowling bag away from her body, she watched the doors slide open and steps unfurl. An Indian man disembarked.

She raised her voice. "Send the chopper back up. I don't know what you're planning on using this for, but I'm guessing you'd rather it be near-mint."

The man complied by waving off the helicopter. It took off in a gust of backwash from its rotors. Nevada shifted her weight as the wind tore at her body, and she saw the man stumbling about before he got his footing. He shook his head and ran his hand through his hair, then cracked his neck as the Sikorsky departed. "Easy Nevada? Hi! Big fan! What are you doing on the roof? Was the room not to your liking?"

"It was tops. I just prefer my doors to lock from the inside."

He was a tall, lanky man, with chocolate-brown hair arranged in a pompadour and a neatly trimmed beard compensating for a rather weak chin. The excessive length of his arms and legs were left exposed by the short white pants and polo shirt he wore, Air Yeezys on his feet and athletic socks crawling up his skinny shins. Nevada could see the power in his limber body. He had a duffel bag slung over one shoulder, and despite its evident weight, lifted it like it was nothing. In his other hand, he held a tennis racquet. Long, jaunty strides carried him across the rooftop to her. When he was close enough, Nevada turned to face him and he stopped in his tracks.

"And the men who picked you up at the airport?" he asked. "Courteous, I trust?"

"Five stars. Just like the guys who picked me up in Belize. In the future, though, I'd prefer a company car to a chauffeur. I kinda like to be in the driver's seat."

"Ah, but I've noticed you have a few reckless driving citations on your record. We wouldn't want any harm to come to you before we've concluded our business."

"Don't worry about me. My last fortune cookie said I was going to die at the age of 92… murdered by a jealous husband."

"An all too common fate."

She shrugged. "Eh, didn't say it was *my* husband. You're Singh?"

"Akbar Akkad Singh, and it is a true pleasure to meet you." He came forward, holding out his hand, and Nevada held the bag higher. "Ah. Business before pleasantries. I totally understand. Very good business practice, no chat-chat-chat, let's talk *money*."

Bending to one knee, he set down the duffel bag. The zipper rasped open and he spread both sides. Inside was the root of all evil. Enough to need a lot of rubber bands.

"A fair price, and good cardio if you're planning on lugging this all the way to the nearest bank. I know, I find online banking is just *the worst*." His voice was light and high-pitched, with a faint, pleasant English accent that Nevada imagined had come straight from Oxford. Overseas education. The jubilant excitement he spoke with, though, would fit in better with a tour guide at Disneyland. Along with the open expressiveness of his face, it gave him a handsome boyishness despite the gray beginning to infiltrate his hair.

"Slide the money over here," Nevada instructed. "Then take a few steps back."

Singh gave the bag a heave; it jostled its way over the hissing concrete and came to a stop a few feet from Nevada. She looked at Singh and he backed up, playing with the tennis racquet for lack of anything else to do with his hands.

Nevada checked over the money. There were no tricks that she could see. No newspaper or ones inside the stacks of cash, just hundred-dollar bills from top to bottom. She counted them, stack by stack, and it quickly became obvious that this was more money than she'd ever seen in her life. She should've closed the zipper, hefted the bag, and walked, but that much money had its own gravitational pull. She was almost in awe of it. God, she'd won the fucking lottery and she hadn't even bought a ticket, just stumbled across a souvenir she thought would look cool next to her stereo.

"Love your work, by the way," Singh said. "I mean, here I was wondering where the hell you'd put my skull. We were all wondering. I was like, *Where is it? Where'd she put it?* Giving it to someone else, putting them up in my own hotel, and picking it up from them when you were ready—that's classic! All my guys, they thought you had a safety deposit box or that you'd buried it in some geocache, but here it was, *right under* my nose the whole time."

"Yeah. And then I set a towel on fire and walked out when the fire alarm unlocked the door."

"That's alright, we expect the towels to be stolen. And the elevator?" Singh wagged a finger at her. "Guests aren't supposed to have access to the roof."

"Swiped an access card off the maid. You aren't supposed to hold people prisoner in a hotel," Nevada chided right back. "The routines are posted on the website."

"Prisoner? In the only seven-star hotel in the world? We let you have all the premium cable channels!"

Nevada closed her eyes and forced herself to review her options. Money didn't spend unless she could walk away with it. The helicopter might've left, but she didn't doubt Singh had a rogue's gallery packing the stairwell, ready to chop her to pieces and mail her wherever the postage was cheapest. He might give the order, he might not. But Nevada couldn't see much of a play besides assuming he wouldn't. She could always shove that tennis racquet down his throat later.

She set the bowling bag down and gave it a shove down the rooftop. Singh snatched it up the moment it was within reach, slipping and falling to his knees in his exuberance, ripping open the bag without bothering with the zipper. He looked inside, then turned his face heavenward consumed with relish, clutching the bag. "Oh, it's real. It is *real*! You can just tell— well, maybe not you—I can tell. Do you know what this is, Easy Nevada? Do you have any idea what we *have*?"

"World's greatest bong?"

Singh looked at her. As open as his gaze was, Nevada had a hard time parsing it. Was he looking at her as a child looked at a new toy, as a player contemplated his next move, or even as a man stared at a beautiful woman? "Fancy a game?"

"This before or after you show me your etchings?"

Singh reached slowly into his pocket, then brought out a remote control. He pressed it and the surface of the helipad irised open. In its place, a tennis court rose into view, the netting taut between them. A second tennis racquet and a tube of balls lay on the ground. Nevada wondered if Singh had planned for this specifically, or if it was one of many outcomes he'd prepared for—and which was more intimidating.

"A nice match!" Singh said, bouncing on his heels, then launching into a series of stretches. All that was missing was a boombox playing YMCA. "Shake off the cobwebs! Get the blood pumping. A little more oxygen to the brain and we can discuss business. It's the twenty-first century—who wants to talk shop over a lousy game of golf?"

"I thought our business was concluded," Nevada said.

"Only if you want it to be."

4

Nevada eyed the roof access door. Either there was a kill squad waiting down the stairs or there wasn't. She didn't see how it decreased her odds to hear him out. "One game."

Singh set the skull down by the net. Nevada set her money down on the other side. She chopped her racquet back and forth in a few practice swings. Her arm registered no aches or pains, just tendons stretching supplely and muscles flexing smoothly.

Singh served. It was an easy serve, and Nevada returned it with equal ease. Singh barely moved from his sphinxlike waiting to send the ball rebounding back. Nevada only had to move a little more to hit it herself.

In the crisp, frail-seeming air at this height, the sound of the ball being struck was as regular as the ticking of a metronome. It didn't echo, of course, not this high up. Instead, the noise seemed to hang suspended in the air, uninterrupted, not lost in any background noise as it dwindled into nothing. Nevada thought uncomfortably of a soul leaving a body, or a child leaving home...

As if sensing how Nevada's mind had wandered, Singh returned the ball with sudden savagery. It soared past her, out into the dizzying drop that separated this perch from solid ground, and she watched it fall into nonexistence. She remembered stories of how you could drop a penny from the Empire State Building and it could shoot right through a man's skull. If that were true, she wondered what a tennis ball at this height could do. Maybe total a parked car.

"Have you ever read about myths, Easy? All of them have a common factor. Hercules, Achilles, Xena—they're all about immensely powerful beings right here on Earth, capable of amazing feats. And not just one, no, not the monotheism that came when Man stripped his beliefs down to make them smaller and more acceptable. There were whole pantheons. An entire race of gods. And where do you think they all went?"

Nevada held up her hands. "Out for cigarettes and said they'd be right back?"

Singh shrugged and went to get another ball. "Honestly, I don't know either. Fifteen-love." He pointed his racquet at the skull. "That's all that's left of whatever they were. That and eleven more. Proof that every story ever told about gods and goddesses was based in fact."

He served, fast and harsh, and Nevada broke a sweat for the first time as she returned it. Singh was going harder now. Nevada ricocheted his shots back, but it was like playing against a wall. Wherever she sent the ball, he was there, and the ball only came at her faster and faster.

He'd been toying with her before, and that only made Nevada more incensed. "I know the rich are eccentric," she said, "but wouldn't it be easier for you to get into green coffee extract?"

Singh was a machine, mercilessly hammering the ball back. "I don't care about losing weight, Easy. I care about the future of humanity. According to legend, if all twelve of the skulls are brought together, the man who does it will be granted one wish."

Nevada smashed the ball hard, sending it almost whistling at his face. "Yeah, I can see how you'd want to improve your circumstances."

Singh knocked the ball back in a wide arc over the court. Nevada made a run for it, saw the ball sloping down past the rim of the court, and skidded to a stop before she could reach it. She saw the ball graze the edge before it dropped away into nothingness.

"Thirty-love," Singh said. He already had another ball. "I've been searching for the skulls for years. You, you aren't even *looking* and you find one. That's not coincidence. You are fated for this search."

He bombarded her with his next serve, the ball whistling through the air.

Nevada threw herself across the court. This time it wouldn't get away from her. She was too damn tired of being Singh's straight man as he amused himself.

Coming up to the drop, she got under the ball and snapped her racquet to knock it back past Singh while she teetered on the edge. The fall gaped open underneath her and Nevada felt like laughing. "Try flying coach sometime. The universe will seem a lot more random."

She recovered her balance, taking a step back from the edge to see Singh throwing his racquet down in a fit of pique.

"Enough games!" he shouted, coming to the net. "I want you to find the other eleven skulls. For each one you deliver, I will pay you ten times what's in that bag. Money like that can open doors for you and your son."

Nevada felt her grip tightening on her racquet. "You say one skull is worth ten times what's in that bag to you?"

"Oh yes."

"Then I'm going to need at least five more bags."

Singh smiled in agreement—a childish grin—and Nevada pictured a little boy in her head.

Nevada didn't have a picture of her kid. What she did have was a CT scan. A cross-section of a brain maybe the size of a bocce ball, incomprehensible in its artistic swells and curves, all except for the ghostly white lump. That she could understand. He was her son, and like her he was imperfect, with a fatal flaw she'd passed on in her blood, the single inheritance he'd taken with him to his new family. And now, like a cuckoo's egg ready to hatch, it swelled and blistered and turned inward. The doctors could irradiate it, but there was no operation, no cure. Unless someone made one. Unless someone paid for one.

Nevada felt unnatural. Didn't every animal care for its young? Every beast but man. She'd given him up, abandoned him to a better life.

Harry Calhoun. That's who he was now. And his new family had two mortgages and an empty college fund, trying to keep him alive. God, what a con she'd pulled.

She told herself she was a heartless bitch. And she tried very hard to make that true.

CHAPTER 1

WITHIN THE MUD AND THATCHED roof of a *tukul*, David Pike awoke covered in sweat. It had nothing to do with the nearly hundred-degree heat and everything to do with the evil that had entered the room.

A white man in his mid-forties, Pike still looked nearly every inch the biker he had been before hearing the call to come to Africa. His hulking body was stout, with the solid bulk of a potbelly like a diesel fuel tank doing little to reduce the physicality of his bearlike six-foot-two frame. A long mane of black hair flecked with gray went down to his shoulders, while the many biker tattoos along his arms and neck had long since been crowded out by ones showcasing crosses, Bible verses, and a select few faces of the Ubangi tribes that had become his adopted family. A horseshoe moustache and little-shaven cheeks gave his wide, flat face an uncut appearance, like rock that had been hewn into the rough shape of a man, but no one had finished chiseling out the details.

Blinking blearily, he saw a face beyond the mosquito netting that surrounded his bed. There was something strange about it, some trick of the eye that he couldn't yet sort out through the midnight shadows and moonlight seeping into the room. It wasn't until he wiped his face with his hand that he realized what was wrong. There was no face, only an invisible force pressing through the gossamer net, leaving an imprint of a man's features where none existed.

Pike backed away from it, nearly off his mattress, feeling now what his animal senses had been warning him about when he'd woken. Turning his head the other direction in an instinctive search for a way to flee from this evil presence, he saw another face there as well, crowding into the mosquito netting. There was another next to it, and another, a legion of faces disturbing the windy sway of the netting. He groped underneath the bed, searching for his flashlight and the Desert Eagle he always kept on hand, when God said, *No. Pray.*

"Something's in the room with me!" Pike replied. His hand was almost clawing at the dirt floor, trying to find a weapon. God spoke again, not more insistent—how could God be more or less insistent?—but more resonant, more showing of His authority.

Start Praying Now.

Pulling his hand away from the dirt like it'd been bitten, Pike threaded his fingers together and prayed. He prayed for his soul, stained by the violence he had done and the crimes he had committed, for the lives of the children he had taken in at Camp Esau, for an end to the bloody war that had put them in danger and taken away so many of their parents, for all those he had harmed in his days as a lost sheep, and even those he had harmed since, trying to stop them from destroying this holy place and these loving people.

He prayed long into the night, the wind stirring the mosquito net around him.

Finally, he slept, and when he woke, he wondered if it had been a dream. Then he looked at the ground. There was a perfect circle around his bed where the dirt floor was undisturbed. The unbroken boundary of that line fit exactly to the mosquito netting draped around his bed. Outside the circle, every inch of the dirt floor was covered in footsteps.

"What happened, Lord?" he asked, his voice quivering.

Satan Was In This Room Last Night. He Tried To Come For You, But I Would Not Let Him Near.

◆

The weight of history fell all over the Earth, but perhaps was most keenly felt in the desert, where time itself crushed down the rock until it was pulverized into sand. The monotony was endless, each moment so identical to the next that Candice could've been trapped in a single second like an insect in amber and never notice it, never see any difference in the wind scouring the sands or the sun beating down with infinite heat or the landscape stretching on in its barrenness until it felt like the whole world had become a wasteland. Thought itself was burned and blasted and dried up, even the simple hope of escape, until only the strongest survived, while lesser men were driven mad.

"I cannot believe you," Candice said.

"Really?" Nevada asked, lowering her sunglasses. "Candice, Sudan is old news. New Sudan now: South Sudan. It's a new chapter in our lives. Hell, it's a whole new book! And we're still doing the 'wow, Nevada, I can't believe you're doing something so shocking and inconsistent with social norms' thing? Move on, lady. I stopped calling you Candy."

"Yes, you've moved on to 'sweetie,' 'darling,' 'doll,' and 'brown sugar.'"

"I'm so affectionate," Nevada said, raising her sunglasses back over her eyes. "I thought you Europeans were into that."

"Let's review. When I went to sleep, because I'd been driving the tank we're on for ten hours straight, I assumed you'd be driving the tank."

"There are sayings about assumption."

"Instead, when I wake up, I find that you are *sunbathing*."

"Oh, that reminds me." Nevada turned over, prompting an almost instinctive averting of Candice's eyes. "What's your damage, sweetheart? I don't know if you've noticed the ratio of melanin between us, but clearly, I need to tan more than you do. Besides, we're still making good time. Ismail's driving."

"Yes, *Ismail's driving*," Candice emphasized, arms crossed.

"Yeah, and he's doing a great job."

"He's twelve!"

"And this is a valuable life skill he's picking up."

"*How to drive an M60 main battle tank?*"

Nevada turned onto her side. "Well, you've got a point there; it is a pretty old model. But I think if he can figure this out, an M1 Abrams shouldn't be too hard."

Candice sat down on the turret with a sigh like a zeppelin deflating. "Tell me we're almost there."

"Yeah, yeah, any day now. We reach this hunting lodge turned refugee camp that the boss made a big donation to, they put us up, Jacques gets there with the plane, we fly out, more crazy adventures and simmering sexual tension." Nevada flopped down onto her belly again. "Hey, there's some suntan lotion in my bag, could you put another layer on my back?"

"You brought suntan lotion on your tomb raiding—of course you did. I'm not even surprised at this point."

"See? New chapter, new book."

"Stop that. You sound like Oprah before she's had her coffee." Candice stood again, hovering over Nevada. "And what do you mean, hunting lodge turned refugee camp?"

"You're in my sun."

"*Nevada.*"

"*Candice.*" Nevada craned her neck to look up to her. "What, it's some missionary operation. They'll even take the kids off our hands—I did ask."

"*Okay,*" Candice said, sliding out of Nevada's sunlight.

"What do you mean, 'okay'?"

"Are you being funny?" Candice asked.

"No, no, you said it in this total *Real Housewives* way like it's not okay, but you're going to put up with it. You're not some Richard Dawkins type, are you?"

"No, I'm not Richard Dawkins. I have a sense of irony. What about you? You're not some Focus on the Family type?"

"Candice, I'm pretty much a sexy cat burglar. Clearly I'm not the most religious person. But it's missionaries. Who has a problem with missionaries?"

"Well, the many millions of indigenous peoples around the world who were forced to convert on pain of death."

"Don't worry," Nevada said condescendingly. "I'll defend you from the big bad youth pastors who don't want you to swear so much."

"And a lot of them don't distribute relief so much as they throw around Bibles and... socks..."

"Candice, we're doing the missionaries' position and that's final."

Candice simmered for a moment on the pun she'd walked into. "I hate you."

"But it's an erotic hate, like James Bond and the villain's sexy henchwoman."

"I'm going back inside," Candice said, pulling the hatch up.

"So you're really not doing my back?" Nevada called after her.

The hatch clanged shut.

"Okay, send Uday up, he has strong hands. Candice? *Hello?*"

———————◆———————

It took a few more days of travel, but eventually the unchallenged dominion of the Sahara sands began to combat the plains and low hills of what locals called the *goz*. The two fought like weary, wounded soldiers, with long stretches of gravel and jagged sandstone broken up by guerrilla attacks of wiry grass or thorny scrub, spreading over the gritty soil until it had taken over the horizon. After the sterility of the desert, it should've been a relief, but the weak and crippled attempts at growth only made the surroundings seem more lifeless. Bleached bones and desiccated corpses were the only landmarks, accompanied by dust devils clawing at the burning sands like red-handed murderers displaying their handiwork.

The sun had disappeared behind evening clouds and the heat was bleeding out of the sand like a fire guttering out when the tank came across a mother elephant and her fallen calf. The child was as big as a St. Bernard, but infinitely more ungainly. Like some cobbled together toy, it refused to function, only stirring slightly as its mother pulled at it with her trunk. It was obvious to Candice that the calf was halfway to being another set of bleached bones, but Nevada stopped the tank, got out, and brought it water in an upside-down helmet. The calf only drank sparingly, but Nevada stayed beside it as ardently as its mother, encouraging it to drink more.

The human children filed out to stretch their legs and relieve themselves, while Candice stayed on the tank in some parody of guardianship, keeping one eye on the children to ensure they wouldn't wander off and another on Nevada. Riding in the tank, she felt like she was being shaken apart. The M60 wasn't much more comfortable when it was parked, but Candice appreciated the stillness.

A week ago, she didn't think she had ever seen a tank in real life. Or heard a gun go off. Or seen any blood that hadn't come from someone's nose. She'd been an archaeologist, working on a dig site in Meroe. She'd been more worried about contaminating her findings than losing her life.

Everything had changed so quickly that it hardly seemed real. More like some TV show where someone got bumped on the head and dreamt they were in the Wild West. The government of Sudan had been decapitated in a terrorist bombing. Another cell of that same terror network, the Khamsin, had come to destroy Candice's dig. Nevada had saved her, then shanghaied her into an expedition inside the tomb her team had uncovered to find a treasure Nevada was set on claiming. There hadn't been any treasure, though. Only a clue to where it had been taken, to be buried in the tomb of Cleopatra herself.

Calling on the resources of Nevada's mysterious employer, they'd finagled their way onto a train evacuating refugees from Khartoum, which had been destroyed midway through the journey. Most of the refugees had been left to hike back to Khartoum and an uncertain fate, while Nevada had used a tank they'd liberated from the Khamsin to drive to safety in South Sudan, taking Candice, the wounded, and the children with her.

Now the plan was to get the refugees to safety and set off on the second leg of this treasure hunt. Candice would find an archaeological treasure trove, with Nevada only taking one small trinket for her trouble.

It felt like she'd sold her soul.

Candice sometimes wished she'd stayed with her first instinct, to drug Nevada and leave her safely behind in the hotel in Khartoum while she went after the treasure... the *find*... herself. But she needed Nevada's street smarts as much as Nevada needed her expertise. And she wanted Nevada to save her kid... assuming he wasn't some con job.

Of course, even if he wasn't, that hardly made things better. You weren't allowed to rob banks just because you donated the money to charity. In Candice's experience, people rarely acted according to justifications anyway; they acted according to their nature. Was the boy Nevada's justification, or an excuse for her to indulge in her nature?

And what's your nature, Candice Cushing? she asked herself. *What is your justification and what is your excuse?*

Something sparked at her eye, almost like a tear. Covering her eyebrows with the chop of her palm, she saw a metallic glimmer on the horizon with a dust storm behind it. Some futile defiance of the sun, rising up to try and blot it out before being sucked away by indifferent winds. In that miasma of torn sands, the metal vehicle gleamed even brighter.

"Easy!" she cried. "We've got company!"

Nevada looked in Candice's direction, which brought her the sight of the woman standing on the tank's cupola, as if she needed to be any taller, and pointing at the southern horizon. Their destination. Nevada looked that way, and there it was, plain as day. And if there was one thing the Sahara had in stock, it was day.

Nevada took her scope out of her pocket and looked through it.

"What do you see?" Candice called.

Nevada adjusted the scope to bring the scene into focus. "Tour bus." Distantly, Nevada heard the whump of sand compacting as Candice hopped down from the tank.

"Tour bus? What's a tour bus doing in a war zone?"

Nevada replaced the scope in her pocket. "Maybe it's the economy tour." She dropped her hand to the gun in her holster to check that its reassuring weight was still there. It wasn't her own pistol, but a revolver she'd taken off one of the Khamsin on the train—so old that she didn't know the make or model. But it fired.

An unfamiliar weight draped across her shoulders, and she looked up to see the mother elephant, its trunk outstretched to curl around her in some gesture of pachyderm emotion she refused to try to read into. Thankfulness or beseeching or even consoling—God, she didn't want to be one of those people who called a pet their "fur baby." Nevada pushed the trunk away.

"It's tough being a mom," she said, as if she'd know, and walked back to the tank.

She slid her dive knife out of its sheath, checking to make sure it would come out without a hitch, then pushed it back inside. Candice was standing in front of the tank, arms crossed, her strong features set with worry. Nevada emptied her own face of emotion, giving Candice a cheeky grin instead. Candice was a tough cookie and she'd taken more than most, but that was no reason to throw anything at her that she didn't absolutely need to catch.

"Get everyone inside the tank," Nevada said confidently. She took her revolver out and checked the chambers. Five of the six were full, the chamber under the hammer left empty to prevent an accidental discharge. She spun a loaded chamber behind the barrel and holstered the pistol again. "Aim the main gun at the bus. If I do this—" Nevada raised her fist into the air and pumped it in a circle. "Blast 'em."

She was turning to walk out to the approaching tour bus when Candice said, "Wait, stop, what if you forget and do the sign accidentally?"

Nevada held up her fist and circled it in the air again. "How many times do you think I do this in the average day? Do you think I'm going to meet Arsenio Hall?"

"Who?"

Nevada laughed. "This is actually about as irritating as I remember commanding a tank crew was."

"I'm sorry, the last time you told me to fire a tank's gun, we blew up a bridge!"

"That worked out well," Nevada reasoned.

Candice stuck her hands to her hips. "We fell off a speeding train."

"I remember that as getting to first base with you."

Candice's elbows spasmed as she pushed her hands harder into her waist. "I suppose it depends on who landed on top and who landed on bottom."

"I'm not touching that one," Nevada said, and started off.

<hr />

Nevada walked out to meet the bus and it grew like the atomic monster in some fifties B-movie. She was walking on bony grit that shifted under her with every step and flew away from her strides like its deadness was repulsed by her life. This sand didn't feel like the good, honest soil of the Mojave she'd grown up with, or even the Arabian Desert. It was more like ashes.

Behind her, she heard the tank's turret pivoting, the main gun taking aim at the bus. If it came down to it, she didn't doubt that Candice would choose the refugees inside over anyone outside. *Me included, most likely.*

The bus stopped forty yards away from her. Peeling paint on the sides announced that it was, or once had been, 'Big Jim's Safari Tours.' It was a big, gas-guzzling, diesel thing, snub-nosed, stippled with rust, and pimpled with bullet holes. The Igor of vehicles. Cargo netting had been strung through the windows and over the roof, a camel hump for luggage. The side windows had been plugged up: plywood, scrap metal, even bricks in one place. To make up for the loss of ventilation, the windshield had been taken out entirely, replaced with chicken wire stretched across the front of the cab like the face mask of a football helmet. Christian rock drooled out of the speakers. Nevada could see a Bible on the dash.

The driver wrestled aside a slab of bullet shield from the driver's side window and pulled his upper body out into open air, seating himself on the bottom of the window panel. He held some sort of machine gun in his lap. Nevada rested her thumb in her belt, near the butt of her pistol.

A passenger worked the lever to open the bus door and stepped out. He had a .45 strapped to his belt, under a white T-shirt with a picture of a fetus on it that read 'BABY.' At least one of the men, Easy judged, was Dinka tribe, the same as Candice's mother. Tall in the elegantly slender way of a Tolkien elf, with starless-night complexions and deep, radiant eyes. Candice definitely took after that side of her family.

The passenger walked out to her. On closer inspection, Nevada could see his shirt had holes along the sleeves. His sandals were a handspan under the cuffs of his too-short jeans, which were themselves wearing thin along the knees. Maybe it was Nevada's imagination, but the sand didn't seem to crunch under him. He stepped over it as lightly as Jesus walking on water.

"I am John Makuei Ladu," he said in a lilting African accent. His English was good, but a bit strange-sounding. His words didn't have a rhythm that Nevada was used to. "I come from the camp. I am here to retrieve you."

"I suppose that makes me here to be retrieved." Nevada glanced at the other man, the one who'd been driving the bus. He wore fatigues, in places more maroon than green or black—splotched with old bloodstains, and she doubted they were his. He had the ritual scarification of the Nuer tribe: beads of scar tissue surrounding his mouth like a second goatee and horizontal *gaar* lines circling his forehead. He was relaxed in a limber sort of way, the machine gun held comfortably in his grip, no nerves, no anxiousness. He didn't expect there to be trouble. At least, not for him. "You have anything more for me to go on than a smile on your face and a song in your heart?"

Ladu looked confused for a moment. His lungs pumped his chest out and then sucked it back in. The sand blew over the hills with a plaintive wail. Nevada felt sweat between her shoulder blades, tingling a path downward like a plucked guitar string.

Shoot him, shoot the guy with the machine gun, get to his body, get his gun...

Nevada tapped her pinky against the butt of her revolver. Doable. Very doable.

"Mr. Pike," Ladu started again, reverence in his voice, "said he had been given a name by your boss-man. The name is Harry Calhoun."

Nevada felt a crack go through her poker face. Her deep, even breathing was interrupted by a sudden intake. She listened to the almost hollow, almost echoing moan of the wind.

Okay, she thought, *okay*.

"We've got kids in the tank. Some walking wounded, a few old fogeys. You can take them?"

"It is a bus," Ladu said reasonably. "I must tell you that there are no weapons allowed at Camp Esau."

Figures. Nevada took out her pistol. Handling the gun between two fingers, she held it up, rolled out the cylinder, and let the bullets tumble onto the shattered ground, rolling into the sands like maggots. "Now it's a paperweight."

She went to tell Candice they were getting bumped up to first class.

———◆———

They left the tank to continue rotting, as it seemingly had been doing even when they were riding in it. In no time at all, it would be stripped, scavenged, salvaged for parts. One more set of old bones being resurrected in the decay economy of South Sudan.

The bus was just as bone-jarring as the tank had been. The music was worse. The driver pushed the gas pedal all the way down and took them up to a speed that seemed nearly suicidal, as if he was determined to kill the suspension once and for all. Through the chained windshield, Nevada could see the sands finally give way fully to browning vegetation, grass, crops, the traditional flattened savannah of Sub-Saharan Africa. It was the dry season, and the occasional brush of green seemed more like an outbreak of some disease than anything else. Farmers performed stubble burning, sending up clouds of greasy smoke and low, orange flames that bleached the landscape to a further monochrome, making it look like just another variation of the desert they had left.

The wooden stock on the FM Mle1915 CSRG the driver had leaning against his right thigh used the same limited palette. The machine gun was big enough for Nevada to make it out all the way from the back of the bus. The crescent-shaped magazine straddling the underside could leave no doubt it was the French Chauchat. It probably dated back to World War I. Made the Browning Automatic Rifle look like cutting-edge tech.

Lines of coagulated blood ran like dry riverbeds along the floor.

Candice came down the aisle holding a knapsack full of Camelbak water bottles. She handed them out to the children and wounded and elderly. When she got to Nevada, she sat down beside her, the bag in her lap. Nevada took a bottle out of it. It was customized with some church logo, a crucifix with the sideways figure-8 of the infinity symbol crossing the arms.

Nevada opened the tab on the bottle and sipped from it. The water on the tank had been staid, as dry as water could be and still be water. This was Nirvana in comparison. Or at least Pearl Jam.

"You feeling okay?" Candice asked, digging out a water bottle of her own.

"I'm great," Nevada said. "Why wouldn't I be?"

"No reason. It's just been a long coupla days."

Nevada swiveled in her seat, resting her back against the window and planting her feet against Candice's thigh. "What about you? Any second thoughts?"

Candice was somber. "Second thoughts, third thoughts, fourth thoughts… nothing serious. If nothing else, we're doing these kids a favor."

"My good deed for the decade," Nevada said, putting her heels up on Candice's lap.

Candice pushed Nevada's boots off, and they clunked down against the floor. "Tell me something. Back on the train, when you went after Farouq—was it to save these people or to get the map off him?"

Nevada let one leg dangle off the seat and put her other foot up on the bench, toes saber-rattling at the border of Candice's ass. "What kind of a question is that? Both. Duh."

"Duh," Candice repeated, imitating Nevada's American accent. She scooted away to the edge of the bench seat.

Nevada pushed her foot out further but didn't bring it into contact with Candice's hip. "Yeah. Duh. People do stuff because they get something out of it. They eat to feel good or they don't eat because thinking of being thin makes them feel good. They even give to charity just to feel good.

Once you realize that and stop feeling *bad* about it, you can stick your nose in the trough and get your fair share, instead of wondering why assholes have all the money."

"And that's all that motivates you? Enlightened self-interest?"

"Aww, you called it enlightened." Nevada smirked. "What else is there?"

"Love, compassion, nobility. Most of human emotions, really."

Nevada prodded her foot in Candice's side. "People do shit because it makes them feel good or they don't do shit because it makes them feel bad."

Candice chopped at Nevada's ankle. "So if Farouq hadn't had the map, would you have just left those people to die?"

Nevada picked her foot up and rested it on the back of the seat, her legs now spread-eagle. "Are you implying I would've felt bad if they died? Because that's kinda my point."

"Could you please put your legs together?"

"Now you sound like my mother." Nevada hopped her other foot up onto the seatback, reclining down with both feet beside Candice's head.

"How can that possibly be comfortable?"

"I'm doing yoga."

"You have your head up your ass."

"I had a swami who could do that once."

"You did not."

"Namaste."

Nevada and Candice slept in shifts as the bus drove through the night, passing the flaming wrecks of other vehicles and those that had long since cooled. Candice didn't know what *she* would do if trouble came, besides wake Nevada up, but then, she didn't even know if Nevada was just in it for the money or not. Hell, she didn't even know why she was doing this. Archaeological knowledge, minus the artifact Nevada had her eye on, or her career? Or both, like Nevada had said?

Or it doesn't even matter, because you already told Nevada where to go so you might as well get used to the idea.

Despite telling herself that, Candice's troubled thoughts let her stay up through the night with ease. Shortly after dawn, they reached their destination.

Camp Esau had started its life as a hunting lodge in colonial times, circular clay buildings with thatch roofs and hardwood floors, the lesser trophies of its occupants decorating the *Out of Africa* surroundings. When the civil war had broken out between the Dinka and the Nuer, it'd been razed to the ground, only to be resurrected in the peaceful lull of South Sudan's new nationhood. When the fighting had resumed, David Pike had converted it into a refugee camp, the lodge now housing a school, a clinic, dormitories, a kitchen, and a library. Tukuls—mud huts ten feet across that could be built in less than a week—had been erected around the lodge for additional housing. Rows of acacia trees—a certain breed that had no leaves, only needle-sharp thorns as long a pencil—grew around the compound, serving as fencing. Outside that was a field of yellow-tipped elephant grass growing waist-high. The bus parked at the edge of the grass. A footpath connected the parking spot to the inner compound.

With the tribesmen hurrying them off the bus, Candice and Nevada found themselves pressed into service as chaperones, Candice staying on the bus to make sure everyone disembarked, and Nevada riding herd on them as they got off,

"Hold up a damn minute, would you? You, back here, now! Stay with the group, ya little monster. Yeah, make a face, it'll freeze like that."

Candice was trying not to get her hopes up, which of course meant tantalizing herself with all the possibilities civilization had to offer. A hot bath. A hot meal. A toilet with actual toilet paper. And clean clothes—the ones she had on she would quite like to burn. Deodorant—

She was suddenly jerked back several thousand years, to a time when all a person could be was prey. Thoughts of the wider world vanished, eclipsed by an awareness of her immediate surroundings. She could feel air currents breaking against her skin, the pattern of the sunlight as it filtered through the clouds. And she knew something was watching her.

"Nevada," she said gently.

"I know," came the terse reply.

Nevada moved between the group and the threat. Candice could almost make it out now. A lion, its tawny fur blending into the wilting grass. It looked bigger than it could possibly be, broken outline sucking up all the shadows and indistinct yellow in its vicinity, drawing that bulk around the sizzling golden eyes that gave an undeniable reality to the fear taking hold of Candice. Nevada put her hand on the butt of her useless, empty pistol.

Candice backed away, a few steps behind Nevada, saying in hushed tones for everyone in the group to stay together. But the lioness had spent far longer than any of them in this primordial state of kill or be killed. She growled, the sound sizzling the air, making it almost too hot to bear. And she swished her tail, which scythed through the grass around her to give a fearful suggestion of her size and nearness. Something half-seen, present but unknown, there and not there. The fear was almost intimate in how deep it was under Candice's skin. It was in the bones of her legs, pulling at them, trying to get her to run. She kept moving at a snail's pace, slow enough for the wounded and the elderly. They were all one big mass, with Nevada the face, staring right at the lioness.

It growled louder and raked its claws through the earth, big scabs of soil coming up under its paws.

"Don't take that fucking tone with me, slut," Nevada said. She took the gun out of her belt. "You see this? YOU SEE THIS, MOTHERFUCKER? THIS IS LIKE A SPRAY BOTTLE TIMES A MILLION!"

———————◆———————

It was barely a rainy season. Everywhere Pike drove, the grass was brown and brittle, the Ankole-Watusi cattle had ribs and shoulders showing almost as prominent as their upturned horns, and the riverbeds had burnt down nearly into rock. There were so few animals now—certainly none of the herds of prancing gazelles that the *mzunga* had once watched from the terrace outside his second-story office. It seemed like one day soon, there would only be vultures to sit and count the minutes he spent resting.

The Dinka Spear Masters made their sacrifices, called upon their animal spirits and upon Nhialic, the god of the sky, but he only answered the prayers of the vultures.

Their god was asleep on the job. Pike wasn't.

The money that his guests' rich benefactor, Mr. Singh, had offered had seemed like a windfall, but the Sudan had a way of swallowing it all up. They needed more water, more food, more everything to keep the camp running as they waited for the dry season to release its stranglehold and allow the rains in. And even that would not be enough. Noah's flood would not be enough—but at least it would make this dirty place *clean*.

I Counted Each Star As I Placed It In The Sky And Foresaw The Path Of Every Wind That Would Cover The Earth. I Have Given You Enough.

"But Lord," Pike replied, "I can't see how we can keep everyone here with not even enough money for half—"

You Are A Worthy Steward, David Pike. You Will Act Wisely With The Gifts I Have Given You. You Will Walk After The Lord Your God. I Shall Roar Like A Lion.

Then he heard it. The throaty, braying bellow of a lion, almost as clear to him as God's voice. And yelling, from outside the entryway to the camp.

Pike left his pen and spreadsheet and went to the gun rack. For a lion, his Sako 85 Kodiak should suffice. It was already loaded with .375 H&H. The Nosler Partition bullets would expand inside the target, like he'd shot his prey with an explosion. Not the kind of doomsday weapon that would take down an elephant or cape buffalo, but just right for four hundred and fifty pounds of predator. It would almost be an even fight. But then, he had the Lord.

Nevada jabbed the revolver at the lioness for emphasis as she continued to curse her out, calling the animal every name under the sun, even a few in Italian. The lioness was keeping her distance, confused by Nevada's boldness and waiting to see who would break from the herd and be easy pickings. But she was getting impatient. Step by step, the group was getting closer to the safety of the compound, and the lioness couldn't have that.

"FUCK YOUR MOTHER, FUCK YOUR FATHER, AND *THE LION KING* RIPPED OFF JAPANESE ANIME! TELL ME I'M WRONG, COCKSUCKER!"

The lioness roared. A full-on MGM Studios roar. Nevada felt the revolver shaking in her hand. This was usually about the time she would improvise something and pretend it had been the plan all along, but she couldn't think of anything to do except hope that she tasted bad. And she hadn't heard any complaints in a very active dating life.

"Anybody have a spray bottle?" Nevada muttered.

Thunder cracked in a staccato rhythm. A pop, then a millisecond of a bolt-action being racked. Pop, racking, pop, racking. Three gouts of blood burst from the lioness's chest in rapid succession, splashing the stalks of grass around her, and then she went down so quietly she might've been lying down with the lamb. Nevada could only watch in disbelief. She could see the three entry wounds. They were grouped together in a circle no bigger than her fist; hit the lioness right in the heart. It must've been like a miniature freight train hitting her out of nowhere.

"Down?" a gritted voice came from on high. Nevada turned to see a tall man standing on a wood-beamed platform on the second floor of the lodge. He wore layers of leather, khaki, and flannel, with a priest's collar around his neck and a bolt-action rifle in his hand.

Nevada gave the lioness a kick. She kept bleeding and being dead. "Way down."

"You must be Nevada."

"And company," Nevada called up, indicating Candice and the others.

"Come on in—let's get this barbecue kicked off!"

He turned to head back inside, and Nevada started toward the compound again, Candice falling in beside her. She had a hand on the shoulder of one of the children, who was holding his ears after the violence of the gunshots. Either not used to the noise or far too used to it.

"You faced down a lion with an empty gun?" Candice asked.

"Lion didn't know it was empty."

"Uh-huh," Candice said, rolling her eyes. "And who was that? Friend of yours?" She gestured up to where Pike had gone back inside.

"The man in charge."

"How can you tell?"

"Africa's the same as anywhere else. The man with the gun makes the rules. Shall we?"

Candice looked at the hunting lodge, seeing its Victorian trappings, and let out a deep breath. "You know it's literally colonial architecture, right?"

Nevada put an arm around Candice's shoulders. "You must be so much fun at Thanksgiving."

"I'm British."

"Oh, that's right, you're never fun."

"Which of our countries invented *Family Guy*?"

"That's a low blow."

On the inside, the compound was more like a village than a refugee camp, its center a bustling town square. A tailor worked on a Singer sewing machine to repair loincloths and robes. Women stripped beans by slapping them against heaps of gunnysacks. Children ran around beating play drums, pushing little clay figurines around on the ground with short sticks. Others were fooling around with gourds filled with water, slapping their bellies after puffing them out.

Candice noticed Nevada's eyes following them. "They're playing *luony kou*."

"He one of those new Star Wars characters? I can't keep track anymore."

Candice gave her an admonishing tap. "It's something they'll do when they become young men. A competition at cattle camp. Over the summer, the richest men with the most cows try to become fat by only drinking milk from their own cows." Candice pointed out one of the boys guzzling from his water-filled gourd. "Whoever is fattest at the end gets the girls."

Nevada shrugged. "Has to be better than *The Bachelor*. But that wasn't what I was looking at."

Candice took a closer look at the boy with the gourd. Then she had to look away. Even a glimpse of his lips and ears was almost too much. "Jesus…"

"Not in the slightest." Pike was coming out of the lodge, ringed by three tribesmen in strangely modern clothing. One had a bandana with a button from the Mitt Romney campaign pinned to it. "The Zuni tribe will swell their ranks by taking in anyone they capture, but first they mark them." He slapped the back of his hand against the chest of one of his men. "Get everyone to the infirmary, have them checked out. Go tell Francis to cook up a big lunch. After they eat, I want them cleaned up, fresh clothes, and bunks for all of them to sleep in."

The one with the Romney button asked something in the Rek dialect, and Pike responded in kind before his men hustled off to herd the incoming children with an experienced professionalism. One of them ran back and hugged Nevada, who patted him on the head reluctantly before he let her go.

Pike crossed his arms contemplatively. "And that is exactly why I'm going to put you up in the lodge. Follow me, I'll show you to your rooms."

Inside the lodge, the furnishings were surprisingly palatial. Wicker furniture, animal-skin rugs, big game mounted and stuffed—with heaps of gunnysacks, supply crates, and stacks of ammunition taking up space. Like a social club taken over by revolutionaries.

"Thank you for your help with the lion," Candice said, her small voice almost swallowed up by the floorboards creaking under their feet and the booming footfalls of Pike's biker boots.

"Weren't nothing. But it was a lioness. No mane. And with lions, it's women who do the hunting."

"I've been to shoe sales like that," Nevada commented.

"To be honest," Pike continued, his gravelly voice like a country singer near the end of a tour, "no matter how much your boss paid, I was leaning towards putting you up in one of the tukuls. I sleep there myself. Roughing it a little is nothing compared to what these folks go to. But hearing about how you took care of the lost sheep out there, the least I can do to repay you is put you up in one of the old *mzungu* rooms. We cleared out all the shit, changed the sheets, even did some vacuuming."

"Oh, no," Candice said, instantly demurring, "with all the people you have here already, we couldn't possibly—"

"Take more than one room!" Nevada interrupted quickly. She put an arm around Candice's waist and pulled her close. "Since it's just us girls, we can share a bed." She smiled at Candice. "It'll be fun. Like having a slumber party."

Pike led them up a flight of stairs that revolved around a chandelier made of antelope horns. Only half the lightbulbs were lit. "Fine by me. I wish we had so many supplies that we couldn't spare the space, but that just ain't so. And speaking of supplies, I'm gonna need your peacemaker."

"I already gave you guys the bullets," Nevada protested, getting an elbow from Candice for her trouble.

"I know that, but you can see how our other guests don't see much of a distinction." Pike stopped at the top of the stairs, chuckling to himself and running his hand over his facial hair. "You know what they tell me? They know that in America, a man only takes one wife. Figure that makes a lotta women left over. So now they're worried you'll—" He made a gun of his fingers and aimed it at Nevada. "Take 'em away and force 'em to marry you."

"They should talk to my cousin," Nevada said, taking the revolver out and handing it to Pike.

He looked it over. "What is this, the gun that killed Liberty Valance?"

"That's what I said."

Pike pointed to a room at the end of the hall. "You're in there. If you want a hot shower, I suggest you get to it before we get the kids washed off. There's fresh clothes in the drawers—the stuff me and the boys don't have much use for. And we really will be having a barbecue this evening to welcome you newcomers. Not our usual fare, but since we're having company over, why the hell not?"

"What is it?" Candice asked. "Cow? Pig?"

"Elephant," Pike replied.

———————◆———————

The room's opulence reminded Nevada of the Burj al Arab, all those years ago. Funny, how dealing with the criminal and the corrupt tended to land you in high society as much as it did the gutter. She picked her way through the antique furniture, the glass-shrouded candles waiting to be lit, the framed drawings and paintings that had given some long-ago adventurer a taste of England. There was even a Victrola in the corner.

"Don't say I never take you anywhere nice," Nevada said to Candice, going through her pockets to set all the contents out on the dresser. She'd be transferring them all into her clean clothes.

Candice looked out the window. The view of the plains had been replaced by the field of tukuls, now lit from the inside as dusk fell and the occupants started fires. With no chimneys, the smoke seeped up through the thatching, making the huts look disturbingly like they were burning to the ground.

"Four-star accommodations in the middle of a warzone. I don't know whether to be impressed or..." Candice trailed off.

"Be impressed," Nevada said. "Liberal guilt is so two thousand and late."

"Honestly, so long as there's shampoo, spoil me rotten. Any more of this humidity and my hair is going to become a member of Mötley Crüe."

Candice started for the bathroom, only for Nevada to hurriedly slide into a blockade, leaning against the doorframe.

"Hey," Nevada said, toying with the hem of her tank top, pulling it up over a row of subtly delineated abdominal muscles, which Candice had to raise an eyebrow at. "Here's a thought. Maybe it's just that that was a choice glam rock reference, but what if we showered together? Save some water… It is the dry season, after all."

Candice took hold of Nevada's shoulder and shoved her to one side of the doorway as she stepped past. "And with lines like that, it's no wonder. Does this combination of arrogance, obnoxiousness, and sexual aggression normally charm women into paroxysms of lust?"

"I wouldn't say paroxysms," Nevada demurred. "Probably because I don't know what that means. But we do have some unfinished business." Nevada ran her thumb over her lower lip. "Now that we've got the kids in daycare, maybe we should follow up on that kiss. Before the shower, I mean, while we're already all sweaty and gross."

"Oh my God," Candice moaned, walking out of the bathroom.

Nevada followed her, jumping onto the bed with some Baywatch-quality jiggle, if she did say so herself. "I know, I know, ladies don't sweat, they glisten. Whatever. Honestly, a little musk is a bit of a turn-on."

"This is not an invitation," Candice said firmly, throwing open a drawer on the empire dresser. The attached mirror showed her curdling expression. "I realized it's probably best to have my clothes ready in the bathroom if I don't want you undressing me with your eyes."

Nevada turned onto her belly, sashaying her ass from side to side. "You *don't* want that," she agreed. "I work much better with my hands."

With a set of underwear, white peasant blouse, and riding skirt folded in her arms, Candice marched back to the bathroom. Nevada reached out as she passed and grabbed her elbow.

"Hey, hey," she said sincerely, soothingly, as she looked up at Candice. Candice looked back at her out of the corner of her eye. "If you're that angry with me, you can be on top."

Candice wrenched her arm away, growling, and proceeded into the bathroom. Nevada rolled out of bed to pursue her, stopping short at the doorway when Candice turned around to block her path.

"I know, I know," Nevada said, laying a palm flat on the stack of clothes to push it down out of the way of their eye contact. "You're thinking, 'That was a really good kiss, but it was with another woman. Does that make me gay?' No, absolutely not, just bisexual. Everyone's a bit bisexual. Not me. I'd rather drown in quicksand than use a dick as a handhold..."

"Let me be clear," Candice replied, drawing herself up to her full height, which almost touched the lintel. "It doesn't matter to me what your orientation is, or your race, or your gender."

"You're very undemanding," Nevada said. "I like that in a woman."

"I find you repellant entirely based on your personality. You are the most greedy, narcissistic, destructive, and obnoxious individual I have ever met. If we were the two last women on Earth, I would choose a life of chastity over sex with you."

Nevada paused for a moment. "You wouldn't even masturbate?"

Candice swept the door shut with her foot; Nevada had to jump back before it smacked her in the face. A moment later, she heard the shower running. A moment after that, she was knocking on the door.

"Candice," she whined, "can I at least use the toilet?"

That night, the lights of the lodge and the tukuls were scant defense against the darkness. It was liquid—Candice felt like she could swim in it—but warm somehow. A fire pit had been lit near the center of the compound. The elephant meat roasted on it, the refugees gathered around. It all reminded Candice of some orgiastic Viking party, but inverted. Solemn and dignified, with portions of meat and vegetables being handed out in silence. Candice took hers: a battered metal plate sectioned into portions, with a fork missing some tines and a spoon made of wood.

Before the fire, several Ubangi performed a dance accompanied only by the sounds of their feet chopping at the ground and their hands slapping their bodies. One of them wore a surgical mask and a white lab coat over his nearly naked body as he went around the onlookers, pretending to examine them.

Up close, the hot coals seemed to throw off a great deal of light, but it dwindled quickly in the face of the infinitely stretching landscape. The ground seemed as flat and monotonous as a sheet of paper—its featurelessness only defeated by the curvature of the earth, which itself was only a faint suggestion in the moonlight.

Candice turned around to look at the hunting lodge, as if for reassurance it was still there in the lunar sterility of the darkly lacquered world, and saw Nevada emerging. She'd picked out a white chiffon dress that evidently did little against the cold; she scooted up right next to the fire before crouching down beside Candice. She didn't seem to have any idea of how to sit down in it either.

"Was there a pumice stone when you showered?" Nevada asked, wringing a last bit of moisture out of her hair. "Because I couldn't find one. I'm not accusing you of anything, but I went in right after you did."

"I remember," Candice said. "You didn't even wait until I was gone to start undressing."

"What? I'm not ashamed of my body."

"I've seen some of your tattoos; you probably should be."

"You wouldn't say that if you could read Korean."

"I *can* read Korean. And now I know how to operate a Samsung dishwasher. By the way, when someone flushes the toilet while you're taking a shower, it tends to result in cold water."

"It's called a courtesy flush," Nevada announced, "and in my country, it's considered polite."

"Did you have to flush the bog roll too?"

"I didn't, just the toilet paper." Nevada was handed her own plate, contents steaming hot from the spit-roast. "Oh. Thanks! Don't mind if I do—"

Candice reached over to grab her wrist. "Don't."

"What, does it have MSG in it? *Do you know what MSG is?*"

Candice rolled her eyes. "It's Dinka tradition—when you eat an elephant, everyone takes their first bite at the same time."

"So, what, is there a countdown or does someone blow a whistle—"

Nevada broke off. She must've noticed, as Candice had, that everyone was watching Pike, forks in hand, their first bites ready to be taken. And as magnanimous as the host of any feast, Pike looked the guests over, speared a morsel on his fork, and bit down. Everyone else took a bite in unison, including Candice and Nevada. Not having had time to cut her meat,

Nevada ripped it right off the bone. As she chewed, she took out her dive knife and savagely cut the meat into portions.

"Tell me you cleaned that knife," Candice said.

"I took a shower, didn't I?"

Pike was on the other side of the fire pit, its sparks dancing across their view of him. Seated on a log, one of the rescued children on his knee, he could've been a Boy Scout troop leader making s'mores before bedtime. It was the dark, Candice thought. He looked at home in it. Maybe at peace.

"So, ladies!" he bellowed across the fire, handing the child his plate. "What do you think of my 'vacation home' here?"

Candice nodded agreeably. "It's really something."

"I would've gone with aluminum siding myself," Nevada said, "but yeah, place is a beaut."

Pike nodded, the light from the fire playing over his features and reflecting in his eyes. "Yeah. Anyone can look at something, but not everyone can see. Me, I can see. I see this place because I saw it before there was so much as a footprint on this ground. Just a boarded-up house. I came here thinking it would make a good picture for my scrapbook. God, though, God thinks bigger than that. He told me this would be where I honored Him. And I heard Him tell me to build here, but I think what He really wanted me to do was believe. Because this place, it's really all God's work. Look at it. No way does this happen without God."

"Well," Candice said, in a sort of British exhalation.

"Well?" Nevada asked, halfway prompting and halfway warning.

"Well—" Candice drew out the last vowel into a hum. "I've read about what you do, how you carry out operations—protecting people, rescuing people, fighting people you see as your enemies."

"My enemies?" Pike asked.

Candice coughed. "I…" She prodded at her meat with her fork. "I just hear about this war and the things each side does, and it's hard for me to believe God is on anyone's side."

Pike smiled disarmingly. "God is on the children's side."

Nevada patted Candice on the shoulder. "I think what Candice means to say—"

"Means to say," Pike interrupted. "I hear that a lot. People mean to say a lot of things. Mostly how complicated this place is. It's like 'hey, even how

I'm talking about it is complicated.' But I think to God, it must be simple. There are people who are doing something about this place and those who aren't. What do you think God means to say to them?"

"I'm sure I wouldn't know," Candice replied.

"I would." Pike sounded completely sure of himself. The kind of certainty people in love used when they talked about being together forever. He fixed Nevada with his fire-lit stare. "Do you believe in God?"

"Still flipping the coin. Ask me in a year."

"Oh, we won't be keeping you that long. I'm told your plane will be here in the morning. Hope you enjoy a good night's sleep before you're on your way."

"I sleep like a baby."

"Clean conscience?"

Nevada inclined her head slightly. "Clean sheets."

A boy came up to her holding sand in his hand, and he pretended to sneeze as he blew it over Nevada's plate. "Why'd you stop eating?" he cried. "Why aren't you eating?"

Pike rose to his feet. "Ezekiel!" he bellowed. "That was very rude!"

Ezekiel ran off, laughing to himself. After a gesture from Pike, one of the men brought her a new plate.

"Kids," Nevada grunted as she took it. "Like it's not bad enough we have to use childproof caps."

———◆———

The fire went out, and refugees dispersed to the smoking tukuls and darkened dormitories. The night was more profound for Candice in their shared bedroom, looking out at the darkness. She could see lights moving in the fields behind the lodge, pinprick fires that could've been as distant as the stars. Her mother had told her about that. The Dinka would dig a hole before a termite mound and burn a bundle of dried grass to draw them out with the light. When the termites came out, a flow of them like water from a sprung leak, they would be swept into the hole with a broom and burnt to death. Then they could be eaten. A traditional dish that Candice had never tasted. She was torn between revulsion and curiosity, not only not knowing what to feel, but not knowing which she *should* feel.

She crossed her arms and watched the fires illuminate termite mounds as tall as a man.

"So like, that was weird, right?" Nevada asked, her mouth full of toothpaste. The bathroom door was open. Candice turned to face her and sat on the windowsill. "The whole 'oh, hey, black guys, just look at me, the white boy, I'll tell you when to eat' *thang*. I mean, I'm not really all that PC…"

"I hadn't noticed," Candice said.

"Sarcasm is right down there with puns and *Saturday Night Live* recurring characters as a source of humor," Nevada informed.

"I had no idea," Candice replied sarcastically.

Nevada spat out her toothpaste. "I don't know, it felt real… Professor Challenger and his native bearers." She poured herself a shot of mouthwash.

"It's an ego trip," Candice said. "It's not acceptable to be the Great White Hunter anymore, so people see how socially conscious they can be. The most charitable, the most good, the most—" Nevada gargled. "—African."

Nevada spat. "Well, he's saved more kids than I have. Can't complain about that."

"I'm not. Everyone indulges their ego in some form. As long as it's done in moderation. But he's acting like some kind of chieftain. It's a warning sign…"

Nevada leaned down to rinse her mouth in the tap water, spat, took another mouthful, swallowed, then came up cracking her neck. "And I thought I was the cynical one."

"How cynical can you be? You're white."

"What? Who told you?" Nevada came to the open doorway and hooked her fingers on the lintel, showing off her arms as she hung down. "Look how big my arms are. Candice, look how strong I am. I'm so strong…"

Candice chuckled. "You know, I think if you grew a social conscience, you might be very much like Mr. Pike. Doing the right thing for… God knows what reason."

"Oh, I'd love to," Nevada said. "But where's the money in it?"

Candice shook her head as she crossed to the bed. "You really are incomprehensible. If you're so greedy, why'd you become an archaeologist in the first place? It's not exactly a growth industry."

"To meet women." Nevada shrugged. "Working so far."

Candice sat on the foot of the bed. "I suppose that brings us to the sleeping arrangements."

"Yes, the offer to top me still stands."

Candice groaned and fell back onto the mattress. "I'm just going to sleep in the bathtub."

Nevada flopped onto the bed next to her. Candice was hard-pressed to ignore the taut ripple that went through her body, outlined as it was by her dress and distinct lack of bra. It felt sourly medieval to give Easy a pass on her crass flirtations simply because she wasn't *horrible* to look at.

"No, no, I won't hear of it," Nevada said. "We're on the same team. And when you're part of my team, you're part of me. I'm not going to let you spend a week sleeping in a *tank* just to put you in a bathtub the moment we reach civilization."

"So you're going to sleep in the bathtub?"

Nevada eyed her blankly. "I might've oversold the team spirit thing. Look..." She turned onto her belly and crawled up the bed to grab one of the many pillows. She slapped it down in the middle of the mattress. "This is a wall. My side, your side. I swear I will not so much as look at anything happening on your side of the bed." She turned onto her flank, facing away from the dividing pillow. "See? I'll pretend you don't exist until you've had your ten hours of sleep. Scout's honor."

"You were a Girl Scout?"

Nevada looked over her shoulder at Candice. "No, but I wore the uniform very well."

"I don't want to know."

"What? I was legal."

"Can't know, *cannot know*—"

Nevada sprang up to sit cross-legged on the mattress, showing impressive flexibility—which also made Candice feel bad about finding her shenanigans even somewhat funny. *If she weren't such a pervert, I'd halfway think she was doing it all to get a laugh out of me.*

Nevada clapped her hands. "*So.* Deal or no deal?"

Candice sighed and crawled up her side of the bed. "What is it with you Americans and walls?"

"What?" Nevada asked theatrically, rolling onto her side again. "Did someone speak to me? I thought I heard something… Grandmama? Is that you? Have you come back to tell me where the family gold is hidden?"

Candice rolled herself under the covers. "*Goodnight*, Nevada."

"What's that, nana? You were *murdered*?"

CHAPTER 2

NEVADA FELT ARMS LOOPING AROUND her sleeping body, warm flesh pressed against her from neck to thigh in a way that couldn't be accidental, could only be someone craving the nearness of her, of being on her, being inside her. A leg, a firm thigh, ran across her lap. *Crystal*, she thought, turning her head and feeling sweet-smelling hair brush against her face. *Tiffany? Amber? Charity? Capri? Yeah, definitely, definitely—I need to meet more college graduates.*

She opened her eyes and saw Candice draped across the pillow, which now looked like the Berlin Wall after David Hasselhoff got through with it. Wearing only a blouse and panties, Candice had managed to entangle herself in both the sheets and Nevada, ending up under one arm with her face nestled in Nevada's neck. She could feel the steady thrum of breathing, swelling out Candice's chest against her torso and then tickling down her pulse with a syrupy warmth that flittered through her body and pooled right by her groin.

The blouse was ruffled as well, twisted up somewhere around Candice's sternum, showing a long expanse of bare back all the way to her cotton panties, which contrasted in lots of interesting ways with the skin above and below and through. Candice had the coloration of a thundercloud, one that could bring either rain or lightning—Nevada wanted to run her hand over the straight, supple muscles of her lower back and find out which it would be.

She just needed to think of a good one-liner to make it official—either rearrange this little tableau with far less clothes or at least prove how witty she was—when Candice murmured in her sleep. She would probably be mortified to find that she'd thrown herself at Nevada like this, even unintentionally. And even if she didn't blame Nevada for the whole thing, it'd probably be one more thing bothering her about this whole situation. She'd brood even more, she'd angst even more—she might even find herself distracted while they were in actual physical danger, and Nevada knew how life-threatening that could be.

On the other hand, it would be very funny.

Sighing, Nevada gently sidled away, practically limbo-ing down the mattress until she slipped off the edge and left Candice wrapped around the pillow. Candice actually moaned slightly, tightening her grip on the pillow as if trying to find out what had happened to the warmer cushioning she'd been enjoying. Nevada spared one last look, then left Candice to hog the covers by her lonesome. At least this meant she'd have first shot at the shower.

She was rinsing her face at the sink when Candice came to, sputtering from giving mouth-to-mouth to her pillow. She rubbed her eyes as Nevada poked her head out of the bathroom.

"Morning, sunshine. Breakfast?"

Candice snorted. "Uh… if there's anyone I could believe could conjure up a bagel with cream cheese…"

"Sorry, I actually meant me. But we do have Pop-Tarts, if you like them cold."

Candice got out of bed, wrapping the comforter around herself and most especially around her bare legs. She trudged to the pantry Nevada had indicated. "No frosting. They make Pop-Tarts that way?"

Nevada shrugged. "Maybe it's just a thing here. Like… sushi-flavored chips."

"Stop. I already want to vomit."

Nevada came out of the bathroom, toweling off her hair. "Toss me one. Any carbs in a storm."

Candice did. Nevada took off the foil wrapping and nibbled on one. "Nn. It's like a strawberry sandwich with graham cracker bread."

Candice opened her own pack. "I had the strangest dream. I was back in Sudan. I was digging again. The ground was hard, but it—turned to sand after I hit it. I'd run my hands through the sand after I dug it up, like I was panning for gold. I didn't *touch* anything, but I felt this… history. Like I was connected to everyone who had ever walked on that sand. It was warm. The sand. It felt like it had a beating heart." She took a big bite from the Pop-Tart and seemed on the verge of gagging. "Yeah. Come up with any good jokes about us sleeping together?"

"Nah. Too easy."

"I know, right?"

"I could probably joke about it more if you played hard to get." Nevada ducked a flying Pop-Tart. "Don't waste almost-food."

"We'll be on your *Magic Carpet* in a few hours. I assume there'll be an in-flight meal."

"*The Flying Carpet*. And yeah, it has a microwave. TV dinners. We'll get you set up."

"Good. I think my appetite for organic food will be *nil* for the foreseeable. Hot water, on the other hand…" Candice started for the bathroom.

"Left you some," Nevada promised. "I'll be checking in with the home office. You might wanna scrub behind your ears and all. First impressions."

Candice turned to face her. "Start without me. I'm beginning to think this is one of those instances where the less I know the better."

"That might be for the best," Nevada said. "Enjoy your shower."

"I'm never going to not enjoy a shower again."

"Let me know if you drop the soap."

Candice firmly shut the door.

They just wouldn't listen.

Pike had taken the bus to a nearby village for supplies, and to check to see if any refugees had found their way there who needed to be relocated to Camp Esau. As his men brought in bundles of firewood, the doctor checked over the ailments of the villagers. Most of it was minor, treatable with antibiotics or Aspirin, but one boy was too sick to even be moved. With Pike and a few of his men as bodyguards, the doctor went to look him over. Parasites. So many that you could see them under the skin, like boils that wouldn't stand still.

He would need intensive treatment, immediate hospitalization back at the compound. The father, Jacob Lol Gatkuoth, wouldn't hear of it. He kept babbling and shaking his head and waving his arms, and all Pike could think was how you tried to be a Good Samaritan, but so many people didn't want to be helped.

God didn't say anything. He didn't have to.

"Get the crate," he told John Ladu. Another of his men went with Ladu; it was a two-man job.

Pike walked in front of the father. He ducked his head and lowered his voice, his words audible only within their shared space. He could've been taking confession. "Have you read the Bible, Jacob?"

Jacob was cowed by Pike's nearness, the muscular frame that towered over him and loomed on either side of his slender body. He only shook his head.

"That's okay," Pike said. "That's honest. Not many people have. Truth be told, there is a shitload of Bible and people only have so much time. That's why there's people like me. Reverends. We chop it down, we space it out, we let you... digest it. Like a meal—we cook it for you. You know what one of my favorite meals is? My signature dish? Matthew, Chapter 18. 'And Jesus said Truly I tell you, unless you change and become like little children, you will never enter the kingdom of heaven. Therefore, whoever takes the lowly position of this child is the greatest in the kingdom of heaven. And whoever welcomes one such child in my name welcomes me. If anyone causes one of these little ones—those who believe in me—to stumble, it would be better for them to have a large millstone hung around their neck and to be drowned in the depths of the sea.'"

Ladu and the other man came back. They carried a footlocker between them. It rattled as they walked.

"Do you know what a millstone is, Jacob?" Pike asked.

The footlocker fell to the floor with a thump that rattled the walls.

"It's part of a mill," Pike said. "Like a windmill. After a farmer harvests his grain, he takes it to a windmill. He places the grain on the bedstone, which is one of the two kinds of millstones. The other kind is the runner stone. That's above the bedstone."

Ladu opened the footlocker. The sound of the lid cantilevering down to the floor was far less violent than the first impact, but no less loud.

"It gets complicated from there—gears and stuff—but the gist of it is, the water or the wind turns a wheel, the wheel turns the runner stone, and the runner grinds against the bedstone to crush anything between the two. It breaks the grain down into flour. So if you want a lot of flour, and you want it crushed down really fine, you need two big, heavy rocks. You can get technical about it, but that's really what we're talking about. A big, heavy rock around someone's neck."

Ladu and another of the men grabbed Jacob's arms, holding him in place and forcing his head down.

Pike walked to the footlocker. His steps were deafening. "A large millstone would be about a ton and a half. Now this…" Pike reached into the footlocker and brought up a length of chain. "Chain… is about fifty pounds. Sixty-six of these around your neck would be like a millstone. And even that would be better than if you caused a little child to stumble."

He was putting the third chain around Jacob's neck when Alexander Tongan came to get him. "Reverend Dave, it's the women. Nevada is calling someone."

Pike gave a nod. "Route it through here." He eyed Ladu. "Keep our friend Jacob down there. Let him feel the weight of his decision for a while."

Outside, the sun beat down on him. He'd trained himself not to feel it, but his pale skin responded instinctively. Sweat swamped his drying clothes. They said Africa was the birthplace of humanity—the Garden of Eden. Maybe that was why it felt like it was so close to hell.

One of his men brought him a tablet. It showed a split screen of two video feeds, Nevada on one side and the other a shaking view of a luxurious bathroom. A bearskin bathmat lay across industrially monochrome black and white tiles, while pop art wallpaper overlooked a Victoria and Albert bathtub.

"I've always thought of porcelain as the poor man's marble." The man's voice came from behind the camera, accent sliding between Indian birth and British education. "That's why in *my* remodel, the toilet is Saint Laurent marble. *Whaaaat?* And the wastebasket you put your toilet paper rolls in? It's by John fucking Brauer."

"That's nice," Nevada said. "New medication working out for you? But really, I have a plane to catch—"

"Hold on, hold on, look at this!" The camera swiveled, aiming at a mirror. Pike recognized the reflection of the man holding the phone. Dubai billionaire Akbar Akkad Singh. "Why have a mirror over the sink when the entire wall can be a mirror? You can check out your knees, your belly, your shoes, all the stuff you just had to wonder about before—now you know! Oh, I'm sorry…" The camera jostled as Singh evidently sat on the toilet, then aimed it back at himself. "What was your thing?"

"The Twitter version? Went to Sudan, it blew up. I killed a bunch of people but they were all bad. Crashed a train, stole a tank, now I'm in South Sudan. Jacques is giving me a ride to the Ennedi Plateau."

Singh's face grew slightly more serious. "Oh, is that where my skull is?"

"That and maybe Cleopatra's tomb, not that you care."

"Who's Cleopatra?" Singh replied.

"I need you to pull some strings, make sure no one asks questions about the flight plan. People around here have this thing called no-fly zones."

Singh sighed heavily. "Well, maybe we'll get lucky and there'll be an elected official in Africa who's open to bribery." He laughed. "It's funny because the vast majority of them are corrupt. Oh, I'm in a good mood, so I'll do it. Look at this antique stool I picked up." The camera swung around to showcase it. "It used to belong to Denise Richards, and before that, James Garfield. Things got *crazy* bidding for that. Some ninja set eBay to increase his bid five bucks every time I bid on it. I spent like twenty seconds just before it sold going higher and higher, like 'Is this gonna be enough, is this gonna be enough?' Anyway, it came with a free checkerboard, if you need one of those."

"I'm good."

"Alright then, go get that bread. From me. For doing my bidding."

"Sure thing," Nevada said, and the transmission ended.

Pike took a comb from his back pocket and ran it through his facial hair, thinking. He was still thinking when John Ladu tapped him on the shoulder. "Reverend, Mr. Jacob has reconsidered. He'd like us to treat his son."

"I thought he might." Pike handed the tablet to Ladu. "God works in mysterious ways."

The airstrip was a simple slash of bare earth, like a well-trod footpath for giants, set next to the dimple of a dried watering hole. Candice supposed it was for navigational reasons. Now the pool only had muddy waters, with a ragged bunch of flamingos sputtering around in it. She and Nevada watched them circle and jab at each other. They squawked dismally and picked at the ankle-deep water.

"You know," Nevada said, "Africa is *nothing* like *The Lion King*."

Candice scanned the horizon. Still no sign of the plane, and it'd been an hour since Pike's men had driven them out here. "Don't start."

"I'm just saying."

"This is the cradle of humanity. The birthplace of mankind. You don't have any observations other than comparing it to a children's cartoon?"

Nevada coughed. "I was wondering why so many people were missing teeth, but I didn't want to be rude."

"It's a tradition. People remove their lower six and two upper front teeth."

"So why haven't you had them out?"

"I just like eating popcorn too much." Candice cracked a kink out of her neck. "It used to be so that they could still eat if they caught lockjaw. Now no one gets lockjaw—but people think it's cute. If a girl still has her teeth, they'll think she's a bad egg. No one will marry her."

"I had my wisdom teeth taken out," Nevada said. "Think that'd do anything for them?"

An insectile humming filled the air and Candice held her hand over her eyes to block out the sun as she scanned the horizon. A Grumman G-111 Albatross flew overhead. With the unlikely grace of a fat clown, it turned in an artful pirouette, cutting speed as its noise crested into a reassuringly diesel sound, like some old tugboat come to rescue a stranded ship. With more ballet, it dropped its landing gear and made its approach, growing into a big-bellied troll of a plane. It came down on the runway, jumped, skipped, and then its wheels caught hold of the surface and seemed to hold it down, the plane's momentum whining slower and slower.

"Shame," Nevada said, "You know Laurence Fishburne's gaptooth? I was about to do a whole bit on that making him a sex symbol."

Candice patted her sympathetically on the shoulder. "Maybe we'll get lucky and find you an open-mic night."

With Nevada leading the way, they walked up to the Albatross as it taxied to a stop, now revealing nose art like a sailor's tattoo. *The Flying Carpet*. Left of the fuselage, a hatch opened and the pilot, Jacques, dropped down a ladder. He had evidently shaved and bathed since Candice had last seen him in Khartoum, but you wouldn't have been able to tell by the scruffy facial hair or the rumpled suit he sported. The Frenchman gave healthy skepticism to the notion of his home country's sophistication, although perhaps not intentionally.

"Madame, mademoiselle, how you wound me!" He clapped his hands together, then clasped them to his heart still joined. "While I have slaved away on your behalf, thinking only of how I may more humbly serve you, you two have done nothing but become more lovely! Look at you! Visions of ravishment! While poor Jacques, he works fingers into bone. But oh, I forgive you. How can a mortal man stay angry when he sees proof there is still *la poésie* in this world of computers and… James Corden?"

Candice found herself smiling. "I am actually glad to see you, Jacques."

"Yeah, he grows on you," Nevada said. "Well, our Uber's here. Shall we?"

"*Ma chère*, please!" Jacques gasped. "Do not speak the German in the presence of my other lady love!" He blew a kiss to his plane's nose art—a tastefully offensive portrait of a belly dancer on a Persian rug—while holding out his other hand to help Candice onboard. She took it and was fairly yanked inside. For all his mannerisms, the Gaul had a firm grip.

On the inside, *The Flying Carpet* had the cramped but cozy spacing of an RV. Enough to put every airline Candice had ever flown to shame, but the luxury didn't edge into snobbery. She could've enjoyed a very nice flight stretched out in one of the bunks, except that every available surface was covered in potted plants. They sported leaves, branches, and flowers that made the Albatross's interior look like a greenhouse, with only a barely visible path leading back to the aircraft's bathroom.

Nevada came onboard, gratefully sucking in the plane's air-conditioned cool. "Hey, Jacques, not to cost you the Good Housekeeping Seal of Approval or anything, but when's the last time you vacuumed?"

"*Mon amie*," Jacques said ruefully, "this is a warzone we fly through, no? What could these people need more than a lovely flower, a fragrant rose, a bouquet of posies? And what could be more French than to provide that?"

"I don't know… Cheese?"

Candice reached into one of the pots, plucking a heat-sealed plastic baggie out of the soil. It was full of white powder. "What's this?"

"Sugar!" Jacques declared as Nevada took the baggie from her. "Everyone knows that sugar keeps a plant healthy and growing, like a woman's love, like a father's approval!"

Nevada ripped a hole in the baggie, raised it to her nose, and snorted some of its contents. A tremor went through her. "Good sugar," she wheezed.

Candice snatched the baggie away. "Is this drug smuggling? Are we drug smugglers now?"

"He's a drug smuggler," Nevada said. "I'm pretty sure you're only an accomplice. Maybe a moll."

In grabbing it from Nevada, Candice had gotten some of the powder on her hand. She frantically brushed it off. "I cannot believe you people!"

"*Ma choupette*, helping Easy on her quest is my solemn duty, my great privilege, my purpose in life—" Jacques hung his head. "But, alas, it does not pay the bills."

"Let's have this discussion in the air," Nevada said, pulling up the ladder from the hatch. "I'm going to feel really silly if someone shoots us with an RPG while we're discussing the manifest."

Jacques fell into lockstep with her, shutting up the hatch with a resounding clang. "*Mieux vaut prévenir que guérir.*"

With Candice trailing behind, they left the cargo compartment and went to the cockpit, which was thankfully less verdant. Jacques took up the pilot's seat and Nevada the co-pilot's. There were two additional seats behind those of the flight crew, and Candice sat herself behind Nevada.

"Guys, c'mon, this is the stuff they teach you in second grade. I'm sure there are a lot of people smuggling drugs around here, but if a lot of people were jumping off a bridge, would you jump off too?"

"British women," Jacques mused with fond resentment while putting his headset on. "They say they have the stiff upper lip, but oh, how those stiff lips move when they have something to say!"

He shoved the fuel mixture knob in, pushed the throttle inward, and otherwise brought *The Flying Carpet* from its idling rest to a full-throated roar of activity.

"Just for the record, I'm a Sudanese immigrant, so at least use the right national stereotype when you want to condescend to me," Candice said bitterly.

Nevada turned to look at Candice as she put on her own headphones. "It's going to be kinda hard to hear with the props going," she yelled over the sound of twin engines revving up. "You're gonna want to use the microphone on the headset. Cuts down on the—you get it." She faced forward again.

"Where's my headset?" Candice looked around. "I don't see another headset."

"That's too bad," Nevada said, switching hers on and putting it on Jacques's channel as she turned back to face front. "So how's your week been?"

They sped down the runway, eating up the same dust Jacques had kicked up on his approach. The flock of flamingos buzzed away from their sputtering, hiccupping horsepower. It made Nevada feel like she was back in Florida.

"Very nice," Jacques answered her. "Katy Perry released a new single. I think it's *très magnifique.*"

"Oh, we should play it later."

"*Oui.*" Jacques pulled back on the yoke, starting their take-off. "And the woman? You have, ah, conquested her yet?"

"Shut up, it's not even like that." Nevada looked back at Candice, who was gesturing somewhat wildly. Nevada gave her a thumbs up.

Inside the vacuum-sealed echo chamber of the cans, the din of the propellers was locked out, leaving only Nevada's own thoughts and Jacques's radio-transmitted voice. Without the headphones, vocal conversation was as impossible as a scientific debate with an anti-vaxxer.

"Oh, ho ho!" Jacques laughed. "But how you would like it to be, *n'est-ce pas?*"

"Shut up," Nevada said again. "Go surrender to something. Did you get my shopping done?"

"*Oui, oui*, I put it by the, how you say, *latrine*. Butch was happy to help."

Nevada smiled humorlessly, refraining from pointing out that latrine was how *he* say. "Was he now?"

Jacques hedged as *The Flying Carpet*'s climb continued, pitching Nevada's digestive system all out of whack—not to mention her eardrums. She should've stayed up later. A good yawn would've come in really handy right about now.

"He may have expressed some *dismay* that you lost his Wilson Combat Sentinel XL when he gave it to you as a gift."

"I didn't lose it!" Nevada said defensively. "I know exactly where it is—approximately. I found the *HMS Endeavour*, I think I can find his stupid—forget it, how's he doing?"

Jacques hedged some more, shrugging as eloquently as he would order wine. "He looked good. He's doing some, ah, ponytail sort of thing with his hair. I don't know, maybe it's the style now. But at least it's not dyed!"

"Small favors," Nevada muttered. She looked back at Candice, who was now ignoring her except to direct a backwards peace sign her way. Nevada smiled at her, turning away before Candice could see.

Jacques noticed the interplay, which Nevada noticed in turn as the Frenchman devoted excessive care to making some final adjustments on his instruments. "So now, if there is nothing going on between the two of you, then you would hardly mind if I…"

"*Casse-toi*," Nevada told him, taking off her headset.

Jacques leveled *The Flying Carpet* off and throttled back the engines, settling them down to a comfortable amount of thrust now that they had reached cruising altitude. The din inside the cockpit dropped off considerably.

Candice was quick to take advantage of that. "Is that duct tape?" she asked, pointing upward.

"Don't be ridiculous," Nevada said. "What kind of operation do you think we're running here? It's electrical tape."

———————◆———————

There was an expanse the size of a walk-in closet in the back of the Albatross; it adjoined the bathroom and the minibar and contained a Pelican case the size of a footlocker. Nevada got down on her knees, threw the latches, and opened it up with a hissing breakage of the airtight seal. Inside, laid precisely into scalpel-cut Kaizen foam, was a CZ Shadow 2 and a CZ Scorpion with an integral suppressor giving the barrel a blunt symmetry, several magazines for both rifle and pistol, and boxes of the 9MM ammunition both guns took. Nevada picked them up, verified they were empty, and did a few quick dry-fire exercises. The action was crisp and clean on both. She wouldn't expect anything less of a craftsman's tools.

Candice appeared in the doorway. There was a tall sunflower planted beside her and she gave it a desultory sniff as she watched Nevada.

"We've done more good than bad," Nevada said, not facing Candice, but letting the words ricochet back to her. She reached down the sides of the Pelican case, found a catch, and slid open a drawer. Inside, for perhaps the first time in his life, Butch had folded clothes. "Saved some kids, put money into a refugee camp. Don't go all Nancy Reagan on me now."

She picked out a reject pile of clothes for Candice. A cotton button-front shirt and boot cut twill pants from Columbia Sportswear, along with a vented Booney hat. Then, for herself, a short-sleeved work shirt, khaki cargo pants, and a *keffiyeh*. The sun hat just wasn't cute enough for her. An M-1951 field jacket would give her some protection from low-flying bullets. There was also a set of boxer briefs. They said BUTCH UNICORN on one side and had a picture of a rhino on the other. No way she was letting Candice wear those.

"Get changed," Nevada said, sliding Candice's pile over to her with a set of briefs on top. "We're nine hundred some miles from Ennedi, we're going at about a hundred and twenty-four miles an hour, so by my calculations—math is hard."

Candice didn't pick up the clothes. "It's not like we're traveling do-gooders. We left people to die in Sudan. Okay, fine, there was nothing we could do, but—I don't think we made it better."

Nevada opened a package of 9MM Parabellum ammo and started loading it into a magazine. "'Officer, I swear, South Sudan was like that when we got here.' We're not making anything worse here. How can we?"

"You have two guns."

"And we're going to Chad!" Nevada loaded the magazine into the Shadow 2, racking a bullet into the chamber and making sure the safety was on before setting the pistol down. "So if anything, we're making South Sudan less dangerous."

Candice stooped down to pick up the clothes. "What do you think we are, though? Survivors? Tourists? Mercenaries? How would you describe us?"

Nevada was loading another magazine for the Scorpion. When she spoke, her voice was as low and steely as the sound of bullets sliding into place. "You're an archaeologist. I'm a businesswoman. I'm doing a job; you're consulting. It is not my problem that the job takes us into bad neighborhoods. What is my problem is making sure we're both alive to enjoy the fruits of our labor." Nevada loaded the Scorpion, racked a bullet up into the chamber, and set the rifle aside. "That problem I am handling. If a plumber gets called into the Bronx, it's not his job to bring up literacy rates. He fixes the toilet and he goes."

"What if that's not enough?"

Nevada stood and faced Candice. For a moment, Nevada almost felt sorry for her. To be so beautiful and to know nothing about the world… maybe one led to the other. "You can't change the past. So why spend time there?"

"Is that what you tell yourself?" Candice asked, and Nevada thought of tiny feet kicking the inside of her womb—angry at her even before she gave him away.

"I don't *have to* tell myself that anymore. Here." She picked up a denim jacket and added it to the pile in Candice's arms. "Sheepskin lining. The desert gets cold at night. And Ennedi is in the middle of the Sahara."

Pike's truck rolled back toward Camp Esau, the frayed tire treads scratching like blunt fingernails on the burnt-out landscape. They barely raised a murmur of dust. In the relative cool of the afternoon, the children were taking a break from their studies, and as the truck came in, they ran over to greet it. Pike sat in the back, playing tail-gunner, but as they began to pass the horde of children, he stowed his rifle and instead came up with a soccer ball he had managed to get his hands on. He threw it out to the mob, starting an animated game that took up half their number. The truck came to a stop and Pike got out. The rest of the children had recently finished an English lesson and were eager to try half-formed knock-knock jokes on him. Pike gamely added 'who?' to each of their set-ups as he pushed the boy he'd taken from Jacob Lol Gatkuoth in a wheelchair.

Inside the compound, he immediately noticed the tension. His men with guns in their hands instead of on their straps. People hiding in their tukuls despite it being the middle of the day. Noises strangely muted, like there was a lion in the center of the village and no one wanted to draw its attention.

He delivered the boy to the infirmary, where Ladu started giving the doctor the patient's background. Neither bothered talking to Pike. They knew he had other problems. A nurse pointed to an acacia tree growing between two tukuls. The tall, thin trunk opened up like an umbrella into widespread branches, the skeletal twigs holding a green hint of leaves. Weaverbirds nested there by the dozen, their spherical nests hanging from drooping branches like Christmas ornaments.

A man sat in the shade, his heavy head sagging, his white robes splattered with the shadows of the branches looming over him. He looked not so much relaxed as like he had fallen from one of those delicately suspended weavings and was now cracked against the ground.

He made no move to get up as Pike approached.

"All are welcome here, brother," Pike said, coming to a stop just outside the shade. If the man attacked, Pike doubted he could cross the distance before Pike drew. "But we'd like to know who we're welcoming."

"Names are unimportant," the man said. "A conceit of men who seek immortality apart from Heaven. What's truly important is how a man serves God."

"Here's where I ask how you serve God."

The man shifted his weight and turned his head to the side, making himself more comfortable—seemingly bored. "Two women came this way. One black, one white. They killed Farouq al-Jabbar, the son of my lord. He wishes them brought to justice."

"Justice," Pike repeated. "Did he use that exact word?"

"We know they're not here. Tell us where they went."

"Leaving aside why I would tell you that, why would they tell *me* in the first place?"

"Not all things are told. Some are overheard."

Pike shook his head. "I wouldn't know where they are."

"Perhaps you're forgetting."

"Perhaps."

"There are good reasons to remember." The man took a pouch from his belt, setting it down on the scorched grass. One pull of the cord revealed the gleaming gold nuggets inside. "And other reasons. Some men serve God as messengers. Others as the message."

God didn't say anything to Pike. Nothing at all.

CHAPTER 3

As the hours passed, the buzzing vibration of *The Flying Carpet*'s engines and the stomach-roiling nausea of its speed passed into something almost comforting to Candice. The dangers of South Sudan were largely abstract; she hadn't actually experienced any of them. But being back on the trail of Cleopatra's tomb felt like returning to the shootouts and chases she'd been in after Meroe. Despite the hundreds of miles that separated Ennedi from the Khamsin, thoughts of the two boiled with coincidences, conspiracies, and wild imaginings. Her hands fervently rolled against each other as she remembered how close she had come to death and how easily the same could happen in Ennedi, in the middle of nowhere. She had thought she was safe in Meroe too…

In the cargo compartment, there were four litters set up bunk-bed style, two to a wall. Candice stretched out on one after moving the plants. She'd found pen and paper among numerous clipboards filled with the paperwork attendant to operating a modern-day tramp steamer. As she lay there, the vibrations of their flight working to both massage her tense muscles and electrify her nerve endings into buzzing neurosis, she tried to compose her thoughts and write. She'd put this off long enough. And having this brief, nervy respite in the sky collapsed down everything she was feeling into guilt over what *her parents* were feeling. What they would feel if she died out in the middle of the desert, thousands of miles from home.

She wrote, but only in hesitant scratches. It all seemed so impossible to explain. She tried to stick to the facts, making a dry accounting of events and her reasoning for continuing, but it all felt so heartless. This was her passion. She was doing what she loved, risking her life for an ideal—and all she could think was how unlikely it'd be that they would even get to bury her.

Nevada came out of the cockpit. She had mostly left Candice to her own devices on the trip, only passing through to use the bathroom and sticking to Jacques like they were some secondary school clique. Now she sat down in the bunk opposite Candice.

"Please tell me you're writing Naruto fanfiction," she said. "You're so close to being the perfect woman."

"Close," Candice replied, with sarcasm so stark it nearly crossed into friendliness. "I'm writing a letter to my parents explaining why I'm dead in case I get shot in the head."

"Ah." Nevada swiveled in her seat, putting her feet up.

Candice carved out another sentence, but doubted it would add any comfort to the message should the letter find itself delivered. "A wise man once said—if a man has not found something worth dying for, he is not fit to live. Here I am, trying to explain that I've found my something… and I'm not sure if that makes me sound more like an idiot or a selfish prat."

Nevada looked at her, dark hair streaking across her face, barely stirred by her breath. "Selfish people don't think they're selfish. They think they're—smart."

"And idiots?"

"I wouldn't know. I'm not an idiot."

Candice stared at the paper. The words jumbled and bunched together in front of her eyes. Empty platitudes, raw clichés, offering no comfort, nothing of what she felt. Her parents deserved an explanation of why she wasn't safe and sound; she could barely give them an epigraph.

"How do I make them understand?"

"They're not going to," Nevada said with blunt certainty. Candice looked at her again. She had picked up a loop of hair from off her cheek and was toying with it. "First of all, because parents just don't understand—as a wise man once said. And second, because you're their little girl. They're not going to care if you died curing cancer. They're only going to want you back."

"So what do I tell them?"

"There's only two things worth doing in this world. What you love doing and what you have to do. Tell them you're doing one of those. And if they don't like it, go to work at Wal-Mart and get hit by a bus. That'll show 'em."

"You're sure you're not an idiot?" Candice asked.

"I have no emotional investment in any aspect of *90 Day Fiancé*, so I like my chances there. We're two hours out, so if you wanna nap, now's the time."

Candice looked at her letter again. Reasoning, justifications, explanations—excuses. She ripped it off the clipboard and crumpled it up. Then she started writing again.

"You don't even care if they do a gay Bachelor?" she asked Nevada.

Nevada rolled out of her bunk. "I think that's my cue to leave." Before she did, though, she crouched down beside Candice. "It's too bad you're against casual sex. This would've been the perfect time to join the Mile-High Club."

"I've never gotten the appeal of that. Sex, but the only thing you can eat after is really bad food."

"You're British. Isn't that all sex for you?" Nevada booped the tip of Candice's nose. "Not for real-real, just for play-play."

With Nevada gone, Candice knew a kind of clarity she didn't want to think about too hard. Right or wrong, Nevada's Falstaffian way of looking at things had a way of boiling life down to its bare essentials. Candice wrote plainly, simply, working hard not to double-down on explanations or try to tell her parents what they wanted to hear. She managed to fit everything from salutation to signature onto the same page. Then, hugging the letter to her chest, she found a brief, dreamless sleep.

She came back to consciousness slowly, sparingly, lingering in a waking dream where her mother was singing to her, cocooning her with miles of ocean and song and love against anything that might want to harm her. Candice woke up with Kamasi Washington's cover of "Cherokee" washing over her, a velvety smooth jazz standard that was brassy enough to be memorable and tender enough to go down sweet.

Getting up, then stretching, she tiptoed around the potted plants and followed the music to the cockpit. The door was open, Jacques still piloting, Nevada in the co-pilot's seat. Neither of them noticed Candice. Nevada had an iPod, too old to be a phone but too new to have a display, connected to a port in the plane's control board. Candice supposed that with all the instruments, dials, gauges, and switches, one of them had to take an aux cord.

Jacques looked over the gauges, then out the windshield, and sighed. "*Sacre bleu*, the monotony of it all. The only thing worse than flying over the desert must be limping through it." He turned to the fuel gauge, tapping on it. The needle stayed resolutely on the right. "We still have plenty of fuel. If you like, perhaps we could find our way off the flightpath, arrive at a more suitable destination."

Nevada had a parachute on her lap and was going through one of its pouches, evidently checking it over. "Such as?"

Jacques took his hands off the yoke to flutter his fingers in the air. "Cambodia!"

"Cambodia?" Nevada repeated dubiously.

"We could get there with two, maybe three stops. Fine food. Friendly people. For pennies on the dollar, I could have a suit made that you would swear came from Saville Row. And, if you happen to have a young woman in your company, it would be far more conductive to showing her a good time than a dusty old desert."

Nevada shook her head. "You don't know women, Jacques."

"*Au contraire! Au contraire!* In this plane alone, I have—"

Nevada conceded the point with a surrendering gesture of her hand. "Well, you don't know this woman. We're going to Ennedi. We're finishing this."

"*Oui*," Jacques said wearily. But he gave the fuel gauge another regretful tap. It remained tauntingly full. "Tell me one thing. Only one—if there is nothing there... if we are too late... if this operation we are paying so much for ends up *tourner au vinaigre*... what will you do?"

"If I can't save my son? Then I'll know for sure there's no God." Nevada looked at him and offered a smile that could've been cut into her face with a razor. "You know how I love being right."

Jacques seemed to have nothing to say to that. He looked over the instrument panel again. "We're almost there. You should wake her."

"She'll be up soon enough." Nevada dug into her pants pocket, coming up with something that she tossed into Jacques's lap too quick for Candice to see. "Here."

"*Quoi—?*"

"Little something I took off Farouq al-Jabbar. It should be enough to convince the State Department that he was taken out. I hear the bounty's something like four hundred thou. That should keep you in snails for a while."

"In five years?" Jacques asked. "When they get around to paying?"

"I might not be around in five years," Nevada said simply. "And without me doing all the hard work around here, there's no way you're going to be able to keep flying. Besides, what else are they going to spend the money on? Healthcare?"

Jacques chuckled. "Very well. I will see what can be done."

"By the way, earlier, when you said Rosa Parks was just a big whiner who was too lazy to get out of her seat..."

"What? I did not say this—" Jacques looked up and saw Candice. "Oh, very funny."

Candice held out an envelope. "Here. My parents live in London. In case I don't... well, you know."

Jacques took it. "It would be my honor. But don't worry. Easy here doesn't let go of people that easily."

Nevada hung an arm over the back of her seat as she turned to look at Candice. "Tunes okay? I thought we could all mellow out a little before we get there. I can change 'em if you want."

"No, I like this song."

"Me too." Nevada nodded.

Candice dropped down into one of the back seats. "Is that a parachute?"

"Good eye, Cushing," Nevada said, closing it up again.

"What are you doing with a parachute?"

"Checking the reserve chute. You should do it every few months, just to be sure."

"But you're only doing that to be safe, right? We're not going to need them? I mean, the plane isn't falling apart?" Candice asked, watching Nevada unplug her iPod and wrap it in its aux cord.

"No, the plane isn't falling apart. It's doing just fine." Nevada tucked the iPod into a pocket.

"So we won't need the parachutes."

Nevada got up. "You should probably try this on, to make sure it fits."

"Of course it's going to fit, I'm not—" Candice found herself pulled up out of her seat and swooshed out of the flight deck. In the more open space of the crew compartment, Nevada helped her into the parachute's shoulder straps. "See, it fits. Can I take it off?"

"In a few minutes," Nevada assured her, belting the rig's harnesses around Candice's chest and thighs. "Once we're on the ground."

"You mean the plane. When we're in the plane and the plane is on the ground."

Nevada snapped her fingers. "You need a helmet! Jacques, where are the helmets?"

"We lost them back in Bora Gora."

Nevada faced Candice again. "Why would you need a helmet? In case you fall on your head? Don't worry about it, forget it, probably just a liability thing."

"Three minutes to the drop zone!" Jacques called back.

"I am not dropping in any zone!" Candice insisted. "We are landing the plane, yeah, and I am walking off it like a sane person!"

Nevada was putting on her own parachute. "And I would love that, I really would, but here's the thing: there's no airports near the Ennedi Plateau. The closest one is in N'Djamena, which is six hundred miles away, so to get to the coordinates, we'd have to get a car, and drive there, and then we'd need camels, and there'd be hiking—trust me, I Googled all of this. Much simpler just to…" Nevada clapped her hands together. "Drop down right on top of it. Just right down. Boom. Done."

"And then how the bloody hell do we get out of the place?" Candice demanded, although her brain felt like it was swelling with all the other concerns that she needed to voice.

"Don't worry about that. It's all taken care of. We'll have plenty of time to find the tomb, we'll be able to leave first thing, and trust me, the skydiving is not that bad. You'll be falling at a hundred and twenty-two miles an hour; it'll be over before you know it."

"When I splatter on the ground like a…like a bug getting hit with a newspaper!"

Nevada blinked at her. "I'd really rather you use the parachute. That's what it's there for."

"One minute!" Jacques yelled back.

Nevada indicated a metal loop on Candice's chest. "This is the ripcord. Deploys the parachute. When I pull mine, you pull yours."

"I am not pulling anything!"

"I thought you didn't want to die, *God*." Nevada tapped a lever on the side of Candice's belt. "If the parachute doesn't work, pull that. It's the breakaway handle and it'll get rid of the main chute. This!" Nevada pointed at another metal ring on Candice's left-hand side. "Reserve ripcord. Pull that after you pull the breakaway handle. It'll deploy your secondary chute, which, you know, just as good."

"You couldn't have explained all of this a few *hours* ago!" Candice demanded.

Nevada grimaced. "I didn't want you to freak out. Didn't you have a nice, relaxing flight thinking we were going to land?"

"I did!"

"And now, okay, sure, you're having a pretty bad five minutes. Excuse me—" Nevada pushed past Candice, walking to the entry hatch. "But it's almost over! All you have to do now is walk through a door. It's easy as falling off a log."

"*The log is fifteen thousand feet in the air!*"

"So, don't look down, ya big baby." She muscled the entry hatch open.

Wind howled into the cabin, slapping against Candice with a cold fervor. She immediately hugged herself against the chill, but it was nothing next to the view through the open door. She could see the curvature of the Earth, clouds on level with her body, the maze-like ridges of the Ennedi Plateau's sandstone rock formations—twisted and scoured by the desert into gnarled fingers with an unsteady grip on the air. They could've been reaching for her. Candice threw herself back from the hatch as far as she could.

"Fuck that! No! No! No! I'm not going! I'm staying with Jacques!"

"Ah-ho!" Jacques cried from the pilot's seat. "The French *joie de vivre* strikes again!"

"You're not helping," Nevada told him.

"There are some goggles in the… where we kept the thing?"

"What thing?" Nevada demanded.

"The red thing," Jacques said.

"Now you're helping," Nevada said, stooping under one of the bunks. "Could you circle around please?" She came up with two sets of goggles, lowering her voice to speak to Candice again. "It's cool, it's not like jet fuel is expensive. That's an urban myth."

Candice didn't hear her, startling as Nevada swept the goggles over her face. "You're going to throw me out of the plane, aren't you?"

"What?" Nevada asked as she put her own goggles on. "What are you talking about?"

Candice backed away from her. "You're going to throw me out of the plane!" she repeated, sounding more sure of herself. "You are! And you're probably going to quote some stupid movie while you do it, like— 'Get off my plane!'"

"Okay, *Air Force One* was a very fun thriller with a seminal performance by Harrison Ford, so let's keep things in perspective here." Nevada took a step toward Candice. Like a startled cat, Candice jumped away from her.

"You're doing it right now!" Candice insisted. "You are just about to throw me off the plane!"

"Candice…" Nevada spread her arms wide. "I wouldn't do something like that to you."

She stepped closer to Candice, who pointed violently at her. "Stop walking!"

"I'm not allowed to walk now?"

"Not when you're going to throw me off the plane!"

"I just told you I wasn't going to throw you off the damn plane!"

"Okay!" Candice raised her voice. "Now you *said it* and the way you said it *just shows me* how much you're going to throw me off the plane!"

"Well, now I want to throw you off the plane because you're being a little bitch about it."

"Did you hear that?" Candice's pointed finger ricocheted between Nevada and Jacques. "Did you hear her say it? She said it!"

"I can't hear anything," Jacques said. "We're at fifteen thousand feet and the door is open."

"A likely story!" Candice gave Nevada a fixed stare. "You are not throwing me off the bloody plane!" she growled, and immediately turned to march out the door and be swept away by the fall.

Nevada stared after her, making a minute adjustment of her goggles. She was speechless, though in the sudden roaring emptiness of the wind-tossed conversation, it was hard to tell.

"I do not understand women," Jacques shouted over the wind.

"Oh, like I do?" Nevada asked, and followed Candice out.

The descent—Candice remembered how it felt. Weightless, and yet she'd been more aware of gravity's pull than she'd ever been in her life. She'd felt motionless but experienced the wind rushing by her as thickly as flowing water.

She fell to her knees, her stomach buckled, and she vomited.

Beside her, Nevada took hold of her hair, keeping it out of the way as Candice's rebellious digestive system had its acrid way.

"Oh, shit, I touched your hair. Sorry, I know you're not supposed to do that with black people, right? Because it's supposed to be lucky? I didn't mean to take your luck. You can have it back."

Candice finished evacuating her gullet by spitting vehemently. "I've been joined to you at the hip for two weeks. How lucky do you think I am?"

Nevada handed her canteen to Candice, who not so graciously used it to wash the bitter taste out of her mouth. Then she guzzled all that she could to try and settle her stomach.

"You did a great job skydiving," Nevada said. "Especially for a beginner. You're like a natural."

"Let's just find this fucking thing." Candice poured a little more water onto her face and then wiped herself off.

They had landed on top of one of the famous rock formations that defined the Ennedi Plateau, a towering mesa of sandstone surrounded by spires, pillars, and arches of rock, protruding from the Sahara sands like the half-buried bones of some gargantuan skeleton. They almost formed a labyrinth, cordoning off the sandy paths below into jagged scars and looping circulations. Candice shook her head. No wonder the desert had inspired the idea of mummification. It certainly made her think of decay.

This wasn't an isolated outcropping. It was an entire forest of stone, spreading out below her and towering above for as far as the eye could see. Candice tried to imagine finding a dig site in all of this.

Beside her, Nevada was booting up her GPS. "Let's review what we know. Amanirenas. Warrior queen of the Kushites. She defeats the Romans in battle, takes the Aegis from them."

"Right," Candice said, "skull thing. Still not clear on that."

"Can we wait until the end before we ask questions?" Nevada demanded. She smacked the GPS unit with the heel of her hand to hurry it along. "The Kushites bury the Aegis with Amanirenas. Natural disasters. Pyramid is falling apart. They assume the Aegis is cursed. Give it back to the Roman-Egyptian tag team. *They* take it to bury it with Cleopatra in a secret tomb, leaving directions in Amanirenas's tomb. Directions which lead..." Consulting the GPS, she pointed to a mouth of the maze. "There, then..." She did some quick mental calculations, her lips moving wordlessly. It was a pleasant change. "To there, to there, to *there*, ending up right about..." She pointed to the sands of a clearing thirty feet down on their left. "There."

Candice squinted. "You mean the featureless expanse of sand and rock that's completely empty?"

Nevada looked down as well. "You're right. It does remind me of your social life. Sha-*zam*!"

Candice prayed that wasn't meant to be a catchphrase. "If I could point out a small flaw in your planning..."

"Why stop now?"

"What if we don't immediately find the tomb? We're in the middle of a desert the size of China with no provisions. What are we going to do for food? What are we going to do for water? What are we going to do for *toilet paper*?"

Nevada clapped Candice on the shoulder. "Oh ye of little faith... I had Jacques put together a supply drop with water, rations, tents, everything we need. He dropped it right after we jumped. It should be landing any minute."

Behind Nevada, a crate streaked down like a comet. It crashed into a stony plateau, its wooden slats instantly disintegrating, its contents scattering across the landscape like the entrails in a gory disembowelment. A sleeping bag exploded against the rock, disgorging its feathery down in a grace note to the otherwise total devastation.

Nevada turned around. "Hunh," she said. "Parachute must not've deployed."

Candice felt a vein trembling along the orbit of her eye. "Parachutes can just *not deploy?*"

"Well, this one sure didn't."

Candice's words leaked out of her like some trailing bile from her recent nausea. "I was just in a parachute!"

"So was I," Nevada reasoned. "And as a wise man once said, two out of three ain't bad."

"That's Meat Loaf. You're quoting Meat Loaf."

"You quoted Martin Luther King."

"What... *what is your point?*"

Nevada thought about it. "Okay, I had one for a minute there, but I lost it. You win this round."

Candice sat down, the rock hard and uncomfortable and overwarm, but she didn't trust herself to be on her feet. "I'm going to die of thirst with the biggest idiot in the world for company."

"Candice, please. If anything, you're probably going to starve to death. We can always get water from that well."

Candice followed Nevada's pointing finger down to a circle of limestone blocks, black with depth in the middle, shards of wood surrounding it like picked-clean bones that had once been a pulley system to pull up a bucket or waterskin. But...

"It's probably dry by now. That design is ancient. Ramses himself could've drunk from that."

Nevada blinked. "You don't say..."

In a flash, she was off, making her way down the steep incline like a mountain goat. Groaning, Candice followed at a much more cautious pace. By the time she was halfway down, Nevada was approaching the well and unfurling a length of rope from her pack. She took out a glow stick, which she cracked and then dropped down the well. Candice fell on her ass and skidded the last few feet to the sands. She had to windmill her arms to keep from being pitched on her face.

"There's something down there," Nevada said. "Some kind of cave. Perfect place to hide something. The well is the only landmark around here, but who'd be stupid enough to climb down a well?"

"You," Candice said dryly.

"Exactly!" Nevada tied the rope around a boulder, using it as an anchor. She gave several rough tugs to check the knot, then tossed the remaining length to Candice. "Here. Belay."

"What?"

Nevada picked up the other end of the rope and tied it around her waist. "Lower me down."

"Okay, stop, no. I'm a serious archaeologist, you're a grave robber."

Nevada looked up with her eyes glowing. "You remembered!"

"If there is something of archaeological interest down there, I should be the one checking it out."

"No, you should be up here, out of harm's way, while I make sure there aren't any death-traps." Nevada checked the Scorpion she had slung over her shoulder and the Shadow 2 she had holstered in her gun belt.

"There aren't any death-traps," Candice said definitively. "There are never death-traps."

"What about Meroe? You step on the wrong tile, big-ass stone crushes you. Classic death-trap."

Candice opened her mouth to protest that that'd been intended as a coronation ceremony, not a way to kill off tomb robbers, but it sounded bad even before she said it. "Okay, so there was one death-trap. That doesn't make it a *thing*. If you met an alien, would that make you believe in Santa Claus?"

"Of *course* you don't believe in Santa Claus." Nevada unslung her pack to lighten herself, then took off her Scorpion and leaned it against the well. "Lower me down. If there's anything down there—besides death-traps—you can take a look too."

With a sigh, Candice took off her jacket. "Your concern is touching," she said, wrapping a length of rope around her forearm to get a good grip on it.

As she begrudgingly lowered Nevada down the well, Candice wondered just how sincere Nevada was about any of this. As peeved as she was over being put on the sidelines, she couldn't think of a reason for Nevada to do it besides some odd, protective feeling. Like how Nevada had put herself between Candice and the lion. She'd even seemed—on second thought—truthful about not throwing Candice off *The Flying Carpet*.

She probably only needs me alive to translate, Candice thought in an enjoyable fit of bitterness. *Or because she wants to get a leg over. Or both. And she was definitely going to throw me out of the plane...*

"Hey, Candice?" Nevada called up, her voice echoing weirdly around the dank contours of the shaft. "Are there crocodiles in the Sahara?"

"Yes, actually." Candice leaned an elbow on the lip of the well. "West African Crocodiles."

"They aren't aquatic?"

"They are," Candice said. "But during the dry season, they stay in caves to keep cool and conserve energy. It's called aestivation."

"What's that?" Nevada asked.

"It's like hibernation."

"Then why don't you just say—never mind. Thanks for the 411," Nevada said. "That's like information."

"Wait, is there a crocodile down there?"

"I wouldn't say that."

The well opened up into an aquifer worn smooth by the water it had once held, maybe fifty feet from end to end and ten feet across. The sweeping, nearly organic curvature to the walls reminded Nevada of the slot canyons of Utah, a gulch with only weak illumination like a faltering spotlight coming down from the well opening. The light reflected off what water remained in the aquifer, throwing up ripples of firefly-like brightness from the ankle-deep water.

The chamber was almost entirely full of crocodiles, lazing in the water end to end and side by side, lazy flicks of their claws and twitches of their tails the only motion. Each one was easily eight feet long, their dappled-gold hides almost blending into the muddy waters. Helplessly, Nevada played the beam of her flashlight over the horde. Their vacant eyes shone back at her, filling the darkness. But at the far end of the chamber, Nevada could make out a change in the angles—a symmetry to the twists and turns the rock took that spoke to her of a human hand. She lowered the flashlight. The crocodiles were nearly carpeting the floor, but there was just enough space between them for a few careful footfalls to carry her closer to what she'd seen.

"Fuck that," Nevada said. Taking out her phone, she opened the camera app, aimed it at the far wall, and zoomed in as far as possible. With her phone in one hand and the flashlight in the other, she could scan the writing like she was right next to it. *Work smarter, not harder.*

One of the crocodiles rolled over a yard from her feet and Nevada drew back her boot. She dropped a hand to her holster. "Okay, buddy, let's just be cool. Keep in mind, I am in the market for a new set of luggage." With the crocodile motionless again, she went back to recording the writing. "Crocs. Why'd it have to be crocs?"

"Nevada?" Candice called down, her voice sounding different. "You, ah—y'all reckon ya almost dun down t'ere?"

Great, Nevada thought. *Now she's had a stroke.*

"Ah surely do would appreciate if it you wou' come back up'in here now," Candice continued in an accent that was possibly the worst thing to happen to the Appalachians since *Deliverance*.

The crocodiles were beginning to stir, disturbed by the flashlight. Nevada shut it off. *If Candice is suddenly talking like an X-Men comic, then maybe it's her subtle way of letting me know not everything is copacetic.* Nevada slotted the flashlight into her belt and dialed Jacques's number.

"Be up in a minute," she shouted. "I think I had some bad fish last night. Might as well dispose of it down here. Trust me, you don't want to be in range of this."

"Ah do appreciate that evah so much!" Candice trilled. "Yuppers, ah suh'ly do!"

I do not sound like that, Nevada thought viciously as Jacques picked up the call. "Frenchie, hey, miss me yet? I need a favor."

———◆———

Candice stared down the muzzle of a gun. In the inky blackness inside the gun barrel, she could barely make out the glint of the chambered round's tip, ready to fly into motion with a little pull and a spark of ignition.

There were two of them, one holding the gun on her, the other covering the well. Only one had brought a gun, a pistol. The other had a club, a long metal pipe that was either rusty or covered in dried blood, but he'd picked up the long gun Nevada had left. They were both, as far as she could tell, Sub-Saharan Africans, dark-skinned and in ragged clothes, with sandals cut out of car tires. They were obviously militia, comfortable with violence to the point of having favorite kinds, but there was no uniform. Just ash smeared across their faces, coating all of their features in white except for a red blotch on their foreheads. Candice swore she felt the madness coming off them, smelled it like some physical malady rotting inside their bodies.

She couldn't stop shaking. It wasn't even for her own sake. She pictured them shooting Nevada, or using that club on her, and that was worse than her own life being in danger. She couldn't imagine being killed herself, but she could imagine Nevada being hurt. Stupid, brave, cocksure Nevada…

Long seconds butted up against each other. The one with the pipe seemed to be getting his grip tighter and tighter. The other held the pistol on her coolly, almost unthinkingly, and the longer it was pointed at her the more unnerving it became. Didn't it require some *thought* to be violent? Some feeling of rage or hatred or… something? He seemed to be prepared to kill her on the flip of a coin.

Then, out of nowhere, the gun barrel was pressed against her forehead. "Enough waiting!" the gunman shouted. "Come up now or she dies!"

"Okay!" Nevada called, her voice echoing up the well. "I'm coming up!"

As she climbed back up the rope, Nevada cursed herself at least half a dozen times for not doing a better job of protecting Candice. She'd left the Scorpion right *there*, but trust *her* not to think to pick it up and use it. Which was on Nevada, really, since she knew Candice was no gunslinger— but honestly, how hard was it to pick up a rifle? And be aware of your environment? Sneaking up on someone in a desert, honestly.

Nevada clambered over the rim of the well, stifling a groan as her own Scorpion was aimed at her by some Coachella reject. It was unprofessional, that's what it was.

She looked at Candice, hiding her own dismay behind a carefully constructed poker face. "You okay?"

"They snuck up on me," Candice said. She bit her lip in embarrassment. Under other circumstances, it'd actually be pretty cute.

"I can see why. They're pretty short. I don't think these guys have ever ridden a roller coaster."

The one with her Scorpion took Nevada's pistol from her holster, keeping her covered with surprising professionalism. The other had what looked like a Steyr-Hahn Model 1911; more proof that Africa was the junk drawer for the world's firearms. He kept it trained on Candice. The message was clear: misbehave and she gets it in the brainpan.

"So what can we help you with?" Nevada asked, looking between them. "If it's applying foundation, I think you're doing a good job already."

"Where's the skull?" Steyr-Hahn asked.

"Top of the spinal cord, can't miss it."

The one with the Scorpion stepped in, clamping his hand down on Nevada's bandaged upper arm. She gritted her teeth, dark explosions popping before her eyes as pain erupted from the wound she'd received back on the train all the way down to her trembling fingers. Nevada was driven to her knees. When he backed off and she was able to look up, Steyr-Hahn had his pistol pressed against Candice's head.

"*Where?*"

"I don't know," Nevada said. "It's not down there."

Steyr-Hahn racked the slide of his pistol and pushed it up against Candice again. It was a cliché, but the way Candice cringed...

Nevada held herself still to keep from shaking with rage. All she could do was hope the glib hero act would get through to Candice and convince her there was nothing to worry about.

"You have ten seconds," Steyr-Hahn said. "One..."

Nevada pulled herself back onto her feet. "Don't waste my fucking time, manlet. You might as well shoot me now because it's not here and if I could pull it out of my ass on a moment's notice, I wouldn't be here. I'd be doing Vegas."

"Where is it?"

Nevada groaned and rolled her eyes. "If I knew that, what would I be doing here? But I'll tell you what, give me back my guns and take a walk, we'll call it a day."

The one with the Scorpion laughed.

"Oh, you like that one? I've got more," Nevada said. "What's the difference between your mouth and a litterbox? My cat won't take a shit in a litter—"

He stepped in and slammed his hand against her bandage. More pain. More dark explosions, bigger, blacker. Nevada blinked and realized, *oh, I'm on my knees again.* The slimy feeling on her arm was probably her ripped stitches oozing blood.

"Just as much fun the second time," she muttered.

"We kill them," Steyr-Hahn announced. "We kill them both."

"That's cool. Except for the part where you get killed a day later." Nevada scooted herself back to lean against the well. "Seems pretty obvious that you're trying to find the treasure by birddogging us. Guess what? We can't find it if we're dead and you can't find it because you're just fucking idiots. So when you go to Nazir al-Jabbar, you can tell him you don't have the skull and you ventilated the only two people who had a chance in Zeus's fuckstick of finding it. It's cool. I'm sure he'll understand—"

"We don't work for the Khalifa."

Nevada blinked. "Say what now?"

"We serve at the pleasure of the Lady Tendai."

"Oh," Nevada said blankly. "She a blonde?"

"Remember on the train?" Candice asked. "The guy said that name before he tried to kill you."

"Oh yeah, right." Nevada snapped her fingers. "She was horrible in that last Spider-Man movie!"

"You said that last time," Candice said.

"And it's still true!" Arms crossed over her belly, Nevada tapped the wrist of her left hand with her right forefinger, hoping Candice would get the message. *Play for time...* "Or did they release a director's cut where their female lead isn't an antisocial shrew played by a Disney Channel pod person doing a third-rate impersonation of Aubrey Plaza?"

"You will—" Steyr-Hahn began.

Candice cut him off. "Just a minute, just a minute," she said. "Let her do this. If you're going to kill us anyway, we might as well get this settled first."

"Thanks, babe," Nevada said. She could see *The Flying Carpet* cresting the horizon. Turning to the soldier holding her pistol, she drew him into the conversation. "You know Spider-Man, right? I mean, there've been about twelve different movies. You gotta know Spider-Man."

"I... I have heard of Spider-Man," the man said, caught off-guard.

"Great! Perfect!" Nevada chopped her hand at him as she addressed him. "Who's he married to?"

The man looked to Steyr-Hahn for confirmation. "Who's he…"

"He's married to Mary Jane Watson," Steyr-Hahn said.

Nevada pressed her hands together and briskly bowed to him. "Thank you, thank *you*. One last question…" She could see *The Flying Carpet* growing from a black dot into a scale model of itself. It was like someone was turning up the magnification on a microscope. The plane grew in leaps and bounds. "Can you describe Mary Jane Watson to me?"

Steyr-Hahn shrugged a bit. "She's a… beautiful woman with red hair—"

Nevada shot up. Steyr-Hahn and the man with the Scorpion both aimed at her. "Boom! That's my point right there." They lowered their guns a little. "First thing you think of. She's one of the most famous redheads in comics. And what does *Spider-Man: 'Homecoming'*—" She made air quotes. "—do? They give her brown hair!"

"But…" the man with the Scorpion said. "She is a redhead."

"Who? Mary Jane Watson? They don't even call her that. They call her Michelle now. And apparently her last name starts with a J, we don't even know what it is, but her nickname or something is MJ, and that's supposed to be some big twist since she doesn't look or act anything like the comics. In a movie that's *called* Homecoming, because it's supposed to be so much more faithful to the comics than the Andrew Garfield movies, but *nope*. They're even less accurate! Flash Thompson is now a bitchy nerd who wants Peter's slot on the academic decathlon team. Drink that in."

"But…" Steyr-Hahn sounded lost. "Flash Thompson is a jock who bullies Peter Parker. Everyone knows this."

"Everyone but Kevin Feige, apparently." *The Flying Carpet* was making its approach now, the sound of it beginning to build. Nevada raised her voice and spoke quicker. "I don't know why you would do Peter Parker in high school, again, *for the second time*, if you're going to get rid of all the classic high school plot points and replace them with generic YA novel bullshit. I guess we don't need the *Daily Bugle* and J. Jonah Jameson. I'm not done yet, this subject is not closed, but Candice, our Uber's here!"

She threw herself to the ground, Candice doing the same as the Albatross roared overhead, an apocalypse of sound and violent wind. Nevada pulled her keffiyeh up over her face. The soldiers took potshots at the plane, but even if they could hit it, it was immediately impossible to aim through the thick cloud of sand that *The Flying Carpet* kicked up in its wake.

Nevada scurried for where Candice had been standing, but she must've moved. The sand in the air and the cloth screen Nevada held over her face made it almost impossible to see. Then the soldiers started firing wildly. Nevada hugged the ground, digging her feet and hands into the sand to break up her outline. She had only a few feet of visibility. She doubted the soldiers had much more.

She heard Steyr-Hahn bark something in an African language she didn't recognize; probably an order for the one with her Scorpion to hold his fire. In this haze, it'd be as easy to shoot friend as foe. *Almost makes me glad I'm unarmed*, Nevada thought wryly.

Coming up into a crouch, she edged her way toward the sound Steyr-Hahn had made. The sand was still in the air, dissipating by degrees, but Nevada pulled her keffiyeh down anyway. She'd need to see as clearly as possible, even if it stung her eyes. The noise of *The Flying Carpet* dwindled into the background. All she could hear was her own heartbeat as it surged against her ribcage like a mad prisoner trying to break free. Her eyes were tearing up. Nevada wiped at them quickly. She could see movement in the dark cloud ahead of her. It could've been the wind beginning to cut into the haze, or—

The soldier saw her, his silhouette resolving itself into a darkened shadow even as he turned to level her own carbine at her. Nevada dropped down to her belly as the hacking reports of the Scorpion told her he was firing. Bullets buzzed like hornets over her. She clambered on her belly across as much ground as she could cover. Simple instinct was that if someone wanted to punch you, stab you, shoot you—they would be standing up to do it. That's what he would be looking for, an upright human figure in all the dust. Nevada stayed down, *low low low*, and circled around him. The sands were starting to part now; torn away as the wind pulled at them. He was aiming where she had been, trying to pick her out of all the swirling particles like he just had to look a little closer, a little closer—

Nevada came up behind him. He still had the Scorpion's sling across one shoulder as he held it in his arms. Nevada took hold of the shoulder strap and pulled *hard*, like she was bringing a dog to heel. The carbine whipped back and smashed against the soldier's face as the momentum of the pull yanked him off his feet, dropped him on his back. Nevada caught the Scorpion in her hands as she stood over him. She supposed the sporting thing to do would be to toss it aside, let him get to his feet, and have a nice honorable fistfight.

She brought the heel of her boot down on his face. His nose broke like an eggshell and the next time he exhaled, his mouth was full of blood. The sands were almost settled now, turning silhouettes into reality, reality into a world painted with orange sand. She reached down, took hold of the soldier's shirt, and hauled him to his feet, holding him in front of her like a human shield.

Steyr-Hahn had his arm around Candice's throat, his elbow jutting out from below her chin, her body in front of his as he aimed his 9MM at Nevada. Nevada pulled her guy against herself. He might've been short, but he was big enough that Steyr-Hahn couldn't shoot her without hitting him.

"I can break her neck like you'd step on a twig," Steyr-Hahn threatened.

Nevada could feel the Shadow 2 that his buddy had taken off her. The soldier had stuffed its barrel down the back of his pants and now it was pressed between their bodies. She folded the Scorpion's stock inward with her chin, then wrapped her arm around her hostage, holding the Scorpion's muzzle up against his jaw. "I can shoot you and him in the fucking face, but that seems rude."

"Drop the gun!"

"No, you!" Nevada replied. "This is a CZ Scorpion, babe. I can shoot through this guy, through her, right into you!"

"Don't shoot through me!" Candice protested.

"I'm not going to shoot through you," Nevada said quickly. "I'm just saying it's an option."

"Like throwing me off the plane was an option?"

"*I didn't throw you off the damn plane, Jesus Christ!*"

"Enough!" Steyr-Hahn roared. "Drop your gun in ten seconds or I shoot your friend."

"You shoot her, I shoot him!" Nevada said, jamming the muzzle up into her hostage's gullet.

The hostage said something she couldn't understand.

"What'd he say?" she demanded of Candice.

"He said don't shoot him."

"Oh."

"Go ahead and shoot!" Steyr-Hahn shouted. "The Ash Army will gladly give our lives for the Lady Tendai! Ten!"

"You're bluffing."

"Nine!"

"I don't think he's bluffing," Candice said.

"Eight!"

"You're going to look real stupid when you finish counting down and you're just fucking bluffing."

"Seven!"

Candice raised her voice. "Easy, he's not bluffing."

"Six!"

"Okay!" Nevada yelled. She dropped the carbine and wrapped her left arm around the hostage's neck. With the chokehold locked in, he was in no shape to break free. Behind his back, she reached down to the Shadow 2. "Now let the girl go."

Steyr-Hahn grinned. "Let him go first."

Nevada eased the Shadow 2 up in her right hand. Her hostage tried to say something. She tightened her left arm around his neck. "You're making me think I can't trust you, guy."

"Five…"

Nevada jammed the Shadow 2 between her hostage's shoulder blades. "You know, back in the States, we'd call this a Mexican Standoff. I've never been to Mexico, but I have been to Texas. That's where I learned to catch a bullet in my teeth. You know the trick to catch a bullet in your teeth?"

The Shadow 2 popped like a champagne bottle, its bullet punching through the hostage's body. It was lost among the splatter of the exit wound for a lethal moment—Nevada could've sworn she saw a glint of it—then it was gone, zipping over Candice's shoulder and into Steyr-Hahn's face, where it ripped open his cheek and chiseled out a row of his teeth. Steyr-Hahn gagged, sunlight hitting the back of his throat.

"Guess not," Nevada finished.

In a spasmodic jerk, Steyr-Hahn returned fire, bullets burrowing into Nevada's shield. She could feel the momentum of the impacts walloping his body, breaking against her own like the tide. In one smooth motion she brought the Shadow 2 out from behind the hostage and slid into a firing stance, the pistol extended out along her straightened arm like a knight's lance, lined up with the world and the horizon and Steyr-Hahn's center mass. As Candice broke away from him, slipped out of his slack grip like a cake of soap in the shower, Nevada fired again, exploding his chest, heart's blood bursting out of his front and running down his back. He rocked on his heels, no strength left to hold his pistol up, and it dangled from limp fingers as he stumbled back, crashed against the well behind him, and somehow miraculously held his balance leaning against the rock. The gun dropped to the ground.

Nevada tossed the hostage aside to enjoy his new orifices, walked up to Steyr-Hahn, and saved some ammo by giving him a shove. "Remember the Alamo," she said as he plummeted fifty feet down to meet his new neighbors. The crocodiles would like the company.

"Nevada!" Candice yelped, and she turned to see that the other guy was still alive despite a half-dozen holes airing out his chest cavity. She fired from the hip, quick as a gunslinger, and took a chunk out of the man's waist. He didn't go down, didn't go into shock. He was scrambling for the carbine that Nevada had dropped, clawing for it like a man climbing out of hell, and Nevada could only think how lucky she was that she'd discarded the two in opposite directions.

She'd fired two shots from the Shadow 2, which left fifteen in the magazine. She kept pumping them into the man, one after the other, but he kept going. Wouldn't lay down and die. *The Ash Army will gladly give our lives for the Lady Tendai.*

He wasn't moving when Nevada fired her pistol into slide-lock. Bulletproof vest. Had to be.

"Is he dead?" Candice asked.

"Let me check," Nevada said. Dropping the Shadow 2 into its holster, she walked up to the body, picked up the carbine, set it to full-auto, and let him have another magazine in the face. "Yes."

She slung the Scorpion over her back and grabbed the body by the hands. "Get his legs."

"Why?" Candice asked, somewhat reasonably.

Nevada was already dragging him toward the well. "We can't just leave him up here."

Lugging the body to the well was a far more formidable task than it looked. In life, he'd had the elfin slenderness of a runner, his weight certainly less than two hundred pounds. But in death, he easily weighed twice that. Candice was out of breath when they came to the well. She and Nevada shared a glance, then they hurled the body over the side in perfect sync.

Sweating, Nevada dropped down against the well, which was just high enough to offer some shade to a sitting body. Candice joined her, as wrung out emotionally as she was physically.

Curiously, though, she didn't feel the same rawness of tender nerves she'd had after her first nightmarish meeting with Easy Nevada, when they'd both nearly starred in an Al Qaeda beheading video. She hadn't been able to stop shaking for so long that she didn't *remember* stopping. Even in the past few days, Candice could recall catching her hands trembling at odd moments.

But this wasn't like that. There was a tremor in her fingers, but it hadn't caused her to let go of the corpse. She felt it as abstractly as if it were happening to someone else. And already it was receding, drawing away from her like the sea at low tide. Candice couldn't explain it. Was she that jaded to the violence already? Or did it have something to do with the calm confidence she'd felt as Nevada had been her usual annoying self to their captors?

Candice still thought Nevada had little-to-no idea what she was doing, but she didn't think the woman would allow her to come to harm. She wasn't sure if the long-lost son story was real, but she believed that Nevada would fight tooth and nail to defend someone once she'd decided they were in her little tribe. And apparently Candice qualified.

If she was going to be hurt, it was going to be after someone had stepped over Nevada's cooling corpse. That probably shouldn't have been reassuring. Yet her hands weren't shaking anymore.

"You sure you're okay?" Nevada asked, looking at Candice oddly. For maybe the first time, Candice wondered what was behind those soft blue eyes. What Nevada was thinking, feeling—covering up with all her quips and constant motion.

"Close enough," Candice said.

Nevada nodded. "Good. I don't think I have time to give you a sensual back massage, although it would be very therapeutic."

"How you can be horny when you just killed two people?"

"One person. I'm pretty sure the crocodiles got the other."

"There are crocodiles now?"

"Uh-huh." By happenstance, the two of them had sat down within arm's reach of where Nevada had dropped her backpack. Nevada took the canteen from it. "More crocs than a Wal-Mart."

"You didn't hurt any of them, did you?" Candice asked, preemptively aghast.

Nevada took a swig of water and gulped. "No, no. What do you think I am, some madwoman who goes around blowing away every bit of wildlife I see?" She held the canteen out to Candice.

"Killed two people," Candice reminded her. "Just now."

"Let's call it one and a half." Nevada got up and quickly sorted through their belongings. It took a second to check out her hurt arm and she seemed pleased; apparently it wasn't as bad as it looked, though Candice blanched at the bruising. Next, she unloaded and reloaded the guns, tucking the empty clips away in her backpack. The soldier's Steyr-Hahn she picked up, safetied, unloaded, and put away in the backpack as well. Finally, she slung one of the pack's straps over her shoulder.

"Good to go?" she asked Candice.

"I'll bloody well walk away from here," Candice replied. "Not that there's anywhere to walk to."

"Oh ye of little faith."

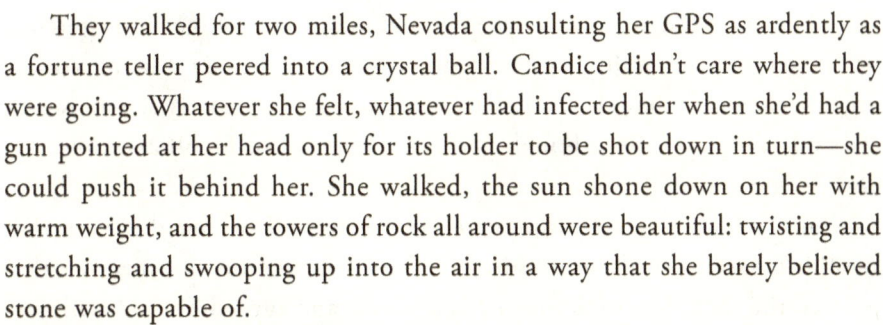

They walked for two miles, Nevada consulting her GPS as ardently as a fortune teller peered into a crystal ball. Candice didn't care where they were going. Whatever she felt, whatever had infected her when she'd had a gun pointed at her head only for its holder to be shot down in turn—she could push it behind her. She walked, the sun shone down on her with warm weight, and the towers of rock all around were beautiful: twisting and stretching and swooping up into the air in a way that she barely believed stone was capable of.

There was still a part of her that resonated on a frequency with the killing and the danger—like she'd hit her funny bone, or her ears hadn't popped on an airplane. She didn't know what to call it: weakness? Compassion? Sanity? But she was getting better at mollifying it. Motion. Exertion. Opening her eyes wide and drinking in the world around her, letting it remind her that she was still alive, still around to enjoy all this. She was sweating and her leg muscles were starting to burn and she was alive. Not dead.

Suddenly Nevada hugged her from behind, an arm across Candice's collarbone, hand patting her sternum enthusiastically. "Here we are!" she declared. They'd emerged from a slot canyon into a clearing of plateaus with a megalith the size of an apartment block in the middle. As impossible as it now seemed, flowing water had carved out the bottom of the stone, leaving it looking like some massive tree trunk that a lumberjack had taken several cleaving whacks at. Nevada pulled Candice into the grotto, where the shade was such an instant relief from the glaring sunlight that it made the space seem refrigerated.

"Pull up a rock," Nevada said, sitting down on one of the several waist-high boulders that littered the ground.

"What are we going to do here?" Candice asked, following Nevada's advice. Sitting down after the long, hot walk felt almost orgasmic. "Hail a cab?"

"All good things to those who wait." Nevada checked her watch. "Give it a few minutes. You'll like this next bit. It's been running through my mind all day."

"Right." Candice knew better than to doubt Nevada, but at the same time, she was hardly in a mood to indulge the woman's dramatics. She looked around, taking in the almost subterranean space that Nevada had led her to.

The cleft in the rock was maybe two and a half meters high, and stretched under that tall ceiling for several yards before stopping in a disconcertingly organic sweep of stone. It reminded Candice of some primary school health class on fallopian tubes, though perhaps that was just Freud at work from beyond the grave.

Then she saw something, some exotic *texture* to the darkness that shouldn't have been there, a misapplied brushstroke on the shadows that painted the rock. She took out her cell phone and turned on its flashlight.

In the light from her two-year-old Nokia, she saw a frail link to a past as distant as the bottom of the sea: maroon and white and ochre paint shaped into cows, camels, lions—engravings depicting men and women that were long dead—cave paintings tens of thousands of years old. Nothing as simple as art, but an attempt to physically capture the raw power of life, nature, the things that dwarfed primitive man. Less writing and language than dreams put down on the only thing that could hold them, some shamanistic, hallucinogenic *thing* invoked like a spell and shattered by time into a million possibilities. Was it decoration? Magic? A diary? After millennia, there was nothing to glean from them but the truth of their existence—the feeling that eons ago, there had been people who had wanted others to see what they saw and feel what they felt. They hadn't been so very different from her.

Candice let out a shrill, unbelieving laugh.

"Yeah," Nevada said. "I thought you'd get a kick out of that."

Candice turned to her. "You… knew?"

"It's on the tour." Nevada glanced up at the paintings. "Fuck, that guy's dick is huge."

Candice looked, then shrugged. "It's probably just the lighting."

Nevada shared a laugh with her. For a moment, she looked weirdly *herself*—not putting on an act, not trying to look cool, but more like a rambunctious kid enjoying a small prank or dumb joke. Then Nevada coughed and dug into her pocket.

"Here," she said, taking out her phone. "More nerd shit for you."

"Seven years in university and I end up a grave robber," Candice lamented.

"It's only robbery if you take something. This is more like grave tourism."

It was a video. Hieroglyphics—possibly a whole dig site down that well. Candice opened her mouth to insist on going down there, then saw the crocodiles. It could wait. Still, she made a note to herself to save the GPS coordinates. This place could be an archaeological treasure once they had the army of assassins off their back.

"What's it say?" Nevada asked.

75

"Play it again," Candice said. She took out a notepad and pen, translating as Nevada held the phone for her. "Do you always rely on some brainiac to do the hard work for you?"

"It's how I got through high school. But don't worry, I made it worth their while. And mine. Something about a girl in glasses…"

"Makes me glad I wear contacts." Candice stopped writing. "Okay, rough translation, but this first line is distance markers, same as back in Meroe. Exactly the same. It's either an accounting of their journey up till then or maybe directions on how to get back. This next line is presumably where they went next. West approximately two hundred and fifty miles, to something called the Doubled Tree. Probably some local landmark they could use for navigation."

Nevada scoffed. "They already went eight hundred miles to get *here*. That wasn't far enough?"

Candice looked at her. "Maybe they didn't want your skull coming back."

Nevada massaged her temples. "Okay, two hundred and fifty miles west, that's…"

"Middle of the desert," Candice said. "Borkou."

"And we have to find a burial site no one else has found in two thousand years." Nevada huffed a sigh. "What we really need is a guide. Someone who knows the desert like the back of their hand, knows what this Doubled Tree is, and knows how to do the whole Lawrence of Arabia thing." Nevada looked at her phone again. "I'm going to check LinkedIn."

"Actually, I may know a guy."

Nevada glanced at Candice as she took out her own cell phone and booted up a map. "You? You know a guy? Candice, you don't know anyone."

"Yeah," Candice said to herself, "Faya-Largeau, that's right on the way to Borkou. Well, it's a place in Borkou—"

"Is he reliable?" Nevada interrupted.

"Reliable? Yes. Sure. He's my granddad."

"Your grandfather?"

Candice nodded.

"We're going to the middle of the Sahara, with two separate groups of crazy people trying to kill us, and you want to bring your pop-pop along?"

Candice stood, stretching, relieved to find that her feet felt much better after their rest. "He's a Hadendoa nomad. He's been traveling the desert his whole life. Right now his tribe's in Faya; I'm sure he'll help us out."

"What, because he's family?" Nevada gave Candice a condescending look. "This is why America invented Thanksgiving, so we'd all remember that families suck."

"We've been writing letters back and forth since I was old enough to read. He's a good guy. And what's your big plan for getting there? Take the bus?"

"I'm an American, Candice. I don't take public transportation." Nevada sighed in frustration. "The treasure's never just in someone's junk drawer. You always have to put together three pieces of a map and travel to the middle of nowhere and solve a puzzle with stones—those guys on *Storage Wars* have no idea how easy they've got it. Okay. Guess who's coming to dinner."

"It'll be fun!" Candice insisted, feeling an unaccountable excitement. She hadn't spent much time with her grandfather, but when her father had taken her to visit him, he'd always struck her as the kind of highly competent sage that gave the elderly a good name; far from the doddering old man Nevada seemed to expect. "You'll like him. He has a scimitar."

Nevada grunted and nodded, staring at the cave paintings.

"So we do still have to get to Faya-Largeau," Candice said. "It's two hundred miles."

"Yes."

"And we're in the middle of the desert."

"Yeah."

"Are we just going to walk?"

"Candice, I already said I'm American. Be patient; I've thought this through."

"Well, which is it: are you American or have you thought this through?"

Nevada shook her head and looked over the cave paintings some more. It was twenty minutes before she spoke again, and then it was just to say, "I think that's Waldo in the upper right corner."

Candice pushed her over into the sand.

It was then they heard the phlegmatic slap of running feet compacting sand into more sand. The sound was echoing through the rocky clefts and

Candice felt the odd animal suspicion of something she could hear but not see. Then the footfalls resolved themselves into a marathon runner rounding the corner. He wore running shoes, running shorts, and a tank top as bright as a robin's breast, with name and number signposted on the front of it. A Camelbak was slung over his shoulders.

Nevada waved her arms in the international signal for distress. He kept going at his cool, collected pace, a white man, skin burnished with sweat and suntan, until he was next to them. He regarded them smilingly, but with concern in his eyes. "You ladies alright?"

"Sure," Nevada said, before Candice could even think of answering. "We just got a little lost. We're tourists."

"Free climbers," Candice said, remembering that Ennedi was a popular rock-climbing destination.

Nevada quickly shot her a look. "Rock-climbing tourists," she confirmed, turning back to the runner. "You must be with Le TREG. I don't suppose there's a bus stop or anything around here, is there?"

"No, but I'm about…" the runner consulted his watch, "three hours out from the next checkpoint. There should be some people there."

"Three hours," Candice repeated dismally. She tried to make herself like the sound of it. "We can do that. I've been meaning to jog more."

"Yeah, jogging," Nevada agreed as noncommittally as possible. "Hey, marathon man, I've always wondered: What happens if one of you guys has a stroke when you're running or something? They can't have doctors *everywhere*, so what happens? Do you just *die*?"

"No, no…" He showed them an armband with an electronic device the size of a beeper on it. "This monitors my vital signs. If there's a big change, they send a medevac chopper to airlift me out. But that probably won't happen. I'm in pretty good health."

"Yeah," Nevada concurred, sizing up his biceps. "You on the Paleo diet?"

"No, can't say that I am."

"Too bad. Cavemen were really well-known for having six-pack abs." Nevada eyed the monitor. "You know what's really interesting about that? It looks almost exactly like that thing."

She pointed over the runner's shoulder. He twisted around to look, and the moment his head was turned, Nevada had one arm around his throat, the other collaring his arms, tying him up in a Gordian knot as she choked the breath out of him.

Candice felt like a slot machine as she watched, spinning through confusion, shock, anger—she settled on acceptance as the runner faded out. Nevada lowered him to the ground and checked his pulse. She gave a resounding nod.

Candice slumped back down onto a rock. "You know what your problem is?"

Nevada checked the device on the man's arm. A light changed on it and it let out a shrill beep. "After seven therapists, you'd think so, wouldn't you?"

"You've got no bloody patience. You can't wait to land the plane; you have to jump out of it. You can't jog a few miles, you have to call in a helicopter! If you could only sit still, be bloody motionless for a *minute* without plotting or planning something—you're going to get someone killed, rushing around like the whole world's on fire."

Nevada stood up. She had a way of seeming taller sometimes. More present in the world than she usually was. "They called me. He's in the hospital. My son is in the hospital. They don't know if he's ever going to leave it." And just like that, she was ten inches tall. "I am so close to having done everything I can. He can't die without me having done everything. I don't want to talk about it. I don't want to be asked how I'm holding up or how I'm doing or how it makes me feel. I don't matter. I have this piece of me that was cut out and I thought it would do better that way and now it's dying. Away from me, it's dying. I don't have time."

Candice couldn't think of what to say. It made a perverse kind of sense—even in vulnerability, Nevada kept her off-balance. She weaponized her own pain and used it to shield herself from criticism. Candice resented it even as she wondered if Nevada knew that she was doing it. And most of all, she was frustrated at not knowing what to say, even more frustrated at Nevada letting her off the hook and not expecting to discuss it at all. She'd always felt so emotionally mature, an old soul, wise beyond her years— Nevada took that and gave Candice a punch to the guts just to prove she wasn't ready to defend against it.

"You'd probably be better off," she finally said, "if you had someone to ask you how you're holding up. How you're doing. How it makes you feel. And if you let them?"

"I think I'm pretty far past healthy life choices by now." Nevada gave Candice an almost pleadingly chipper look. "New Year's resolution. I'm going to learn Italian and aim for not being emotionally dead inside."

Candice forced a laugh, but silence fell anyway. Just them, the unconscious body, and the wait. It was a quiet arrangement. Nevada brooded like she was nursing a wound. After five minutes, Candice found the waiting unbearable—the irony, somewhat less so.

"So what is it with you and *Spider-Man: Homecoming*?" she asked.

Nevada gave her a weak smile. "To answer that, I'll have to ask you to journey back in time with me. The year is 2007 and an underappreciated classic by the name of *Spider-Man 3* is about to be released…"

As Nevada talked, Candice stared up at the clear blue sky, at the barely existing clouds in wisps of papery white. Somewhere up there was the helicopter, and she waited for it like her ancestors might've waited for rain.

Had they waited for rain? She knew the Sahara hadn't always been so big—Lake Chad to the southwest had once been an inland sea, a million square kilometers instead of a mere thirteen hundred, but did that mean her people had once been farmers, shepherds? She'd gone to Sudan in the first place to reconnect with her heritage, but she had less idea of what it was now than ever. It couldn't be the Khamsin, who seemed determined to turn her homeland into nothing more than a vision of their own warped ideology. But then what was it? Beja nomad? Dinka pastoralist? The more she brushed up against her supposed people, the less of a connection she felt to them—to anything. Did that mean she couldn't connect to them or they couldn't connect to her?

Maybe at Cleopatra's tomb, she would have her answer. She'd always believed that everyone had something of themselves in the past. Maybe her piece was out there in the Sahara, waiting for her to uncover it.

"And that's why all the Tom Holland movies are a cinematic apology tour by Marvel for not using Miles Morales," Nevada concluded confidently. At some point, she'd started smoking. The cigarette hung out of the corner of her mouth like she was a soldier biting the bullet during surgery. "Which they shouldn't apologize for, since Miles Morales sucks."

"Hot take," Candice said distantly.

"No one even knows what his origin story is," Nevada argued. "Batman, parents died. Superman, planet blew up. Miles Morales, it's a fucking mystery. We know more about Wolverine's backstory. *Wolverine*."

"So we're definitely talking about this, yeah? Yeah."

Above the sound of Nevada's opinions—which seemed to go on and on like a clown pulling a handkerchief out of his sleeve—Candice heard the steady chop of a helicopter's rotors through the air. She looked up while Nevada tapped some ash off her cigarette. There was the helicopter, sidling down into the clearing Nevada had brought them to, the sound of its rotors becoming a bellowing cacophony that Candice covered her ears against. The wake slalomed down the surrounding rock to stir up the sand. Candice turned away from the instant sandstorm pouring in from the outside world, her elbow raised to ward off the grit from her face. Nevada's cigarette was snatched out of her fingers. The helicopter seemed to downshift, idling its engine, or at least the rotorcraft equivalent.

"Have you ever heard of someone hijacking a helicopter?" Nevada asked in the relative quiet.

The helicopter's cabin door slid open, and two medics emerged with a stretcher. They wore street clothes instead of a uniform but looked like they knew what they were doing.

"No," Candice said as they approached.

"Good. They shouldn't be expecting it then."

Nevada got up and, while the medics checked out the unconscious runner, approached the helicopter. Candice trailed after her. One of these days, Nevada was going to get herself shot. If nothing else, Candice wanted a good look when that happened.

Nevada leaned against the helicopter's fiberglass nose, looking up at the pilot. He wore a professional-looking flight jacket and had woolly hair and a beard that went down to his collar.

"English?" Nevada asked.

The pilot said nothing, barely even paying attention to the medics transferring the downed runner onto their stretcher.

Nevada pulled open her jacket and displayed her holstered gun to him. "American English," she clarified.

The pilot looked at her with a bit more interest, giving a confused but nonthreatening spread of his hands. "What the hell?"

Nevada dropped her jacket shut again. "Relax, this question's multiple choice. Either I hijack this chopper and you give my friend and I a ride to Faya-Largeau, or—" She dipped a hand into her pocket and came up with a clear plastic baggie. The contents were white. "I hijack this chopper, you give my friend and I a ride to Faya-Largeau, and you forget what we look like."

The pilot craned his neck closer to the canopy. "What is that, a dime bag? It'd be worth my job, flying you to Faya. What do you take me for?"

"A businessman," Nevada replied. She took off her backpack, held it in front of herself, and pulled open one of the compartments.

More baggies. Candice had seen piñatas that were less full.

The pilot rubbed his chin as he thought it over. "Fire one round so they know you've got a gun."

Nevada flashed Candice a grin. "Just gotta know how to talk to 'em."

Then she took out her gun and fired it into the ground.

Five minutes later they were airborne, on their way to Faya-Largeau.

"I can't believe we left those medics behind," Candice said, watching them dwindle away in the maze of Ennedi rock. "It is literally a marathon back to civilization."

"Don't worry. With help, they'll probably recover from being the kind of people who run marathons."

———◆———

Pike watched a Range Rover lead a caravan of buses and vans to Camp Esau. A half-mile out, the buses turned off the road to wait as the jeep continued on. It pulled to a stop in front of him, and through the windshield he saw John Ladu matching his stare. It only took that eye contact for both of them to be assured: Pike that the caravan was safe to let into the compound, and Ladu that the compound was ready to take on new refugees.

Yesterday, negotiations between the government and rebel forces had resulted in one of the factions surrendering. Their child soldiers would be given over to NGOs like Pike's, to feed and house until they could be reunited with their families. For many of them, that wouldn't be possible. But it was better to be an orphan than a soldier.

Pike clapped his hand triumphantly on the hood of the jeep. Ladu shut off the engine and got out, waving the first of the buses forward. It rolled up, stopped, and the children began to disembark. Some of Pike's female followers were already there to put a friendly face on their new home. The refugees were told to set their weapons on a tarp, where God willing Pike would be able to put them to use against some of the bastards who had given them to the kids in the first place. In exchange, the children were given fresh clothes. Their green fatigues—most crudely hacked up to make them short enough for children—would be burned.

Some internet assholes had donated a hundred child-sized shirts with Cookie Monster on them, saying 'Me So Hungry.' It was the kind of thing that made Pike wish he could work to civilize the home front with the same brutal efficiency he did this place. They weren't so genteel back home; they just found different ways to be savage. But with the offending words painted over, he could make use of the shirts. The boys would look like kids again.

It wasn't a happy occasion, not a celebration, but Pike took satisfaction in it. He imagined it was something like a surgeon would feel after stitching someone up. There was still blood and bandages, but the cutting was over. The healing could begin.

He could feel God's hand on his shoulder.

He looked over at Ladu. The man was gray-faced, looking out at the procession of children with blind eyes.

"What is it? You look like you just found your son playing with toy ponies."

Ladu looked back at him. His eyes were bloodshot. "Nazir al-Jabbar sent someone to talk to you. They wanted to know where the girls went."

Pike felt his belly pitch and yaw like a ship in a storm. "I didn't tell that man anything."

"But they know *you know*," John insisted. "Not al-Jabbar. *Her.*"

"Who?" Pike asked.

"They were at the exchange—I had to talk to them—they wouldn't let us leave until I talked to them."

"*Who?*" Pike demanded.

"Lady Tendai." Ladu shook his head. It looked more like some invisible beast was biting down on his neck, shaking him, than like he was doing it. "You can't say no to her, David. You can't do that."

"You told her where they went?"

"Yes. But… she said that wouldn't make any difference." His voice was small now. Lost. "She said all of us were going to die but you. God wouldn't let you die. God wants you to suffer."

Pike laughed uneasily. "Now why would God want a thing like that?"

"I asked her. I didn't say no, but I asked her. And she asked me if I would like it better if that wasn't what God wanted. If God couldn't stop it."

Pike heard an engine roar. One of the vans had broken formation—it drove for the camp so fast that its tires clawed at the road, jostling and shaking the vehicle like it was an animal too angry to hold still. Ladu just stood there, the strongest man Pike knew looking like he'd walked a million miles and no longer had the strength to lift his hands an inch.

Pike moved, pulling his rifle from its sling and lifting it to brace against his shoulder. Maybe he should've thought about it, considered his options, but it was like that van held all the doom he'd seen in Ladu's eyes. He fired through the windshield, his shots chiseling away the image of the driver, and without a master the van swerved to the side. Children ran out of the way, his people shepherding them to the sides, and the van impacted the bus, rocking the massive weight all along its suspension. Both came to a rest, deformed from the impact, shaken heavily, but intact. The van's tires scratched impotently at the ground but were unable to push any momentum into the bus.

Pike's men formed on him instinctively, all but Ladu. Guns held at the ready, they advanced on the van. He could see through the bus's window that the children still inside were getting up, and Pike told himself it would only be bruises and a few broken bones. The only life the driver had taken would be his own, when he decided to try to mess with Pike's church, his family. It would all be like any other day in South Sudan. A little gunfire, a little craziness, but nothing he and God couldn't handle.

The bomb going off was nothing like the 15,000 pounds of TNT it would later be found equivalent to—not to Pike. To him, it was like a hole being cut in the world, a shroud being torn, and through it, there was only hell.

CHAPTER 4

IN NEVADA'S EXPERIENCE, SECURITY IN third-world countries was one of two extremes. Either fanatical, hair-trigger paranoia or the twenty-four-hour siesta of low-morale forces. Fortunately for her, Faya-Largeau proved to be the latter. The intrusion of an unauthorized flight into their airspace was resolved with the pilot exchanging words with air traffic control for maybe thirty seconds. From what Nevada could grasp of his Arabic, he'd simply offered a bribe, and one that seemed insultingly low at that. *Talk about your budget vacations.*

From the air, Faya-Largeau wasn't much to look at. A six-mile sprawl of low, mudbrick buildings built with desert anonymity. When Candice and Nevada walked through it, they could've been anywhere from Tangiers to Iraq. Nevada stowed the Scorpion in her backpack but wore the Shadow 2 on her hip. No one took any issue with it, except maybe Candice, who kept pointedly looking away from it like Nevada was smoking weed in a mall.

With the Beja camp at the outskirts of town, scavengers, peddlers, artists, and merchants had come from both sides to turn the neutral territory between city and nomads into an open-air bazaar. The city-dwellers had set up wooden stalls or sold their wares through windows in the buildings. The Hadendoa simply tied up their camels and unpacked their saddle bags onto pieces of cloth on the sand like they were having a picnic.

There was loot straight from the crisis in Libya, goods and jewelry sold for safe passage or offered in obscure trade, alongside home appliances still in the shipping boxes they'd been in when they were swiped from the docks in Egypt or Nigeria. Cassette players and VCRs, along with good old-fashioned Chinese knockoffs of anything and everything.

The hawkers were an ungodly combination of mosquitos, try-it-free salespeople at the mall, and Mormon missionaries. Nevada put herself between Candice and them, projecting a studied don't-fuck-with-me vibe. Behind them, the mob of street merchants closed up again, everyone auctioning fake Rolexes and real elephant tusks to everyone else. Candice looked at the whole thing with a tourist's curiosity, like she might actually be interested in any of this crap. If she put any more blood in the water, Nevada worried they'd have to shoot their way out.

"Your guy picked a nice meet," Nevada commented acidly, eye-fucking a vendor into submission before he could try any harder to sell her a blender.

"Easy to find, you have to admit. Here! The races." Grabbing Nevada by the hand, Candice pulled her to a roped-off circle, one of two. The one on the left had gathered a ring of white expats around it, watching as horses were put through their paces for prospective buyers. On the right, camels were doing the same, but were infinitely more ungainly. Ridden by young boys, they galumphed back and forth, barely able to walk in straight lines for any amount of time before swerving into each other. It was more a demolition derby than a race.

"Fast camels," Nevada commented, then caught scent of delicious barbecue among the sweat, body odor, and animal flesh that mingled together to form the smell of the market. Nearby, meat and vegetables were roasting on a grill, drawing clouds of black flies like neon signs. "I haven't eaten all day—what is that?"

"Slow camels," Candice replied. When Nevada broke off to go to the grill, she called out "Where are you going?" in a perfect teacher's pet voice.

"You're so clingy," Nevada chided her, pulling out a wad of Central African francs.

Candice followed her to the grill, where Nevada paid for a hunk of meat that turned out to be as gamey as chewing gum—made of grease.

"We're supposed to wait at the camel market," Candice insisted.

"Now we're waiting at the camel market with food." Nevada let Candice lead her back to the racetrack. Mangy dogs darted in and around the crowd, adding to the confusion as they barked at the camels, who responded as theatrically as pro wrestlers. The children riding the camels were hard-pressed to keep them from breaking out into the audience, but none of the adults in attendance intervened. Nevada guessed this was as much floorshow as it was auction.

"Someday I really am going to give up on figuring you out," Candice said. "I really am."

"What's so tough to figure out? I like money, I hate getting shot, and I'm a very good lay. What more do you need to know?"

"Why'd you swipe the cocaine? You were all gung-ho about being a drug smuggler this morning."

"I don't think—do I look like someone who thinks these things out? I just thought you kinda got shanghaied into all this and you deserved a vote."

Candice leaned against one of the posts holding the ropes up. "And obviously Jacques would vote for his plan, since it was his plan, so you—"

Nevada grabbed hold of one of the ropes. She leaned back and let it take her weight. "Yeah, I just liked the thought of knowing you were wrong about me."

"Or you wanted to seduce me."

"Honestly, Candice, look at me. I'm super cute, I have big arms, and this is me not even wearing lipstick. If you're not seduced yet, that's on you."

Candice laughed. "Of course, we could've buried the drugs. Now that pilot's just going to sell them."

Nevada pulled herself upright. "You haven't met many pilots, have you? He's going to have a crazy weekend and that'll be the end of that. Besides, throwing them away? Terrible for the environment. We'd end up with a bunch of raging cokehead camels."

"I don't think there'd be much difference," Candice observed. Inside the ring, two of the camels were spitting at each other. "Of course, now you're going to have to explain to Jacques how you're nice all of a sudden."

"He's got the reward money for Farouq coming in. He'll be fine. And do *not*," Nevada insisted with sudden stringency, "go around telling people I'm nice. Maybe that's okay in Britain, but if word of that gets out in the States, people start getting on you to put your groceries in tote bags and give blood."

"So you let everyone think you're a cast-iron bitch?"

"Works for New Yorkers."

Candice chuckled harshly. "It's so cute how you Americans think New York is hardcore. New York has *Broadway*. Now, spend a weekend in Glasgow—"

"Honey bean, I'd spend a weekend with you anywhere." Nevada gave Candice her most charming grin. She could see that Candice barely eked out being amused over being charmed. "So, grandad. How will we know him?"

"CANDICE CUSHING!"

The voice boomed out like a foghorn. Nevada's hand automatically dropped to her gun at the loud noise, and she turned to see the crowd clearing, making way for the man who had spoken. He was elderly but vital, a youthful energy melting away the years. He could've passed for a man in his forties. His body, tall and spindly, was clad in the traditional white jellabiya and dark vest, but instead of a turban or skullcap, he had a New York Yankees cap on his head. His beard fell down to his chest, as white as city snow, with soot tracing down his chin and the edges of his mustache. A similarly unruly head of hair, bushy and fuzzy, was partially pulled back into a bun behind his head, while the rest fell down his back in graying dreadlocks a foot long. On his face, round spectacles set in wide, old-fashioned frames gave him an even more scholarly, chipper air. A scar wrapped around his head and covered one eye like a set of half-glasses. It looked like it had been made by a sword.

He repeated the call, arms thrown wide into the air as he marched down the corridor the crowd had made for him. "My darling granddaughter!" he announced to everyone present, and in near-earth orbit. "Gone from me fifteen years! I see her again now!" Now within range of Candice, he clapped his hands on her shoulders. "I see my son's eyes looking at me once more. Subhan Allah!"

A scattered chorus of *subhan Allah* went up among the crowd as Candice's grandfather hugged her. Evidently unsatisfied with this, he drove one fist up into the air while keeping his other arm around her.

"Subhan Allah!"

"*Subhan Allah!*" the crowd echoed back loudly, and he finally released Candice and turned to Nevada.

"And you must be her associate," he continued in a smaller, almost reedy voice. Nevada held out her hand and he trapped it in both of his, shaking it effusively. "It is no less a pleasure to meet you, of course."

"You speak very good English for a Hadendoa," she said, a little suspicious.

"Thank you! You speak very good English for an American!"

"Ha!" Candice burst out.

Her grandfather appeared to politely not notice. "You may call me Usama."

"Oh," Nevada said, chagrinned, "like the—"

"Like the famous terrorist, yes." Usama shrugged. "Naming a child, it is, how would you put it—a 'crapshoot,' yes?"

"Yeah," Nevada agreed. "I had a roommate once named John Tesh... maybe I should call you by your last name."

"Yes, that would be Hussein."

"Nevada," Candice said gently, "maybe we should be considerate of our host's feelings, since he's going to be helping us so much?"

"Of course!" Putting an arm around each of them, Usama led them through the crowd. "I have consulted the tribal maps since I received your message, and there was once a doubled tree in the area you spoke of. Apparently a cedar tree was growing in the desert when a bird dropped a seed on top of it. The seed grew into an acacia tree, with roots going down the cedar tree."

"An epiphyte," Candice said, nodding. "That makes sense. It's rare, but not unheard of."

"You Googled that," Nevada said accusingly. "Usama, can you take us there?"

"It would be my esteemed pleasure! As the Qur'an says, 'and to parents do good and to relatives, orphans, and the needy. And speak to people good and establish prayer and give *zakah*.'"

"Thanks, Usama." Nevada saw a sheen of refracted sunlight shooting through the dusty market and craned her neck to see a row of cars lined up for sale alongside a herd of goats. Patting Usama on the back, she broke loose from him. "You two catch up. I'll get us a ride."

"Do you even speak the language?" Candice asked.

Nevada held up a wad of bills. "They speak mine."

"That's not going to be enough for a car," Candice said.

"I know. You have money, right?"

Candice unthinkingly reached for the money belt under her clothes. "For emergencies."

"This is an emergency. I'm cash-poor."

"What does that mean?"

"I'm poor," Nevada said bluntly. "C'mon, what else are you gonna do, give it to charity?"

"You are a charity." Candice took a stack of bills out of her belt and slapped it into Nevada's hand. "And I want change!"

"So did Barack Obama, and look how well that worked out." Nevada flicked through the stack. "Wow, this is enough to get Julia Roberts to kiss you on the mouth."

"Go!" Candice insisted.

Nevada disappeared into the crowd and Candice wheeled on Usama in disbelief. "You see what I've been dealing with."

Usama gave a sage nod. "I have traveled the deserts all my life. I would very much like to do so once more... with air conditioning."

———◆———

With nightfall, the Beja in the marketplace concluded their sales and their haggling, rolling up their merchandise or packing up their purchases for the pilgrimage back home. They lugged their unsold straw mats, wool rugs, and firewood like they were carrying prized possessions.

There was something... invigorating about being in their midst as Candice walked with Usama. Though she doubted many of them had Dinka blood, she still recognized much of her family in their features, the way they moved and carried themselves, even the way they talked. Maybe they didn't speak her native English tongue, but this was a sound that felt as familiar as an old nursery rhyme.

And yet, the men wore jellabiyas identical to Usama's, and the women conservative but colorful thawbs. How could Candice not feel out of place in her shirt, pants, and sun hat? It made her think of the expression 'stranger in a strange land.' But was she a stranger in a familiar land or the other way around?

The Beja camp was a good half-hour's walk from the city, and as they walked, she updated Usama on how her parents were doing, and he told her about her various cousins, nephews, and nieces among the Hadendoa. Candice was unable to find it very interesting, not after she'd seen two men shot under the same sun that was now setting—one more way she felt like she didn't belong even when she *should*. But she let Usama talk and gave every indication of listening. He was a man who liked to talk about his family. She wouldn't deprive him of his chance.

Around dusk, they reached the camp, an elaborate colony of tents. They were made of everything from palm fronds to goatskin to straw mats, with even some modern nylon tents looking ridiculously colorful among the darker shades of the traditional tents and the brown sands. The women were tidying up for the night, bringing in dates that had dried in the sun and solar panels that had finished recharging batteries. Now, with those batteries plugged in, lamps came on and radio music fluttered through the campsite.

Usama led Candice to his *arish* at the center of camp, a portable house made from the split trunks, stems, and fronds of palm trees, with mangrove poles holding it together. A *barjeel* soared up to catch cool, clean air from high above the hot sands and funnel it down into the arish, making it sweetly temperate inside. Once they'd stepped through the wool flaps protecting the interior of the dwelling, Usama seated himself under the barjeel and groaned happily to have its manmade wind blowing the desert heat off him. It was so much how any old man would rest his tired bones that Candice felt a swell of affection for him. There were so many grandparents in the world; he was hers.

Usama opened his eyes. "When I heard word of your coming, I prepared a feast that I think even your Western tongue will agree with. Behold." He gestured to a brass tray with stubby legs holding it off the floor. "Pizza from the Domino's. One large pepperoni and one large cheese. With Pepsi alongside."

"Thanks," Candice said, taking a slice. She sat down across from him on a cushion—one of the sparse furnishings in the room; its opulence was in its size. "It wasn't very nice, playing a joke like that on Nevada."

"What joke?" Usama asked as he prepared tea in welcoming ritual. He used an electric hot plate to heat it, but other than that, it was the oddest preparation Candice had ever seen. For a filter, he lay grass across the opening of the coffee pot.

"Usama Hussein?"

Usama spread his hands equivocatingly. "It is bad luck for a Hadendoa to give his true name to a stranger. Everyone knows that."

"You couldn't have picked a better name?"

"What name could be better at putting that funny look on her face?"

Candice smiled despite herself. "Oh, you two are going to get along famously... You know she's doing the same thing?"

"Her name is false?" Usama asked, leaving the tea alone to brew.

"Easy Nevada?"

Usama reached for the pizza boxes. "It seems a reasonable name for an American. I am told there is a very famous woman whose parents named her Lady Gaga."

"Easy's not quite that unlucky. I've heard her real name."

Her grandfather pried a slice of pepperoni pizza away from the pie, looking distrustfully at the trail of cheese it left behind. "This Domino gentleman is a strange baker... A Hadendoa, of course, only tells their true name to family."

"We're not that close," Candice assured him, thinking privately, *Thea and I.* Taking that thought back and keeping it to herself. "The only thing we have in common with family is that she drives me insane."

"I try now to think about something which I do not care about which still has the power to drive me insane." Usama took a bite of pizza. "*Bismillah!* What a fine way of delivering cheese!"

"It's pretty good," Candice agreed.

"And if your friend is keeping her name a secret, we are doubly lucky."

"Guess that leaves me the odd man out."

"Odd man...?" Usama shook his head. "You are not an odd man..."

"It's an expression," Candice said quickly. "It means... you and Easy both have something in common, and I don't. Because I use my real name."

"Then Candice Cushing is your real name?"

Candice dropped her hands to her lap. "Oh, we're getting philosophical?"

Usama sprang up, pouring the tea into two demitasse cups and adding pepper to the brew. "Your name now is Candice Cushing, because you were taken to a strange land when you were small, and that name was easily spoken there. But now you are here in the desert, and the land of the name Candice Cushing is far behind you. Perhaps there is another name you are known by here. Something you were called as your mother and father dreamt of you, long before you had flesh or blood."

Candice took the full cup he offered her, wondering if this was some put-on, but he was too intense to write it off as a joke. "If there is a name like that, it doesn't apply to me. Candice is the only name I've ever known."

"But is it the only name you ever *will* know? You have heard where this name, Candice, comes from, yes?"

"*Kandake*," she said, and took a sip. Somehow, his eclectically prepared tea tasted wonderful—perfectly suited to her taste buds. "It's the word for 'queen' in Nubian."

"You talk like you have forgotten the desert. But it is in the very sound of your name."

A gunshot rang out. Frigid water poured into Candice's veins. It brought a fearful tremor with it, but also propelled her into motion. She hurled herself into Usama, knocking them both to the ground and covering him with her body as two more gunshots cracked, sharp as ice breaking. Then she heard brake pads hissing against tires, dragging some huffing, chugging beast of a car into stillness.

Usama laughed richly. "Not that I would cast aspirations on a woman's figure, Candice, but you are getting a bit big to hug me so recklessly."

"I thought…" Candice trailed off as she got up and helped him to his feet without another word.

"Merely a car backfiring," he said. "You're becoming skittish. Most definitely in need of tea."

"Yeah," Candice said. "Skittish." She remembered how she had cast her eyes about, looking for a weapon in that moment of panic. She hadn't felt skittish.

Outside, the sun's heat had been replaced by the moon's icy glare. Candice hugged herself to keep warm. Many of the Hadendoa were unimpressed with the commotion; others had formed a crowd at the edge of camp surrounding a white Land Cruiser. It was the kind of vehicle that looked like it had taken steroids at some point—a clunky, boxy thing that could've come out of Mad Max, with scratched paint, pitted metal, cracked glass, and threadbare tires.

Candice caught the breath she'd lost. "Please tell me you did not pay money for that thing."

"Barely." Nevada leaned out of the driver's window, elbow resting on the doorframe. "I drove a real hard bargain."

"What, did you promise to drop it off at the junkyard for them? It doesn't even have a rearview mirror."

Nevada looked at the stump where one should've gone. "You worried about tailgating?"

Candice put her hands on her hips. "How old is that? Was it even built this century?"

"It's not the years, honey, it's the mileage," Nevada told her.

"What's the mileage?"

Nevada paused for a long moment. "The tires are very nice," she finally said. "These are great tires... radio works..." She turned it on. A quavering broadcast of Maître Gazonga's mellow "Les Jaloux Saboteurs" played. Nevada bopped her head slightly. "Of course, I'm guessing your grandpa might not be much for modern music. I don't know much about Islam, but I figure it works on the same basic principle as that town in the eighties that wouldn't let Kevin Bacon dance."

"You nailed it," Candice said.

"Thanks. Anyway, I decided to make a playlist with songs we could listen to that aren't about drugs, drinking, or sex." She reached down and opened the console between the driver's seat and the passenger's seat. "So I got a bunch of Hank the Cowdog tapes."

"We're going to be listening to a bunch of children's stories about talking animals?"

"In Texas!"

"I know you like to condescend to me, but isn't this taking it a bit far?"

"I do not condescend to you," Nevada said firmly. "Now have you gone potty? It's going to be a long car ride."

Usama came out of the crowd, cleaning his glasses with a handkerchief. "Do you mean to leave now? It is almost nightfall."

"Truck has headlights," Nevada replied.

"We should not travel at night. The desert is easily angered."

"Are you gonna anthropomorphize the desert the whole time?"

Candice patted her arm. "Be nice. But also, good word use."

"*Danke.*"

Usama arranged his glasses on his ears and across the bridge of his nose before speaking. "Whatever you hope to find, it will still be there in the morning, and better appreciated with a good night's rest and a vessel fully loaded with supplies. Come. There's tea."

Nevada glanced at Candice. "No wonder your family did so well in Britain—"

"Shut up," Candice said, reaching past her to turn up the radio, which had cut to a news report in Arabic.

"What is it?" Nevada asked. The way she said it made everything worse—all full of concern and sympathy. Candice could only imagine the stricken look on her own face that had prompted it.

"It's Pike's camp," Candice said. "A truck bomb went off next to it— Khamsin's claiming responsibility—and they're still... They're not even done counting the bodies."

———◆———

With the camp's recycling bin tucked under one arm, Nevada walked along the length of a dune, jamming empty cans and bottles down into the sand so they stood upright in a row. When she was done, she tossed the bin aside, walked up to Candice, and pulled a gun from her belt.

"Browning Hi Power. Oldie but a goodie—one of your grandad's toys. I already cleaned it, dry-fired it, should shoot fine. You know how to load it?"

"It's not exactly assembling a cabinet from IKEA."

Candice didn't feel the lighthearted banter, which usually inspired a weird blend of assurance and irksomeness. Whatever she said, Nevada would always knock it right back at her like a volleyball, but at least there was consistency in that. Maybe that was why they kept it up, despite Candice being able to see in her eyes that Nevada didn't feel it any more than she did.

Nevada demonstrated how the magazine went in. "Slide it in, slam it home with the heel of your hand, then rack the slide. That takes the first bullet out of the magazine, puts it in the chamber. You're ready to rock and roll. I don't suppose I have to go over basic gun safety with you?"

Candice tried to keep things light, think of some quip, but it was like climbing up a mountain. It was weird to think of things being easy with Nevada—possibly the most aggravating, frustrating individual she had ever met—but in comparison to this, anything would be easy. "Why don't you anyway?"

"Why don't I?" Nevada repeated. She showed Candice the safety catch. "Safety's here, right by your thumb. Keep the safety on at all times. Do not take the safety off until you're literally about to shoot someone."

"Yeah, I got it."

"Magazine release is next to the trigger." Nevada thumbed it, slid the magazine out, then popped it back in. "Still leaves one in the chamber, though, so it can still shoot. Shit like that is why you treat every gun like it's loaded, all the time. I don't want to see you goofing around with one of these things, acting like it's a water pistol, okay?"

"Are we gonna talk about it?"

Nevada came up short, paused a moment, then barreled forward. "We can talk in the car. It's gonna be a long drive."

"Maybe I wanna talk now."

"Right now you have to know how to shoot. Second rule: never aim at anything you don't intend to shoot, and never shoot something you don't want dead. Forget about the Lone Ranger shooting guns out of people's hands, winging them, kneecapping them—that's bullshit. Aim for the center mass. You can be off by a foot and still hit something they'll miss having."

"Have you ever thought about it?" Candice asked.

"Thought about what?"

"That they might be following us?" Candice wrapped her arms around herself. "Khamsin could've tracked us to that camp, which means they could follow us here—"

"We won't be here much longer," Nevada interrupted.

"That's not the *point*, Thea."

Nevada grabbed Candice's right hand, wrenched it out of her self-embrace, and forced the Browning into it. "You wanna feel bad, feel bad on your own time. You need to know this stuff. I'm expecting you to watch my back."

"That's what it's all about, right? Your back?"

Nevada forced Candice's hand up. "Two sights. You have the front sight at the end of the barrel and the rear sights at the top of the grip. You line them up, nice and level, and wherever they're pointed, the bullet's going to go. Front sight right between the rear sights. Only all the sights are on top of the gun and the bullet comes out below them, so whatever you want to hit, aim at the top of it. Bullet'll drop."

Candice shoved the gun down. "Can you give me something here? Please?"

"What do you want to hear? That it's not your fault? It's not. Khamsin did it. And if they did it because we went there, then I took us there. So blame me. But you didn't do anything. I dragged you along."

"Maybe that's enough. Maybe I let myself get dragged along and that's bad enough."

"Fine!" Nevada cried. "You're a horrible person. Congratulations. We can eat at Chick-fil-A. But if they do come, it'll be a lot more useful to know how to shoot them in the face than to tell them how bad you feel about everything."

"You're a wanker," Candice said. Her throat felt huge, like she was choking back tears without knowing it.

"If you're going to insult me, please use a real curse word and not one of your made-up Harry Potter words."

Candice hiccupped a sob, then smiled despite herself. "You're a bitch."

"Thank you," Nevada lifted the Browning again. "Focus on the front sight. Use the pad of your first knuckle to pull the trigger—not the tip, not the crease." Candice wiggled her forefinger through the trigger guard, laying the pad of her finger against the trigger. "That's good, but don't touch the trigger unless you're firing. Put your finger outside the trigger guard, right here along the slide." Candice did. "Good. Keep it there. Line up your shot—first can on the left."

Candice obligingly stood as she'd seen Nevada do, holding the gun out in front of her like it was a knife and she was warding off some home invader.

"Deep breath," Nevada said. "Hold. Aim."

Candice did. Her sights lined up three in a row, hovering over the can. The barrel projected out from her; it could've been a blade she was thrusting into someone's chest.

"Good. Now what I want you to do is squeeze the trigger—pull it all the way back—then slowly release the pressure." Candice opened her mouth to protest, but Nevada was quick to speak over her. "The gun won't fire more than once no matter how long you hold the trigger down. It's semi-automatic—it won't fire again until you release the trigger and it resets. You'll hear a click."

Nevada put her fingers into her ears. Candice guessed that meant it was time for her to shoot.

She took a deep breath, holding it as she aimed, just as she had done before. This time she squeezed the trigger. There was a loud crack as the slide jumped back, the whole gun pushing against Candice's grip—then the plastic bottle she was aiming at jolted in place, knocked nearly horizontal as the bullet punched through it and slapped into the sand behind. The sand burst upward where it'd been hit, a crude circle rippling a few inches out from the impact.

The sound echoed through the empty desert like rolling thunder.

Candice released the trigger as she'd been told, heard a click, and lowered the gun. Half of the bottle had been torn away. Sand seeped over the jagged edges, disconcertingly like blood as it trickled inside.

"Good," Nevada said, taking her fingers out of her ears and flicking off a bit of wax. "But if you're really defending yourself, you'll want to fire two or three times. That'll put anyone down."

Candice nodded tersely. She felt a little better, somehow. Like the gunshot was a scream she couldn't let out any other way. "I hope they are following us. I hope they catch up with us. Because if they do, they're mine."

"Oh no," Nevada said, shaking her head. "We split 'em fifty-fifty."

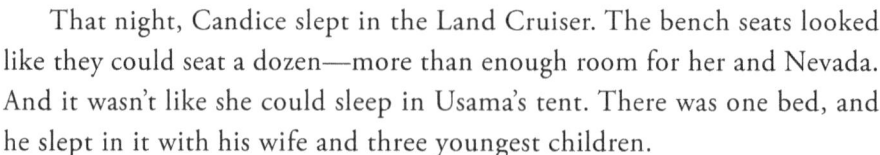

That night, Candice slept in the Land Cruiser. The bench seats looked like they could seat a dozen—more than enough room for her and Nevada. And it wasn't like she could sleep in Usama's tent. There was one bed, and he slept in it with his wife and three youngest children.

Nevada didn't snore, but Candice still couldn't sleep. The very serenity of her slumber pinged Candice all wrong. She thought of herself sleeping that peacefully and felt nauseous.

In the middle of the night, she pulled on her boots and outerwear, then stepped outside with her blanket wrapped around her as a shawl. The night was cold, but it felt hot—the sweat of the day turned rancid and slimy under her clothes. Walking away from the camp, Candice crouched behind a sand dune to use it as a windbreak. The temperature became reasonable. She could hear jackals yipping and laughing in the distance as they searched for prey—the wind making the tents breathe with its pressure—and the peculiar quiet of loneliness, resonating at a frequency as stripped and barren as the sands themselves. She felt like the only person on Earth… the only one who cared.

Uncapping her canteen, she poured out a small quantity of water onto a washcloth, then ran it under her clothes. It was probably doing little more for her filth than smearing it around, but the cool water felt good. Even the electric tingle of the wind over her wet flesh felt nice. Like something a living person would feel.

She heard Usama's footfalls approaching from behind, the sand barely seeming to mind his weight. It didn't crunch, but rather was softly smothered under his feet. He set a coat around her shoulders, its heavy down shielding her from the cold far better than the blanket, then sat down beside her.

"The desert is cold at night. The fool curses the wind, while the wise man finds a fire."

Candice shrugged equitably. "No fire to be found."

"I was not speaking literally," Usama said gently. "That was more of an aphorism. In this case, I would be more referring to space heaters."

"I was being a bit metaphorical myself."

"Ah." Usama nodded. "Perhaps I should improve my English before we speak with this much subtext."

"I could be more direct." Candice lay back, catching her head on top of her hands and staring up at the stars. In England, with all the lights, they left people alone, but out in the desert, the stars crowded the sky and demanded to be seen. The night sky was a black diamond and it was sparkling everywhere. "I spent my entire adult life in Britain. Never saw anyone shot or stabbed or anything. Then I come out here and I am knee-deep in blood. And I can't help but think—what if they're right about us? What if we're barbarians?"

"What if we are?" Usama looked at her, his glasses reflecting the moonlight to become a second and third moon. "What if all of us are responsible for this killing? What if you were, Candice Cushing, my *kandake*? What would you do if somehow it were all your fault?"

"I... I don't know." The stars seemed sharp now, like spikes hanging overhead. She supposed that's what they were—spikes of light from a billion miles away. "I suppose I'd try to make up for it. Help people."

Usama turned onto his side, his arm under his head as he looked at her. The two moons of his eyes held no judgment, no expectation. They seemed to see only what she was. "And is that not what a good person would do anyway?"

"It's not that simple."

"Isn't it?" Usama scooped up a handful of sand and let it trickle out into the wind. "Some of this sand could've come from a meteor, once as far away as the furthest light in our sky, and some of it could've been vomited from deep within the Earth. But now, all of it is only sand. And only a fool would try to sort sand into this row or that. Some people say that men should praise God so he won't cast them out. I believe we should do it because it is good for men to praise God. Do not sort the sands, Candice. Just walk on it while you look at higher things."

Reaching into his pocket, Usama brought out an amulet. Hanging from the leather cord was an elaborately detailed metal casing. "Before you came here, I went to see my sheik and told him of your troubles. He wrote a verse of the Qur'an on a piece of paper inside this. I gave *hijbat* just like it to your mother and father before they left. It will protect you."

Candice accepted it when he handed it to her. "What verse?"

"Surah Al-Ma'idah, verse 100. 'Not equal are the evil and the good, although the abundance of evil might impress you.'"

With the rising of the sun, a fine mist of sand was revealed, hanging over the desert like a veil. Every grain the wind could pick up glinted like a shard of crystal in the newfound sunlight. The sand soon darkened the sun itself, turning it from yellow to orange to red, like a bloodshot eye.

They breakfasted outside the tents. Usama built a fire and held a frying pan over it, pouring batter into the skillet. Before it could fully turn into a pancake, he added something like shredded beef jerky and a few pinches of insane-smelling spices. A baby camel, trying to nurse, accidentally grasped at the udder of a camel who hadn't birthed it. The unaffiliated adult returned the favor, nipping at the baby and sending it racing around with a distressed bellow. Usama laughed as he watched.

"You know why camels live in the desert, of course?" he prompted. Candice and Nevada looked at him in confusion. He took a deep breath and said portentously, "On the day of Creation, the camel looked into a lake and saw itself in the water. And it was so embarrassed to be that ugly, it went and hid itself in the desert!" He laughed again, so joyously that Candice joined in and even Nevada smirked.

Candice burned her mouth on her pancake. The next time her tongue made a sweep, she felt a bump rising on the roof of her mouth and knew she wouldn't be able to stop tonguing the bloody thing until it finally went away.

"Hey, Gramps," Nevada said. "Ever heard of someone called Tendai?"

Usama stopped laughing, stopped smiling, stopped making any expression whatsoever. He took a handkerchief out of his vest and extravagantly used it to mop up his lips and hands before finally wiping the sweat from his brow, then returned it to his pocket.

"There are ill omens which should not come before a long journey. Speaking of things such as this—there are few omens so black."

"Grandpa, please," Candice said. "It's important."

"Very well." Reaching into the sand, Usama started pouring handfuls of it onto the fire to douse it. "Many years ago, there was man named Stephen Obanna. A colonel who attempted to seize control of the government but did not succeed. Fleeing their judgment, he revived an old evil—the Zuni tribe." Usama focused his gaze on Candice as the fire finally went out, leaving only smoke between them. "You have heard of them?"

"Stories from my parents," Candice nodded. "On Halloween. Or... when I wouldn't behave..."

"They didn't tell you the half of it, I assure you. Even now, it is not something to be spoken of when one has care for another's ears."

"Okay, am I missing something?" Nevada asked. "What's so bad about the Zuni?"

"They were voracious slave traders, long before the white man showed up," Candice explained. "They would wage war endlessly on other tribes, taking in new members with ritual mutilation of the lips and ears. Then you add in religious indoctrination and drug addiction—anyone they captured would be turned into shock troops to continue their war."

"They flourished under the colonial powers," Usama continued, "supplying an endless influx of slave labor to the Europeans. But eventually they grew too demented even for those cruel overlords. The tribe was put down and disbanded, scattered to the four winds—until Obanna revived them. And the old ways."

Usama ran a hand across his forehead. He'd started sweating again.

"Okay, an African warlord with his own personal death cult," Nevada prompted. "So far, so horrible. Where's Tendai come in?"

"I will come to that," Usama assured her. He didn't seem to relish the prospect. "With his Zuni legions in tow, Obanna traveled from country to country, claiming to fight for God, for country, for freedom. But in his chaos, all that could be seen was… hate. Then the woman you spoke of came in. No one knows where she came from, but she beguiled Obanna, seduced him. It was like they fed on each other, two horrible parasites draining what little good remained out of one another. She convinced Obanna that he was a living god and became in turn his high priestess. They say she knew dark magic—old, forbidden rites that made her followers invincible in battle. It seemed the Zuni would sweep over all of Africa like a dark tide, but then the man Obanna was killed. Some say the Americans did it with a drone strike, others that Tendai killed him—some even say that God Himself could not stand his wickedness another moment and struck him dead. The Lady Tendai disappeared, with all her followers, and has not been heard from since. And you will not find anyone, not even the most foolish of men, who is not grateful to let that name be forgotten." Usama dusted his hands of sand. "I also understand that there is an American actress of the same name who gave a very bad performance in the last Spider-Man movie."

"Yes!" Nevada cried. "Thank you!"

"It seems to me she treats the Spider-Man very badly. I'm not at all sure why he would be into her."

"*Preach!*" Nevada cheered.

Candice got up and stretched the kinks out of her back. "Are you done? Can we go now, or would you rather complain about... I don't know, Daredevil?"

"What's to complain about?" Nevada asked innocently.

Candice held out her hand. "I'll start the air conditioning."

Nevada tossed her the keys. "Don't mess with the radio, I've got the presets just the way I like 'em."

Candice rolled her eyes and moved out.

———————◆———————

When Nevada went to follow her, she found an umbrella blocking her path. Usama was holding it in her way.

"That new?" Nevada asked. "Way to accessorize."

Usama set it down. "I will enjoy going on this journey simply to spend time with my granddaughter. But there still remains the matter of your price to be paid."

"Look, I'm flattered, but you're not my type. I don't go in for May-leap year relationships."

Usama canted his head. "I have heard you speak of Khamsin. You believe they pursue you?"

Nevada rolled her shoulders. "That's one theory."

"I have heard of their treatment of women. It is a shameful thing. I... cannot imagine my granddaughter going through that." Usama picked the umbrella up again and staked it in the ground. "You must promise me that if it comes to it—if there is no hope—you will not allow Candice to suffer that fate."

"Yeah, of course," Nevada said blithely. She held her jacket away from her holstered pistol. "Why do you think I carry this bad boy?"

"Anyone can kill an enemy. I mean for you to prevent suffering. If the moment comes when they have her—do not let them take her."

Nevada kept a grin on her face, but it was distinctly humorless. "You seem like the hands-on type. Why not do it yourself?"

"I care for her too much. She's my blood. *Astaghfirullah*. But to you, she's just another life. And life is cheap for you, isn't it?"

After a moment, Nevada nodded. "Yeah. Strictly dollar store."

Nevada felt an almost sexual charge as she started the Land Cruiser's ignition and moved them out. Ever since Candice had relayed that news report, she'd felt the walls closing in, but back in the driver's seat, she felt independent again, unfettered again. It was an American thing, she decided, being behind the wheel of a car. You could be on the highway to hell, but at least you had your foot on the gas. And she was so close—to Candice, to the treasure. So close and so far away.

But it wasn't a quick drive, even without traffic. The dunes loomed up as high as hills, and as Usama cautioned, they could only be summited carefully. A shifting patch of sand could bog down the tires or slip out from under them entirely, sending the Cruiser into a deadly roll. But going slow and steady wasn't an option either—it took real speed for them to make their way up a steep dune.

Usama proved invaluable there, pointing out firm passages over and around the dunes. He seemed to have a sixth sense for exactly how fast the Cruiser should go to make its destination without overshooting the mark. And he loved listening to Hank the Cowdog audiobooks.

"This Drover, he dishonors himself by blaming his cowardice on his wounded leg instead of overcoming his fears!" Usama slapped his knee without a hint of irony. "Ha, what a thing for a dog to do!"

"Yeah, he's a caution." Scanning the horizon, Nevada caught a glimpse of something dark among the light-colored sand. She pulled the Cruiser to a halt at the top of a dune and stopped the tape. "That it?"

"*In Shaa Allah*," Usama said, taking a collapsible telescope from his vest and extending it before putting it to his eye. "No. It's a Libyan T-55."

"A *tank?*" Nevada asked. She took the telescope from Usama. Through it, she could see a half-buried tank surrounded by speckles of disintegrated metal, its cannon jutting upward like Ozymandias's shin. "Fucking tank," she confirmed.

"Men will fight, even over deserts," Usama said.

Nevada reached to play the tape again, but Usama stopped her.

"You could wake her," he warned, and Nevada looked back to see that Candice was slumped over where she sat, lulled to sleep against the cool glass of the window.

Nevada worked the gearshift and they took off again. When next she spoke, it was in a politely hushed tone.

"So. Nomad. Kind of an ironic gig out here, isn't it?"

"How is this so?"

"You don't have any home, you're not tied down, you can go wherever you want..." Nevada shifted gears, giving them an extra burst of power to get over the dune in front of them. "But it's all kinda sorta desert, right?"

Usama braced himself against the dashboard as the engine rumbled its way up the steep incline. "That is not misspoken. But wherever you go, you are not the same person. Even if the destination does not change you, the journey does."

"Use the oh-shit handle," Nevada advised, and pulled down her own to show him how. Usama gratefully pulled down the one on his side, clinging to it. "Seems like a lot of trouble to go to when you're still in a desert at the end of the day."

"Then do you not change in all your travels?"

"I'm pretty great to begin with."

"Yes, you seem very pleased with being as you are—like an American movie woman, the ones who are always either kissing someone or shooting someone."

Nevada took the description in stride. "Hope for kissing, plan for shooting."

Usama told her to take a turn that would loop around a mountainous dune and she curved them too hard, the Cruiser fishtailing, tires spewing sand like they were as sick of it as Nevada was. Finally, the wheels caught and they rambled forward again, cruising over the desert's looping dunes like a sailboat cresting the waves. Only a sailboat wouldn't feel so heavy, so leaden—a fact Nevada relished. She felt like she was digging through the sand, just as she would for any treasure, only horizontally instead of vertically, the entire four-wheel drive her implacable will punching forward. It could be diverted or delayed, but it couldn't be stopped. It would keep coming until it hit home.

Then, among a fortune of golden sands, she saw her treasure—a splotch of green, rising up into a wide-brimmed cloud on top of a faded trunk.

Nevada stopped the Cruiser. "Telescope," she said to Usama.

"Tell a... what?"

Nevada rolled her eyes. Like she didn't have enough language problems with Candice. *This is why geniuses are never understood in their own time.* "The looking glass, dude."

Usama handed it to her. She focused on the tree. The two trees. Above the wide canopy of the cedar tree, an acacia shot straight up with only a few fronds to mar its vertical ascent. Between the two trunks, the acacia tree's leaves looked a bit like an olive stuck on a toothpick.

Nevada could've gone for a martini right about then.

She tossed the telescope back into Candice's lap, waking her. "Put your shoes on, honey, we're at Grandma's."

They parked several yards away. While Candice and her grandfather marveled over the sight, Nevada opened the rear door and brought out her toy. It was the size of a fire extinguisher, with wheels on the bottom that she folded out and a handle that she telescoped out. Candice gave it a sidelong glance when she saw Nevada pulling it toward the tree.

"What's that?"

"You ever play video games?" Nevada asked.

Candice waved a hand dismally. "I have Candy Crush on my phone."

"Yes, but I asked if you played video games?"

"No," Candice said firmly.

"Well, I do. And you know what I really love about them?" At the base of the tree trunk, Nevada powered the device on. "Cheat codes."

Candice looked skyward, realizing. "Ground-penetrating radar."

Usama snapped his fingers in recognition. "Like at the beginning of *Jurassic Park*!"

Nevada pointed a finger-gun at him. "See? Usama gets it!"

She lugged the radar device around the tree in a spiral, like she was dragging around a Radio Flyer. With her free hand she checked her phone, watching an app in real-time scan what was going on in the underlying geology.

"You know," Candice said, "before we do that, we really should set up a grid system."

"Oh, should we?" Nevada asked sarcastically. "*Nerd.*"

Candice planted her hands on her hips. "That's the way every archaeologist in the business does it."

Nevada circled the tree again. "Yeah, well, they're nerds and I'm cool, so…"

"Yeah, well," Candice replied in an imitation of Nevada's American accent, "they work out of colleges and you work out of a biplane, so—"

"Found it!" Nevada cried cheerily.

Candice simmered.

"I do not know what a nerd is," Usama said, "but I think I would not like to be one."

Candice simmered more.

Nevada dragged the radar past them on her way back to the Cruiser. "Six feet down. Cheery. Looks like we're in for some digging. My big muscles are going to get so sore and sweaty…"

"Did you at least mark the site?"

"Did I mark the site?" Nevada repeated dubiously. "I don't need to, babe, I remember where to dig. It's right…"

She gestured to the double tree. Tamarisk shrubs grew in the shade of the canopy, their bright pink flowers catching the light that filtered through the leaves.

"You know what?" Nevada said. "I think I'm gonna need to do another sweep with the radar, just to be sure it's not a false positive."

"I'll bring the shovels."

———◆———

They crossed the shovels over the spot where they'd dig, but before they started, Usama insisted on everyone having a hearty meal. Grandparents would grandparent, Candice figured. In the shade of the acacia tree, they ate lunch: dried dates, mushy *durra*, and salted goat meat. While they ate, Nevada tried to catch Usama up on *Jurassic Park*'s sequels. Usama was increasingly dubious that people would keep going back to the one island in the world with dinosaurs on it.

Then they worked. By unspoken consent, Usama was relegated to standing watch, the old-timer leaning against the tree and holding a Lee–Enfield rifle while Nevada and Candice dug. Thankfully, the dig was underneath the acacia's shade, though all that meant was that it was microwave-hot instead of oven-hot. Candice was careful to call for a water break every half-hour.

It was on their third such break that she remembered something: "Hey, Easy, you never gave me back my change."

"Huh?" Nevada asked, drinking from one of Usama's leathery *gerba*.

"My change from buying the Land Cruiser."

"Oh, right. Usama, could you hand me my pack?"

By now they were waist-deep in the plot they were digging, making it simpler for Usama to pick Nevada's backpack up and bring it to her than for Nevada to climb out. He set it down at the edge of the dig and Nevada reached into it.

"Tell me, Candice: would you rather have your change *or...?*"

She displayed a small toy monkey with a pair of cymbals. Nevada wound the monkey up and it bashed the cymbals together while she displayed it delightedly.

"You spent all the change on that?" Candice demanded.

"No, I spent like five bucks on it." Nevada reached back into her pack and brought out a money clip, which she handed to Candice. "There. And you can have custody of the monkey whenever you want. Little something to remind you of home when you go back to London."

Candice pointed at the monkey. "Those are made in Japan and they cannot be worth more than a dollar."

"You could probably get ten of them for a dollar on the eBay," Usama said.

Disgruntled, Nevada picked up her shovel and drove it into the ground. "Not if it's haunted," she protested, levering another spade's worth of sand up and out of the pit. "Then you can get a hundred for it easy. And this thing is definitely a little haunted."

"Please, the death-traps were enough," Candice demurred. "Don't start on curses now."

"I'm not saying I believe in curses, but I don't go around breaking mirrors either."

"Of course not. Mirrors are expensive."

Usama nodded sagely. "Pray to Allah, but tie your camel first," he quoted.

"Not really the same—" Candice started, breaking off when Nevada's shovel made a sharp cracking noise. "Oh, God, I knew we should've had a grid system."

"Relax," Nevada told her. Dropping onto her knees, she cleared the sand away by hand. "Just chipped it a little—I suppose it was too much to hope for a giant garage door opener…"

Even working by hand, with Candice urging caution every second, it only took a few moments to clear off the artifact. It was a tablet, a slab of petrified wood with black wax in the center. Candice had seen the type before. After the wax solidified, it was marked with a metal stylus, much like a blackboard would be written on with chalk. She blew the last layer of sand off the wax and saw writing pristinely etched into it, the thoughts and feelings of someone dead for two thousand years—

"Candice?" Nevada prodded, interrupting her astonishment. "I know you like to have a moment with these kinds of things, but—what's it say?"

Candice cleared her throat. "It says… Hey, do you think we should take it with us? We do get shot at a lot? But if we leave it here and then get shot ourselves, no one's going to find it—"

"Candice," Nevada pressed.

"Maybe we could make a quick round-trip to Faya, put it in a safety deposit box, then fill out a will—"

"*Candice!*" Nevada took a deep, fuming breath. "C'mon. It's really hot out here."

Candice coughed. "I'll just… yeah. It says… well, it's the directions from before, and now it says they went north."

"North," Nevada repeated.

"North. About a hundred and fifty miles."

Nevada sagged against the side of the pit they'd dug. "I swear, I hope the Egyptians got it right with all their afterlife crap, because when I kick off, I really wanna find everyone who planned this little field trip and—I mean, it doesn't even make sense! Why go a thousand miles west, then turn north all of a sudden? Shortest distance, two points, straight line. Even I know that. You'd think the pyramid boys could've figured it out…"

"Maybe not…" Candice noticed Usama offering his hand to help her out of the pit. She took it, the tablet cradled under her other arm, and let herself be pulled up. "In fact, it makes perfect sense. Thousands of years ago, Lake Chad was over a hundred and fifty *thousand* square miles in size. It was actually a paleolake called Lake Mega-Chad."

"Okay, hilarious." Nevada got a running start and pulled herself out of the pit. "What's that have to do with the price of tea in China? Wait, what's the price of tea in China have to do with *anything*?"

Candice ignored her. "Mega-Chad shrank, the Sahara grew, but before it got to where it is today, some academics believe there was a river network linking Chad, the Sudan, Nigeria, maybe even the Nile. The Egyptians could've been moving your treasure by boat, and this was the only point where the river turned north. That would actually explain these checkpoints. They could've left them at forks in the river to mark which path they took, either for when they made a return voyage or for someone following after them."

"So what we seek is a boat in the middle of the desert?" Usama asked.

"Possibly. Going north takes us straight to the Tibesti Mountains, and water doesn't flow uphill. Could be they ditched the boat to finish the journey on foot."

"Please tell me we're not going to have to climb a mountain," Nevada moaned.

"I doubt it. The Tibesti is a mountain range about nine, ten thousand feet tall, guarded by Toubou warriors. At that height, to desert dwellers like the Egyptians, it'd be like swimming in liquid nitrogen. No, I think they'd stop there, in the foothills."

Nevada wore a half-grin. "Is that a hunch, college girl?"

Candice bit her lip to keep from smiling back. "Call it an educated guess."

Nevada took out her satphone. "Well, if it's a hunch from you, I'll take it. And I still have a signal, so this seems like a good time to call the home office and let them know to get their checkbook ready. I'm not finding this damned thing and getting told that all their assets are tied up in craft beer. Not that that's ever happened to me..."

<hr />

John Gore watched as two of the Khamsin held down a camel, its legs tied as they sewed pieces of wet leather to its wounded soles. The camel being operated on, the other camels and horses in the herd, and the Khamsin themselves all seemed equally disinterested in the process. Gore was interested enough in the act, but through his mediatory calm, it was hard to tell. He only moved from his lizard-like stillness when he felt a burning on his left hand.

He was sweating there, the black oils that came from his defective glands staining his palm and absorbing the light as any dark color would. Ironic, he thought, that a biological process meant to cool him down could instead roast him alive. Gore brought a handkerchief out of his pocket and wiped his hand clean.

When he turned his attention back to the tablet, its electronics had finally gotten on the same page as the satellite uplink. He was getting an image: a massive pool formed into a slice of simulated beach, waves curving from the little end to the big end. Rows of colored lights underneath the water shone up into the waves, blurring and distorting inside their pregnant heft as they curved onto the artificial shore. Despite it being nighttime over there, the lights allowed surfers to ride the water, bodies and boards darkly glistening as they slashed the waves into white foam.

After a few moments, the camera turned to face Akbar Akkad Singh, who smiled like he'd tasted something sweet. "It's something, isn't it? Artificial waves so you can surf at night without all that sun, *finally*. As soon as I buy the place, we're adding in jet skis…"

"Can they see us?" came a voice behind Gore.

He turned his head slightly, more to acknowledge the voice than to see who was behind him. He knew what Nazir al-Jabbar looked like. "No. We're tapped into their signal. We can see what they're sending, hear what they're saying, but to them it's a private conversation."

He'd talked over Nevada and Singh exchanging pleasantries. Now he turned his attention back to the tablet, sensing they were getting down to business. Nevada talked about trees in the desert and river systems and boats. Gore heard it, absorbed it, but his attention was on the reflection in the glass screen—Nazir was listening intently, but the light from the sun had caught his glasses, turning them into blank, shining discs. It gave him an eyeless effect that made even Gore shudder.

These are the people in your neighborhood, he thought, sing-song, a mental process as absurd as someone laughing when they were afraid. *They're the people that you meet each day.*

The only one who didn't seem to be paying attention was Singh, who nodded along like an undermedicated schoolchild, the gesture almost becoming a tic as he waited for his turn to speak. "So you know where it is?" he asked at last, straining to keep a level tone. "You just have to go there and get it—"

"And you have to pay me my money," Nevada interrupted.

"Yes, yes, I'll have all the paperwork filled out. But you just gotta have the skull. Otherwise—I don't know, I've been feeling very anxious lately, I have night sweats. Don't kick me when I'm down, Easy. Just get me my skull."

"It's a boat in the middle of the desert, boss. Not exactly a needle in a haystack."

Nevada signed off there, leaving the screen black. In the sudden darkness, Nazir's glowing glasses could've been two flames.

"Then that is where your treasure is," Nazir said.

"Yeah." Gore felt his palm burning again. He reached down, picked up a handful of sand, and ground it inside his fist. The sand trickled out as black as pitch.

"It seems to me," Nazir continued, "that the women are now—what's the American expression—surplus to requirement. You've kept them alive to lead you to the treasure; now you know I have it. Give them to me. I want justice for my son."

Gore threw what was left of the sand away. "My employer will want to come here personally to take possession. It will take time for the travel arrangements to be worked out."

"It will take time for my men to hunt down the infidels. Give me their location. As a show of good faith."

Gore chuckled. "*Good faith*. And they say Muslims don't have a sense of humor." He dusted his hands clean. "You'll get it. But if I were you, well..."

"Well?" Nazir prompted.

"What's the American expression?" Gore asked sarcastically. "Don't hunt what you can't kill."

CHAPTER 5

HER CALL CONCLUDED, NEVADA MOVED on to tallying their resources with gung-ho efficiency. She quickly decided they had enough for the remainder of the trip, and with hours of daylight yet, she was equally enthusiastic to get moving again. Candice tried to defer to Usama's health, but he was in high spirits and quickly swept along by Nevada's fervor, so Candice found herself going along as well. She couldn't think of any way to get Usama out of the expedition without precluding herself from it.

Back behind the wheel of the Land Cruiser, Nevada was like a bloodhound on a scent. As if in deference to her will, the desert sands had spread out into long, flat expanses, and Nevada pushed the gas pedal horizontal. The ground was still unpaved, though, and after the first two hours of bumpy driving, Candice wondered if internal organs could have migratory habits. Usama seemed to be enjoying himself, though. Candice supposed when you were used to riding a camel, any amount of suspension was an improvement.

The sun crept down, lighting up the landscape into a chiaroscuro of reaching shadows and burning golds. The fading light burnished the clouds, burnt the dunes, cast the shadows into strong relief until they could've been as deep as wells. Nevada flicked on the headlights, their incandescent white igniting the ground ahead in rude detail. Stirring sands drifted like a swarm of insects inside the headlights' glare; Candice saw Nevada reach for the windshield wipers before realizing how pointless it was.

"Maybe we should call it quits for the night," Candice suggested. On their left, the sun was kneeling, sucking its light down below the horizon.

The desert gold became blue and black and maroon, pushing in oppressively on their burning headlights.

"Quit?" Nevada asked. "I don't wanna quit. Usama, you wanna quit?"

"*Ma'alesh*," he replied.

The dusk gave way to the glow of the moon, painting the dunes and clouds silver with the same brush. And as if the moon could exert as much of a pull on the sands as it did on the tides, the ground curled in a series of humps now. Pitching up and down with the headlights only able to expose a fraction of what was in front of them made the vast desert feel somehow claustrophobic.

Then Nevada hit the brakes, grinding the locked tires into the sand until a haze of yellow static pressed in on them on all sides. Ahead, the rolling hills were replaced by an almost sheer slope, a mountainous dune that plunged down from on high like a plummeting roller coaster track. It had to be a hundred feet high, at least, with the incline only a third as wide.

Nevada rolled down her window. A searchlight was mounted on the side mirror and she flared it. Its light made the headlights look anemic, shooting out like a pillar of fire. Nevada turned the light to the left and to the right. The wall they faced stretched on for miles in either direction.

"Now can we stop?" Candice asked. "We'll find a way around it in the morning."

Usama nodded agreement. "The desert is easily angered at night—"

"Yeah, I heard that one," Nevada snapped. "It's not that high. We can make it."

She spun the searchlight around, searching behind them until she found a flat stretch of sand between two dunes. Bringing the Land Cruiser around, she sped them through that, then made a tight turn to face the slope again.

"Everyone belted in?" Nevada asked, revving the engine.

Candice self-consciously checked her seatbelt, then Usama's. "Yeah."

Nevada laughed. "Pussies."

She gunned the engine. The tires slashed at the desert floor before catching, and then they were catapulted forward, the acceleration pressing Candice back in her seat. Her tongue thoughtlessly brushed over the bump in her mouth. She was surprised it hadn't gone down yet. Probably cancer, she told herself.

They hit the slope, tires butting right into the sand before disintegrating it, slapping it down under them. The hood pitched upward—Nevada shifted gears with a grinding grunt. The engine roared, full-throated, and they slugged their way up the incline, engine chugging, the Cruiser nearly vertical.

"So Usama, hey, how are the kids?" Nevada asked, grinding the gears like a fiend.

"Pretty well. Five of them got together trying to sell solar panels, but I think it may be a scam."

The Cruiser dropped back suddenly and Nevada stomped the brakes and twisted the steering wheel, popping the clutch before they trudged upward again.

"Wait, five of them? That's not all? How many kids do you have?"

"Twenty-three," Usama answered. "Counting all four wives."

Nevada slammed the gearshift again. "Candice, you sure this guy is your grandfather? Maybe this is just how thirty-year-olds look when they have more than a dozen kids."

Usama laughed, his eyes shifting around nervously. "What about you, Ms. Nevada? Any husbands?"

"Not a one," Nevada replied. "I always worry that the moment I get into a committed relationship, the producers of *The Bachelor* are *finally* going to call me back. I don't think I could take that kind of heartbreak."

They were almost to the summit, Nevada nursing the Cruiser every step of the way. It was give and take, a tug of war with gravity, and Nevada was determined to chisel away every last foot of altitude standing in her way. Braking, shifting, working the gas to gain a few feet wherever she could. The engine sounded like it was dying a slow and painful death, but Nevada coaxed more out of it. Candice was beginning to think the woman could get blood from a stone.

"What about you, granddaughter?" Usama asked, breathing easier as the summit's edge and the night sky beyond swept into view of the headlights. "We haven't spoken about your personal life. Have you met anyone special?"

Candice was tight-lipped, but Nevada said, "I think I saw her kissing someone a little while ago."

Candice's lips pressed even tighter together as the wheels spun tirelessly on the incline, taking them nowhere. "Oh, that's nothing," she said after a moment. "Not really a good match."

Usama spoke up. "Sometimes a match is as good as you make it."

"You have a positive attitude, Usama," Nevada said. "I respect that." She worked the gearshift determinedly. "Although it's hard to be positive when this Toyota crapola can't get over a little speedbump. I don't know how the Japanese kicked Detroit's ass with cars like this. There had to be—"

The wheels suddenly caught something, some hardness under the sand they were sweeping at, and the Land Cruiser lurched into motion, bringing them up over the summit to see that there was nothing on the other side but the night sky and a sheer drop.

"Shit," Nevada cursed, standing on the brakes, but the Cruiser had rolled over the spine of the dune and was now momentarily suspended on it, balanced on its undercarriage, both sets of wheels in the air as it tilted forward with the weight of the engine. "Shit!"

The sand compacted under the Cruiser, lowering it, and they sidled forward until the back wheels broke through the top of the dune. The front tires came down on the slope with an exhausted *whuff*. The sand instantly parted, locked tires slitting through it as they careened downhill. Nevada swerved, trying to break their momentum, but the slightest curve tipped the Land Cruiser onto two wheels, threatening to send them into a rollover. She straightened the wheel and they plummeted like an anchor, headlights showing the bottom of the dune approaching in harrowing detail. Candice swore she could've counted the grains of sand that waited to meet them.

The slope evened out, bringing them level in time for another sand dune to loom in their path. There was no chance of traveling up it at the speed they were going. They slammed into the sand, the Land Cruiser burying itself up to the windshield. Nevada's head careened into the steering wheel while a toolbox detached from the cargo area and whistled by Candice's ear before cracking the windshield.

Candice felt a tightness across her chest where the seatbelt had cut into it and knew it would absolutely bruise, but otherwise she was unharmed. She looked around. Nevada pulled her head up from the steering wheel, a gash across the bridge of her bloody nose, while Usama looked like he'd just gotten off a roller coaster.

"Nice parking space you found us," Candice said.

"Eh. Women drivers," Nevada replied. "Is my nose broken?"

"Let me check," Candice said, and flicked her in the nose. Nevada cringed. "No."

At Candice's insistence, they all submitted to be inspected for injuries. They couldn't find anything more severe than a bruise. Candice chalked it up to luck, though a part of her she was too frustrated to give voice to insisted that Nevada's skillful handling of the vehicle had prevented more severe injuries.

Nevada wanted to dig the Land Cruiser out and keep going, but Candice flatly refused and Usama backed her. With the air of a poker player with a bad hand, she agreed to bunk down for the night.

That was when Usama took his leave, explaining that while it was only natural for two young, unmarried women to share the same resting place, it would be improper for him to be there too. Taking his pack, he unrolled his sleeping bag and set up a small fire within walking distance.

After Candice had prepared for bed—another night spent camping in the Land Cruiser—she stared out the window at Usama's fire, telling herself he must have roughed it the same way thousands of times in his life. She still felt delinquent, leaving the elderly man to the elements. But she doubted either he or Nevada would agree to him sleeping in the jeep while the women slept outside.

"I'm worried about him," she said, only half aware that she'd spoken aloud. She slept on the floor, Nevada in the middle seat. They'd crammed the backseat with supplies until it was completely impassible.

In the darkness, the bandage across Nevada's nose shone white. "What are you worried about? It's a desert. Do you think Tusken Raiders are gonna get him?"

Candice scowled. Served her right for going to Easy Nevada for sympathy. "Just, he's old! He should be in a retirement home."

She heard Nevada turn, and her voice sounded closer. "Pretty sure these guys don't believe in retirement homes. When it's your time, they probably just put you on an iceberg, push it out to sea—Goodnight, Gracie."

Sensing she was being watched, Candice turned onto her back to look up at Nevada. "Iceberg? What are you talking about?"

"You know, a thing, for old people. They gotta have a thing."

"Like taking the Long Walk to bring law to the lawless."

"Yeah. Whatever you said."

Candice turned onto her side, facing away from Nevada again. "You're right, I'm being silly. It's probably the sleeping arrangements."

"What, do I snore? I don't snore."

"You don't snore. It's just—"

"It's just like before. You sleep there, I sleep here, you miss out on some top-notch oral, my nubile young body goes to waste in its sexual prime."

The crack in the windshield was letting in little drips of sand with the breathing of the Earth. "It's not that I don't trust you, I'm sure you'll be a perfect gentleman… woman… at least when it comes to this. It's just weird that we're doing this again."

Nevada dropped her hand down to run a finger along the curve of Candice's ear. "Worried you can't resist temptation a second time?"

Candice turned over so that Nevada's finger was hanging in front of her face. "Believe me, the more I get to know you, the less temptation there is. Take that finger away or I'm going to bite it."

Nevada folded her arms back under her head. "I think we should agree on a safe word first."

Candice ignored her. "My mother used to say that before you have sex with someone, you should sleep in the same bed as them. Just sleep. No funny business."

"What possible reason could there be for that? To make sure they don't turn into a dog at night or something?"

"To see if you're compatible, if you can be intimate without sex."

"God, that's stupid."

"My mother's advice on love is stupid?" Candice rapped her knuckles against Nevada's seat. "My mother who's been married for forty years?"

"Oh, how hard was it to be married forty years ago? Didn't the man basically own you? If you can fix a pot roast and work a laundry machine, boom, healthy relationship."

Candice shook her head. "I really wanna meet your parents someday."

"Me too. But that's the problem with dating, everyone has a bunch of dumb tests and hoops to jump through because they have to find The One. Women acting like fucking Morpheus—'Are you the One?' Like it's that hard to find someone who can hold down a job and eat pussy."

"Just for the record, you are single, correct?"

"Yes, thanks for asking. Gay men, now they have the right idea. Fuck on the first date, and if the sex is good, let the other stuff work itself out. It's like finding a roommate for them, just with condoms. And I would know. My cousin was gay. Well, he moisturized."

Candice rolled her eyes. "I feel like someday there's going to be a psychological test named after you."

"He might've just sweated a lot… What?" Nevada asked, lolling her head over the side of the middle seat again, her hair hanging down.

Candice blew it away from her face. "Your approach works fine if you're some charismatic, beautiful, somewhat slutty woman… who isn't afraid of axe murderers…"

"That's why God invented open-carry laws," Nevada reasoned.

"But if you're a little more introverted than that, you like the thought of someone getting to know you. Really appreciating you beyond just a warm body. Not giving up on you no matter how hard it gets, because they don't want to give up on you. Not sex roommates, but friends."

Nevada hummed in consideration. "Have you thought about how unfair your approach is compared to mine?"

"Oh?"

Nevada raked her hand through her dangling hair, suspending it behind her ear, and Candice felt a curious sense of loss. It had smelled nice. "Yeah, the more you get to know me, the more annoying I get. Meanwhile, you're still sexy. I still want to fuck you. It's totally unfair. Check your privilege."

Candice rolled over again, staring back at the cracked windshield and its slowly penetrating sand. She had a feeling Nevada was about to get all smug again when she said, "You're not that annoying."

"Really?" Nevada asked smugly.

"Well, you are, but there are certain redeeming qualities."

"Such as?"

"The way you never ever fish for compliments."

Nevada chuckled. "I must be rubbing off on you—you're actually starting to be funny."

Candice rolled onto her back, staring out the window upside-down. The desert was beautiful at night, the arid wasteland a thin sheet suspended over a bottomless expanse of stars. All it took was a flip of perspective and what was once desolate became breathtaking.

———————◆———————

In her dream, Candice flew over the desert. She was going as fast as a jet, but the desert stretched on and on endlessly. Still, she was flying.

She came awake slowly, becoming aware of her body, a sensation of warmth in her hand that wasn't of her own flesh. Still half-asleep, it felt like a place to land somehow. She opened her eyes. Nevada's arm was dangling from the middle seat to hold her hand. Candice looked at Nevada's face, saw the eyes lazily closed, the expression slack. She was unconscious, her only motion rubbing her thumb against Candice's hand like someone would rub a rabbit's foot.

Candice gave her hand a squeeze and Nevada came awake. "What?" she mumbled blearily. "What, what, what?"

"You were holding my hand."

"What?" Nevada asked, rubbing the sleep out of her eyes with her free hand. "No. Was I? Sorry."

"It's okay," Candice said. "It's obvious you're feeling a little fragile at the moment and subconsciously you see me as a source of comfort."

"No, I don't," Nevada said quickly.

"It's flattering, really."

"I'm not fragile. I'm a badass." Nevada snatched her hand back. "How do we know you didn't hold my hand? That seems like the kinda girly thing you'd be into."

"I was sleeping on the floor! You think I reached up, in my sleep, and took your hand?"

"Yeah, you're like a very needy person. Seems like a thing that you would do." Nevada sat up, yawning and stretching. "Hey, wasn't there a really old guy with us last night?"

Candice looked out the window. Usama's little camp was still there, but the man himself was nowhere in sight.

"Bollocks," she muttered.

"This is why you're supposed to hang your old people up in a tree when you're camping," Nevada said. "Make sure a bear doesn't get them."

Candice threw a side door open. "Would you come on?"

Moments later, boots on and pulling on their outerwear, they walked up to the campsite. The fire had been reduced to sparking ashes; beside it, stones spelled out BRB.

"I'm not sure which we should be more worried about," Nevada said. "That he's missing or that apparently he used to be on AOL."

Candice heaved a sigh. "I think he did something like this when I was thirteen. Just disappeared for a few hours. My dad didn't think it was weird. I suppose it's something of a thing."

"More importantly, he left his campfire going, which is exactly how you get forest fires."

Candice looked at her. "What is with you and the hiking jokes this morning?"

"I had a weird dream about a forest. Guess it put me in a mood."

Candice shrugged. "I dreamt that I was flying."

"Oh, I can't beat that," Nevada said sardonically. "C'mon. While Usama's playing hooky, we can at least get the jeep dug out."

That work took the better part of an hour, Nevada and Candice once more putting their shovels to work. The sun was a constant, nagging enemy, but it was tolerable. Candice knew that by the middle of the day, trying to do physical labor would be like subjecting themselves to a blast furnace.

With every pile of sand they moved from the top of the Land Cruiser to the desert floor, Candice tongued the bump on the roof of her mouth. Still wasn't gone. Probably heal faster if she stopped tonguing it. She touched it again anyway. *Dammit.*

Candice stabbed her shovel into the sand and flung it over her shoulder. All at once she heard a click and felt a sharp pain in her back. *Double dammit.*

"What's wrong?" Nevada asked, having heard Candice's pained gasp.

"Nothing," Candice replied, holding her lower back. "I think I pulled something. I'll be fine."

Nevada skidded down the dune, dropping her shovel to take Candice by the shoulders and lead her into the shade the jeep cast. "Sit down, take a load off. I'll finish up." She reached through an open window and brought out one of Usama's waterskins, dropping it in Candice's lap. "I'll rub some Ben Gay on you later. It's a lot more platonic than it sounds."

"I'll bet." Candice shifted to get comfortable.

Nevada picked up her shovel, slinging it over her shoulder. "And after that, we'll see how things go. But it is called rub and tug, not rub and *don't* tug."

Candice sighed as she uncorked the gerba. "You do of course know why you keep hitting on me, don't you?"

Nevada steadily ate into the sand with her shovel. "Because eventually you're going to be overcome with lust and throw yourself at me, so we'd better get your feelings for me on the table first or else I'll feel like a slut."

"I think you want me to fall for you because it'll give you some validation that you're this lovable person who's… capable of being loved."

Nevada stopped digging. "Wow."

"Which you are!" Candice added hurriedly as Nevada started digging again. "But you don't need to have sex with me to prove that to yourself."

"Yes, but I *want to*," Nevada stressed. "You have a really nice ass and these tits that are just top-notch, so, respectfully, and with the fullest regards for your intelligence and your talent and your overall nice personality… I really want to fuck you." She finished off with a shrug.

"'Overall nice personality'?" Candice asked.

"You have some quirks."

"You kill people for a living!"

"I rob graves for a living. The dead people are more of a hobby." Nevada staked her shovel into the ground. "Okay, that should do it."

They deflated the tires, then took the floor mats out and laid them behind the tires. It was slow-going, but Nevada managed to back the jeep out of the dune. When she put it into first gear and twisted the wheel to take them to the side, there Usama was, standing right in front of the grille holding a cat.

"Where have you been?" Nevada demanded, launching herself out of the front seat.

"Finding this one," Usama replied, holding up the cat. It wasn't a breed Candice recognized, but it resembled an orange tabby, or maybe a tiny caracal. "He's a sand cat. I found him chasing scorpions. It's good luck to catch a sand cat."

"You're not going to hurt him, are you?" Candice asked suspiciously.

"No, no," Usama demurred, and indeed, he held the cat gently. It submitted to being petted with feline contentment. "You let them go once they've caught all your bad luck in their fur. They take it with them."

Candice gave in, crowding up to Usama to pet the cat. Even Nevada leaned in to tickle its chin.

"I suppose he can stay until after breakfast," Nevada said. "You missed out on all the fun, exhuming our ride."

"Then it is working once more?"

"Yeah," Nevada nodded. "Air conditioning and everything. I take it all back about the Japanese. Their car takes a beating and keeps on going. It's a regular Irish housewife."

Candice glanced at her. "Not funny."

"Haven't you heard? Comedy isn't supposed to be funny these days. Comedians just talk about how they were abused as children and can't get dates. You go to a comedy club, it's like being someone's therapist with a two-drink minimum."

"Any therapist you have would need two drinks, minimum," Candice retorted.

Usama handed her the cat. "I believe I will fix breakfast."

Breakfast ended up being kofta—ground beef rolled up into balls with egg yolk, bread, and spices, something like giant meatballs if the spaghetti were replaced with rice and gravy that was practically in drag as curry. Usama apologized for serving it cold, but Nevada came up with an ingenuous way of heating it on the Land Cruiser's engine—Candice didn't want to know *how* she had learned that trick.

It tasted good, but Candice couldn't really comprehend the logic of eating something so spicy in a desert. She was sure she used up twice as much water as usual just washing the meal down.

Candice drove, Usama in the front seat quizzing her on what the different dials meant and how the controls worked. Nevada sat in the back, her arms crossed impatiently until the shuffling of the Land Cruiser lulled her to sleep. She didn't look peaceful, her teeth grinding together and her head slumped to the side as if she'd taken a punch.

Every time they crested a dune, the desert stretched on to eternity ahead of them. The scalloped hills only made it look more endless—without them, Candice could've convinced herself that infinity was a trick of the eye. But there really did seem to be no end to how much sand was laid out in front of them. The more she drove, the more Candice felt a dreamlike haze descend over her. The dunes blurred together until she was seeing them without seeing them: seeing through them to the undying wind that sculpted them into the delicate yet imposing mounds that broke up her journey. And seeing inside them to the impregnable rock they'd once been, before time had broken the sand down like a blacksmith's hammer at work for eternity.

The engine kept up an invigorated roar, pushing the four-wheel drive through the soft, giving sand that tried to bog them down, and making it splash out like an exhale of cigarette smoke. But no matter how exclamatory their wake was, it didn't last long before the wind had its way with it—tearing down their tire tracks and kicked-up sand alike into the same unvarying ripples that lay ahead of them. At times, Candice saw a glimmer of metal in the distance and wondered if it weren't their own vehicle, the Land Cruiser somehow following itself through a desert that was one big circle.

When she realized she was nodding off, she shook her head to clear it. "Say, Grandpa... where did you get that rifle?"

Usama hefted his Lee-Enfield, an almost quaint-looking bolt-action rifle, so wooden it looked more like a walking stick than a gun. "It was my father's," he said simply.

"Your father?"

"Yes. Here. Look at this." Under the muzzle of the rifle was the bayonet mount, but there was no spike, only a jagged metal end half an inch long. "It broke off. Father showed me that the first time he let me use it."

"Wow." Candice looked it over. Military history wasn't her specialty, but if she'd added up the dates right, she'd guess her great-grandfather fought in the First World War. "British?"

"Yes. The colonial government of Sudan at the time. Not so popular these days, but my father vowed loyalty to them. He was very proud to have such a fine weapon and very proud to have a son to take it. Why do you ask?"

Candice didn't quite know even as she spoke. "No reason, really. I've just been thinking lately about—archaeology, I guess. How we see the Egyptians and the Nubians from where we're standing. And how people are going to see us in the future. As these terrorists or..."

Usama considered this, dropping the rifle onto his lap. "It is a little presumptuous, is it not?" he asked finally.

"What is?"

"To imagine how you'll be seen so many years in the future. Granddaughter, as long as our lineage stretches back, the desert has been here longer. It is the only thing I truly own. And next to it, I'm nothing. This heritage you try so hard to form in your mind—perhaps it's not meant to be held there. Perhaps it's something you touch."

"You really think that's all it is?" Candice asked. "Me caring about you and you caring about your father, all the way back?"

"I think people can choose their heritage. Either hate and fear and ignorance, or love. There's more than enough of all of them in everyone's blood."

Candice thought on that for a moment. She could agree with Usama's sentiment, but there was something in it she took issue with, something she felt compelled to voice. "I used to *love*..." Candice drew out the word like she was slowly biting into a piece of chocolate, "coming to visit you. I never quite felt I fit in in London. All the cars, the people, radios and subway cars. The desert was so quiet. And everyone looked at me like... I don't know. Never any second looks, nothing out of the corner of the eye..." She glanced at Nevada's fleeting reflection in the windshield. "The way they must look at her wherever she's from. And now I look at the desert and... it's death."

"It's both," Usama said simply.

"I wish I could go back to it just being the first one."

Candice saw another glint of metal, this time much closer. She stepped on the brakes.

Nevada woke with the sudden change in motion. "Eh?" she asked, her confusion somehow irritated.

"Over there." Candice pointed. Fifty feet away was a low, rippling sand dune, little more than a fold in the fabric of the Earth. A metal cylinder laid across its backbone, forty feet long, maybe the height and width of a subway car, with a crude lean-to at one end. Candice couldn't make out what it was until she saw the tail fin at the other end. "It's a plane," she said.

Nevada crowded in between the front seats, settling her elbows next to the headrests. "Looks like a B-17 Flying Fortress. Must be a couple decades old. Sucks to be them. Let's go."

Candice looked at her incredulously. "You don't want to check it out?"

"We don't have time," Nevada insisted, looking at the Cruiser's GPS. "We're twenty miles out and you wanna stop?"

"I would like to stop," Usama said. "For... male business."

"Number one or number two?" Nevada asked.

Usama drew himself up. "I would not bring it up if it was number one."

"Okay, fine," Nevada said. "But I'm eating a sandwich while we're stopped."

Nevada grabbed her Scorpion and Shadow 2, while Usama took his Lee-Enfield. Candice guessed it was something they had in common, though Nevada wasn't so paranoid that she held a weapon at the ready like Usama did. True to her word, she took a ham on rye from the cooler in the back and bit into it as they walked up to the wreck.

Cresting the hill that the back half of the plane was embedded in, they saw a wing jutting out of the hollow between dunes, climbing up nearly fifty feet. There was no sign of the other one. Nevada guessed that was why the thing had crashed in the first place. They came to the lean-to, a tent constructed out of what looked like parachute canopy, a ghostly membrane still pulsing and fluttering with the wind. Usama went first, brushing it aside with his rifle. With the first step, he nearly fell in—Nevada's free hand lashed out, grabbed the back of his shirt, and hauled him backward.

Kneeling, Candice took out a flashlight and turned the beam downward. It was like a mineshaft going straight down, its mouth covered by the tent. Nevada crouched down beside her. "Radio compartment, bomb bay, flight deck—" She glanced upward. "She must've come down in a nosedive, smashed straight into the sand, then the back half broke off and fell over..." She directed Candice's flashlight upward to see into the aboveground portion of the plane. It was an empty circular shaft, olive-green, with two gunnery positions on the side and an open door. Though mostly dark, light flooded in through the waist gunner windows and door, sparkling almost mockingly on the dusting of sand that had seeped in to cover the floor. "Waist section," Nevada said. "Tail gunner will be at the back."

Candice stood up and backed out of the tent, looking at the exterior of the bomber. The metal was rusted and pitted, but it was mostly intact. The driving sand had only vandalized the craft, unable to make it rot or decay. "You think anyone could've survived that?"

Nevada took hold of the parachute fabric that'd been used to make the tent protecting the interior from the elements and gave it a rustle. "This didn't build itself."

Candice looked down the buried half of the airplane—it reminded her of a grain silo, plunging straight down thirty feet through narrowing, constricting passages of metal to terminate in the nose section. She could barely make out the bottom, but it looked like the glass in the flight deck had shattered, mingling with the sand that had punched its way inside on impact. Her flashlight beam threw back glints of light when she looked down.

"This is my first time in an airplane," Usama said.

"Beats flying in coach," Nevada replied.

"There is no danger here?"

"Tetanus, maybe."

"I will take my leave then." He held the rifle across his chest in a mild salute. "I will return, having attended to my business."

"Remember to take a hall pass," Nevada quipped.

Usama looked quizzically at Candice.

"Ignore her," she said. "She's being American."

Usama strolled back to the Land Cruiser, where he dug into the back for a spade, a roll of toilet paper, and a beach umbrella, Candice was amused to see. He took all three with him behind a sand dune, where there was plenty of privacy to be had.

"Alone at last," Nevada said in a playfully suggestive tone.

"Stop it," Candice said bluntly, but with no venom in her voice.

"Can't help it. Something about airplane crashes. Always gets me going." Nevada stepped back under the tent, skirting the edges of the abyss to step into the horizontal portion of the Flying Fortress. "Come on, you wanted the grand tour..."

Candice wondered for a moment at Nevada's motivations. She knew how impatient Nevada must be to press on, even when they all needed a break, and it didn't seem like her to be so magnanimous when she wasn't getting her way. Usually Candice would think Nevada was trying to seduce her, but there was something so joking about that last flirtation that Candice didn't think she was taking the prospect seriously.

Maybe she's just being nice, she thought as she followed Nevada's path, joining her in the waist section. But why would Nevada be nice when she had a chance to drop cheesy pick-up lines and show off her body?

Inside, the darkened wreck felt like it was holding its breath, warped and deformed by the crash, keeping stubbornly quiet while Candice sensed the groan of metal waiting to be voiced.

"There are the .50-cals," Nevada said, pointing to blackened parts scattered across the sandy floor. Candice took Nevada's word for it. Whatever they had once been, the crash had shattered them, and they now reminded her of beetles that had been stepped on and then scraped off on the ground. "Wonder if the tail gun's any better…"

Nevada led the way through the wreck's fuselage, through pools of light radiating from the shafts that cut in from the windows and door. The metal underfoot thrummed hollowly, impotently, with their footfalls. It seemed less noisy than the sand that crunched beneath their heels. Once or twice, a footstep sent a few metal cartridges arcing through the air or rolling across the sand. Candice guessed they were ammo from the waist guns. There could've been kilos of it buried ankle-deep in the sand.

"Ten crewmen," Nevada said, her voice echoing through the tomblike space. "Maybe some bailed out, maybe not. Maybe some died in the crash, maybe not. Some of them, at least, survived, built shelter, waited for rescue. Buried whatever dead there were—" She looked back at Candice, answering an unasked question. "No bodies."

Candice suppressed a shudder. As brave as she was feeling at the moment, she didn't know how brave she'd be with corpses lying around. At this point, of course, they'd probably be as skeletal as the remains in any pyramid, but there was a difference between the long-dead, wrapped in linen or sacrificed in arcane ritual, and someone who had gone to the cinema, breathed smog, read a newspaper.

Ahead of her, Nevada stooped down before an open hatch to the outside. Using her hands and one strong breath, she cleared away the sand from the bottom of the doorframe. The floor she excavated was corrugated metal, and there was a boot print in blood, the toe facing out the door.

"No rescue," Nevada said. "They left."

The way she said it, Candice could almost picture the next footstep, and the next, an endless trail leading out into the sand. The sand that was now as clear as an innocent conscience.

"Do you think they made it?" Candice asked.

"Who knows?" Nevada replied. Then, apropos of nothing: "You're staring at me."

"No, I'm not," Candice said automatically.

Nevada pressed on. "And I'm not even doing anything interesting with my hips. Or breathing hard." Reaching the end of the waist section, she stopped next to a twisted lump of metal whose purpose Candice couldn't fathom—perhaps a compartment to hold the rear landing gear while in flight?—and looked back, taking a deep breath that strained her breasts against her shirt.

Candice looked her in the eyes. "Have I ever thanked you?"

"Well, I wouldn't say I've done anything too fun to you so far—"

"For saving my life," Candice said. "The couple of times you saved my life."

"Probably," Nevada shrugged. "You're a very polite person. And I'm kinda uncomfortable with affection, so don't give a big speech. You'll trigger me."

"Thank you," Candice said, sincerely.

"You're welcome," Nevada said, flatly. "And thank you for translating those hieroglyphics and stuff. I probably could've done it myself, but you saved me a lot of time. And I didn't have to do math. Where were we?"

"Tail gun."

"Yes." Nevada kept going through a doorway that took them into another compartment, this one marginally lit by a bubble of glass canopy that was so cloudy with caked sand it was almost tinted. "Here we go!" Nevada said, sitting down under it. "M2 Browning. Looks like it's still in pretty good shape. They built these things to last. Good thing, too. Apparently you never know when you're going to need to shoot some Nazis."

Candice leaned against a battered metal wall as Nevada fussed over the glass, knocking away some of the sand with a pounding fist. "Nevada— Easy—have you given any thought to what you're going to do when all this is over?"

"What, like over-over? Six seasons and a movie over? No more clues written in a rock inside a skull beneath a cairn…"

"Yeah," Candice said. "You said you have to get twelve skulls. You've already gotten eleven, so this is the last one—after this, you're all done."

"Weird thought," Nevada admitted. She took a closer look at the machine gun itself. "This is really well-preserved. You could get a fortune for it on eBay…"

"Well?" Candice prompted.

"Well?" Nevada retorted.

"You haven't put any thought into what you're going to do after this? You're just going to take the money and—what? Retire? Hope someone hires you to go after femurs? What?"

"You know—the kid. Surgery. All that very noble mama bear stuff." Nevada shrugged. "There didn't seem much point in thinking it out after that. Never actually thought I'd get this far. I've been doing this for six years, and that's just for Singh." Nevada pulled the trigger on the Browning. It clicked resoundingly. "Firing pin's still good, but the thing isn't loaded." She shook her head. "What about you? You were on a bona fide archaeological expedition. What were you going to do when you got back?"

"You know—try to get published, try to get hired on for another dig…"

"You don't know," Nevada said smugly.

"I had meant to figure it out, but then a civil war broke out, and that seemed to take precedence."

"Excuses, excuses." Nevada picked up a long chain of ammunition that Candice guessed fed into the gun somehow. "Maybe you were hoping for some dashing rogue to show up and whisk you off to a life of adventure."

"Maybe you were hoping to meet someone just sane enough to settle down with."

"You offering?"

"You know any dashing rogues?"

Nevada chuckled under her breath. "The closest thing I can think of would be you."

"I'm not a rogue," Candice said.

"It's not like we have a permit to do any of this." Nevada reached up to a handle on the tail gunner's canopy, hanging from it as she faced Candice. "And you did sort of whisk me away on a life of adventure. I was just trying to loot a hole in the ground. You're the one who dragged me out into the Sahara Desert with your faithful sidekick."

Candice stood up to her, jabbing an accusing finger. "You're the one with the faithful sidekick who jumped out of a plane!"

"You jumped too."

"You were going to push me."

"It is so unfair that you keep throwing that in my face when I didn't even get the satisfaction of actually defenestrating you."

They were both standing up in the glass canopy now, Candice having to incline her head to keep the sun out of her eyes. "You know what?" she said. "Forget it."

"Forget what? You didn't say anything. You just stared at me a lot and for once showed a degree of gratitude for all the times I saved your life."

"Oh, I throw stuff in your face? You're throwing that in my face and I just thanked you for it."

"What were you going to say?" Nevada insisted.

"*Nothing!*"

"You were getting some big pitch ready, and now I'm curious. I wanna hear it."

"You're delusional."

"Was it a green card?" Nevada asked.

"What?"

"Were you going to marry me and get me a green card into Britain?"

"No! It wasn't a green card!"

"So it was something."

"It was nothing," Candice cried. "I swear to God!"

The Land Cruiser exploded.

First, Candice heard a sound like a giant bringing its palms together, then a keen whistling. She turned her head in time to see a blur of motion strike the Cruiser. Flames rippled out from underneath the vehicle as it leapt into the air, doors flying open, hood and trunk wrenched apart, the glass in the windows disappearing as fire licked out of the interior.

The Cruiser had been so solid and dependable when they were in it, but now it was a cheap toy, first yanked up into the air by the explosion and then dropped back down. It slammed into the dune under it in a burst of sand and rolled down the slope, flinging away the supplies inside as flaring embers. The flames got a rush of air as it turned end over end, and they roared, covering the Land Cruiser until it was nothing but a fireball, finally coming to a stop at the bottom of the dune in an immediate haze of black, oily smoke.

It had all taken only seconds. Then Nevada reacted, shoving Candice down with a whispered command: "*Stay low!*"

She took her scope out of her pocket and eased her head upward until she was aiming the end through the glass canopy.

"What do you see?" Candice asked. Nevada shushed her. "Do you see my grandfather?"

"No," Nevada whispered back. "He's probably keeping his head down, like you should be doing."

"Yeah, right," Candice retorted, starting to rise.

Nevada shoved her back down. "Technical. Three-man crew. SPG-9 recoilless rifle."

"*What?*"

Nevada dropped the scope into her hands. "Fine! Look!"

As Nevada ducked down to the machine gun, Candice poked her head up and looked into the scope. A hundred feet away a rusty old pick-up was parked on top of a dune. There was something that looked like an oversized bazooka on a tripod in the truck bed, like a harpoon gun on a whaling ship, one person manning it, two others getting out of the truck's cab. Candice recognized their stringy builds, bristly hair, swords, and old AK-47s. Khamsin.

While the man in the back stayed with the truck, the other two were coming their way. Candice ducked back down to see Nevada doing something to the Browning, a Swiss Army knife in hand.

"They're coming over here!" she said in a fearful hush.

"There's not exactly a lot of other places to look for us," Nevada replied, not looking up from her work. "You have your gun on you?"

"No!"

"Oh, right, you're British." Still not looking up, Nevada took the Shadow from her gun belt and held it out. "Take this and go to the hatch. If they try to come in, shoot them."

Candice looked at the pistol like Nevada was offering her a handful of earthworms. "I thought we kinda delegated the shooting people to you."

Nevada turned her full attention to Candice, shoving the gun into her hand and locking her other hand around it. "The moment they know for sure we're in here, they're going to shell us. If I can get the Browning working, maybe I can take out the technical from here."

"The pick-up?"

"Yes, the pick-up," Nevada said patiently. "Just don't let them shoot me before I can shoot them." Candice looked askew at the gun in her hand, then felt Nevada squeeze her shoulder. "You can do this, Cushing. I mean, they can shoot people, and I'm pretty sure they have nowhere near as many degrees as you do."

"Yes, but..." Candice ground her teeth together. "I'm terrified!"

"So be terrified and shoot the motherfuckers."

Crouching low, almost going on her hands and knees, Candice moved to the hatch. It was facing the technical and the pair of approaching men, but she didn't dare stick her head out. Her heart pounded, her lungs working like bellows. It was impossible that she could've been lightly conversing with Nevada a couple of minutes ago. It felt like hours must've passed.

She edged closer to the frame of the hatch, still not poking her head out, but straining her ears to hear anything. She could make out a metal on metal sound, but that was Nevada's work traveling distantly through the fuselage. No trace of the men's footsteps or conversation. Maybe they were taking their time. In this heat, they'd want to conserve energy. Or maybe they'd turned back, assuming their enemies had died in the Land Cruiser.

Almost unthinkingly, Candice moved to check before she stopped herself. She wanted to cry out to Nevada, ask if she'd finished with the Browning yet, say anything to get a response proving she was still there. Sweat ran out of her palms, into the cold, hard weight of the Shadow. Candice looked down at it. It didn't look *right* there, the symmetry not fitting the graceful curves of her slender fingers. It was like some tumor growing out of her palm, filling her hand.

Now Candice could hear them, voices carried on the wind. Laughter. A joke being told. Candice could barely think to translate it with the blood pounding in her ears between each thought. Something about Jew York. The sand puffed lightly with each of their steps, the sound surprisingly feminine. She looked again at the gun in her hand, like a tool this time.

Tried to remember Nevada's instructions: rear sights and front sights, safeties.

She thumbed the safety off. Wrapping her free hand around the unfamiliar heft of the slide, she racked it back and let it spring forward. There was a bullet in the chamber now—potent venom that gave her an immediate contact high. Her ears were supersensitive, hearing the hand settling on the side of the plane to steady a body as it came inside, the huff of exertion as he lugged himself off the ground...

Candice whirled and pivoted, pointing herself at the hatch with the Shadow at the ready. She saw the man filling the doorframe, filling her sights, and she pulled the trigger as fast as she could. Bullets went into him, scooped out handfuls of blood that splashed onto the sand behind him. She kept pulling, no, *squeezing* the trigger. He staggered backwards, holes filling his chest, gun smoke and arterial spray like a bucket of paint dumped over the picture that had once been all white robes and golden sand. He fell on his back, but she was still pulling the trigger, bullets digging up the sand around him, the air full of smoke a shade of blue she'd never seen before. She kept squeezing the trigger with an aching finger. The gun clicked.

There was a pressure in her ears like she was underwater, but they were still so sensitive. She could hear the metal ring of a sword clearing a scabbard, then a high, animal yowl shaped into a human ululation. She thumbed the mag release and the clip dropped away. Candice tried to think of where more ammunition was, but the second man was in the hatch now, coming at her with that trilling howl and a flashing scimitar.

She held her hands up to block the blow and the blade came down right next to the trigger guard on her upturned pistol, slamming the gun down against her chest. Its metal frame kept the sword from entering her body and she pushed back, her strength against his, shoving the blade away while he tried to force it into her, still ululating, the sound filling the wreck like a thousand screeching bats in some dark cave—

"Hey!" Nevada called, and they both turned to see her with the Scorpion raised high. "You'll wake the neighbors."

She fired a short burst, no more than three bullets, but they wrenched the Khamsin away so quickly that Candice was suddenly unbalanced without him straining against her. He flew back, toppling to the ground and skidding across the floor, the sand parting around him.

Nevada let the Scorpion drop, hanging from its strap as she turned back to the Browning. "Cover your ears," she said.

Candice slapped her hands against her head as Nevada let it rip, a bridge of tracer fire immediately connecting the gun and the technical. Candice could see it through the open door. Bullets the size of butter knives poured into the truck even as the last man standing tried to turn the recoilless rifle on them. Before he could, the truck's hood flew up over a bloom of flame and smoke, and then the whole vehicle went up—Candice could see the blast picking up the nearby sand, pushing it along the desert floor in a liquid ripple, and sending gales of it up into the air, hiding all but the light from the flaming wreck.

Nevada took her finger off the trigger, the gun hissing and cooling and leaking smoke. "What'd I tell you?" she cooed to it. "I know you were in the Nazi killing business, but these guys hate Jews and have shit taste in facial hair too. What's the difference?"

Bullets thudded against the plane like hail on a tin shack. Nevada ducked as more bullets sparked off the struts of the canopy, shattering the glass over her. Crouching, she spun the Browning to face the other way and opened up, working the gunfire back and forth blindly. A moment later, more bullets came from the other way—Candice saw them dimple the hull.

Candice poked her head out the door. At least ten Khamsin, both on foot and mounted on horseback, were coming over the same rise the technical had been on. She ducked back behind cover as a barrage chiseled at where her head had been a moment ago.

Nevada took her finger off the trigger. "I think they may be doing a pincer maneuver," she said.

"Is that bad?" Candice asked.

"Well... do you like pincers? Watch my six."

Where's your six? Candice was about to ask, when Nevada popped back up, took quick aim through the shredded canopy, and fired. Her line of tracers walked across the ground, kicking up gouts of sand and knocking the Khamsin down, replacing them with clouds of arterial red.

Some vestigial memory of bad action movies sparked, telling Candice that Nevada's six was behind her, and she wondered how she was supposed to look through the solid metal of the hull before remembering the waist gunner windows. She sprinted to the one looking out on the other side, dropping down against the metal below, and looked gingerly through the window. More bad guys coming over the sand dune there, hooves thundering as the horsemen rode hard for the plane, puffs of smoke blotting the air with each bullet they fired. Candice threw herself down on the floor.

"Easy! There are more of them!"

Nevada ducked down again, covering her head as a volley of return fire punched out more glass in the canopy, the shards raining down on her. "That sucks. If only you had like a gun or something…"

"I ran out of ammo!"

"Ran out?" Nevada demanded, jumping back up to fire a quick burst from the Browning. Candice heard a dying wail from outside. "There were seventeen bullets in the magazine! Who were you shooting, Rasputin?"

"I panicked, okay?"

Nevada took another magazine off her belt and slid it across the floor. "Could you maybe panic only three or four shots at a time?"

Candice picked up the magazine and her hands seemed to know just what to do, popping it into the butt of the pistol and racking the slide. She looked through the window again. In only a minute of chaotic action, the landscape had become clogged with flying sand and lingering gun smoke, the Khamsin roving through it like sharks in a feeding frenzy—a riot of their ululating war cries.

She tried to take aim and fire, spacing out her shots one at a time, but still didn't think she hit anything. They were moving too fast. She got an answer of gunfire ricocheting off the hull all around her. The metal dimpled inward. A foot above her head, it was easy to remember those were bullets trying to get at her.

Candice wanted to curl up in a ball and wait for Nevada to make all the bad men go away, but she couldn't shut off the adrenaline coursing through her, almost shaking her apart trying to get out. It was pure life force, wanting to defend itself, wanting to survive.

She heard the whiplash sound of disturbed fabric in the middle of all the carnage and turned to see one of them pulling aside the tent to get into the plane. Candice aimed and fired, three bullets punching into the silhouette. He went limp, weight settling against the parachute canopy as blood spread through the silk. She knew, intellectually, that she should feel traumatized and sorrowful and horrified, but she grinned fiercely, a laugh welling up in her breast.

"Get some! Get some! Get some!" Nevada shouted over the roar of the machine gun, spent shells fluttering out of the breech and chittering to the floor.

Candice shook her head and looked out the window again. The horsemen rode in a great circle around the plane, while the Khamsin on foot advanced slowly, firing on—Candice ducked her head—any hint of movement. The horsemen were bigger targets, making Candice briefly consider the ethics of shooting horses. She didn't want to. But she didn't want to die either.

Candice jumped up, ready to fire when she saw another pick-up truck cresting the dune on her side of the plane. This one didn't have a bazooka on its back; it looked more like a bunch of tubes tied together, sort of a...

"Nevada!" Candice called. "I think they have rockets!"

"I highly doubt they have—"

The second technical let out a throaty cough, one of the barrels lighting up as it freed a fireball roaring sideways. Candice heard Nevada swear, saw her jump down from the tail gun as the rocket hit. The noise of the explosion crashed into Candice's ears, compacting itself down into a dull, tinny *tone* against her eardrums as fiery claws slashed into the hull, caving in the tail end of the plane. More than that, the impact shoved the plane over, dislodged it from its perch on top of the sand dune and sent it rolling downhill.

The ground slid out from under Candice, rolling her body across the fuselage as the plane careened out of control. She saw the window spinning down to meet her, blaring light in the whirlwind of darkness, and had a nightmare vision of falling partway through it and having her body scissored in half by the plane's revolution. She threw out her arms, catching the window's sides, but her momentum still shoved her facedown into the sand. The plane's roll pulled to a stop, checked by the twisted metal still connecting it to its other, buried half, and it swept sideways instead, digging into the unresisting sand before finally coming to a halt.

Candice spat sand and looked in both directions. The front end of the fuselage was still attached to the buried wreckage, though some of the connections had been sheared off; the rest uttered tortured groans as they held the two halves of the plane together. The back end of the fuselage had disintegrated, the tail ripped off, the compartment open to the elements.

Nevada rose up, bleeding from a gash on her forehead, clutching the Shadow. She looked as bad as Candice—bruised, battered, and in places, bloodied.

"I am never putting my dryer on spin cycle again," she moaned, clutching her bicep.

Over Nevada's shoulder, Candice saw a group of six horsemen wheel around and ride full-tilt for the plane, a cacophony of war cries, cracking rifles, and blasting horse nostrils. Nevada twisted and dropped to one knee, bringing the Shadow up as she faced them. She fired a short burst, and pink mist exploded from the chest of the lead horseman. He toppled from his mount.

The others rode through it, his blood marking their robes. They kept firing—bullets chipped at the ground around Nevada, tore through the sand that still hung heavy in the air from the rollover. Candice threw herself facedown on the ground, looking up to see the Nevada swivel a fraction of an inch to the left, fire another burst, a fraction of an inch to the right, three more bullets.

The second horseman went down, planting himself in sand which sucked him in as the sea welcomed a drowning man. Bullets punched through the third horseman, center mass, severing an artery that quickly painted his chest red. He hung limp in the saddle, shifting out of place more and more with each gallop of the horse. Finally, he fell, his foot catching on the stirrup, the horse dragging his body as it broke away.

The horsemen were scattering like bowling pins now, pulling away before they could get any closer to point-blank range. Except for the one in the back. Streaked with the blood of his comrades, he dismounted as Nevada fired at him, her bullets ripping harmlessly through his cape. He hit the ground running, his rifle coughing smoke as it fired. The bullet combed Nevada's hair. She pulled her own trigger, but the gun clicked empty.

He charged at her, not bothering to rack his rifle's bolt-action, but holding its bayonet out for Nevada's heart. She had no time to reload; her hand dipped into her boot and flashed silver as she came up with her dive knife. She flung it into his chest from six feet away. It thudded into his breastbone. He staggered, but kept coming. The knife had broken his stride, though. When he got within arm's reach of Nevada, she easily ducked out of the way of the bayonet and gave him a hip-toss that landed him on the knife's handle. His weight drove it into his heart, hilt and all.

"I've been meaning to get a new knife anyway," Nevada said.

Candice heard a belch of ignition and the full-throated ripping of a rocket in flight. The technical. It must've lost them when they'd rolled down the dune, but now it had targeted them again. Nevada had already realized this even as Candice froze. She ran as a rocket hit the fuselage behind her, the explosion ripping away more of the hull, and another rocket hit next to it, and another, and another—a series of booming *thumps* like a hammer banging on the world.

Candice lost her balance, each explosion jerking the ground out from under her. She fell and Nevada grabbed her around the waist, lugging her off her feet. Another rocket hit just behind them—Candice felt a wave of pressure break over her, the heat of the explosion sizzling on her skin. She ran as best she could, trying to keep up as Nevada dragged her along. She heard a roar of flames behind her and could only imagine how close the explosions were. Shockwaves hit her like heavyweight punches, nearly ripping her off the ground, and she was so concerned with staying on her feet that she didn't see the abyss looming in front of them until Nevada jumped into it, pulling her along for the ride.

For a second, the chill of rushing air felt good on Candice's overheated skin. Then she realized she was falling thirty feet straight down to the buried cockpit.

Nevada landed in a svelte crouch. Candice landed on her face. Rearing up, she spat out her second helping of sand for the day.

"I hate sand," she muttered.

"I know, right? It's coarse and rough and irritating and it gets everywhere."

"If you're going to quote Star Wars, at least quote one of the good ones..." Candice looked up. A nearly impenetrable cloud of black smoke hung in the air above them. She doubted the B-17 was still in one piece up there. "It's incredible. We managed to crash a plane that's still on the ground."

"If anyone asks, it was like this when we got here." Nevada reached out and grabbed the Shadow that Candice hadn't realized she was still gripping. "Please and thank you."

They looked around. It was like being at the bottom of a well with striations on the walls that could've served as handholds. Candice tried grabbing one and immediately snatched her hand back. In the desert sun, the metal was as hot as a lit skillet.

"Hmm," Nevada said.

"What is it?" Candice asked. She tried to adopt a joking tone, "Don't tell me I'm finally here to see you proven wrong about something."

"Oh no, not at all." Nevada bent down to sit on the sand. She rested her back against the wall as she rubbed the spot on her arm she'd hurt earlier. "This is better than being out in the open with people shooting rockets at us. But, ah—not by much."

Candice looked up nervously. There still had to be, what, a dozen Khamsin up there? She doubted there'd be much confusion about where their targets had disappeared to.

Nevada rotated her shoulder a few times, hissing breath through her teeth. "Yeah, landed on this all wrong. Gonna be sore in the morning."

"Nevada, seriously, *what do we do?*"

Nevada dug into a pocket and came up with a small bottled water. "One of two things: either they kill us right here, right now, or they take us."

Candice could only stand there as Nevada took a gulp. "What happens if they take us?" she asked in a small voice.

"Ever seen a true-crime show? Think girl in the black and white photos who everyone is saying nice things about." Nevada held out the bottle. "Here. Drink. Dehydration is a bitch."

There wasn't much room to pace, so Candice really just kicked one side of the plane and then kicked the other. "So we're buggered? That's it? We're going to be killed and raped and tortured, is that it?"

"Maybe not in that order." Nevada shook the bottle. "Hydrate. It's good for your skin."

Candice took the bottle and drank. It was cool, refreshing, and she found herself gulping it down, desperate for all she could get. She heard voices up above, shouting to one another in harsh Arabic.

She hit the last drop too soon.

"You don't have to be here for it," Nevada said.

Candice looked at her.

Nevada held up the gun. "When you're wounded and left on Afghanistan's plains," she quoted Kipling's *The Young British Soldier*.

For a moment, Candice was dumbfounded. It seemed impossible that there could be anything that would make her welcome death, but intellectually, a bullet to the head had to be better than what the Khamsin had planned for them. And it did seem they were running low on impossible escapes. They'd been lucky, incredibly lucky, but—maybe there was something to be said for cashing out when the cards were against them.

"Reciting poetry to me," Candice said drolly. "When you crush, you crush hard."

Nevada lowered the pistol. "If you think that's good, I know the lyrics to every Britney Spears song."

Candice smiled. "Think you can get us out of this one? Stall for time, make a dumb joke, smoke a cigarette?"

"I don't know."

"Thea—"

"*I don't know,*" Nevada stressed. "If I had money, I wouldn't put it on me."

"I would," Candice said.

Nevada hung her head, but despite the gesture, she seemed to light up somehow. Something about the set of her shoulders. Then Candice realized—she was smiling.

"I never much liked that name."

"What?" Candice asked.

"Thea. But you say it pretty nice."

"It's the accent. Everything sounds better British."

Nevada brought her head up and Candice saw how rueful her smile was. "I don't think I could've killed you anyway." She got up, tossed her gun to the ground, and shouted up to the sky. "Hey! Can you come take us prisoner already? I haven't got all day!"

CHAPTER 6

A ROPE WAS DROPPED DOWN and they were hauled to the surface. There, they were roughly searched, bound, and gagged, their ropes tied to the saddles of the horsemen with a lead of a few feet. The horses were whipped to a cant, and Nevada and Candice were pulled along. It was walk or be dragged.

They walked. They walked and walked and walked. They fell and got back up, the sand sticking to sweat-damp skin, and they walked.

The Khamsin rode ahead of them, sitting in their saddles with a haughty grace, moving in sloping rhythm to their mounts' swaying gaits. It was almost hypnotic. Nevada had no doubt that if she or Candice could not keep up, the riders would be happy to rake the desert floor with them.

They walked.

The sun beat at their clothes, got through them, needled into their bodies and swelled inside them until it was shouldering aside thoughts, memories—anything and everything but the cruel knowledge that they were not meant to be under this heat.

Blisters formed on their feet and their lips cracked for want of water; the blisters burst and the sky itself turned so red it could've been bleeding. The sun hid behind the horizon, but the heat stayed, burning in their sore muscles, in their boiling sweat. The emptiness of the desert seemed to mock them now, full as they were with aches and fatigue and regret.

Finally, some invisible signal passed through the Khamsin, calling a halt. Without permission, Candice collapsed to the sand. Nevada followed, telling herself it was in some sort of solidarity. The cold was little better on their bruised flesh than the heat had been, but they let it take its turn. The Khamsin dismounted and took advantage of the break, feeding their horses, relieving themselves, fixing quick meals—their routines indifferently arrayed around the two women.

Nevada forced her desiccated lips to part, though her mouth felt like old parchment and every movement without water felt like it would tear. "Water… water…" she begged. The thirst inside her was too big to allow dignity to fit alongside it. But the Khamsin ignored her, their callousness almost impressive. It was barely even cruel. More like a meditation predicated on ignoring them.

Nevada kept mumbling the word long after she was out of breath to make herself heard, but the only attention she got was when a horse blanket was thrown over her and Candice. It provided enough protection from the nightly chill for that concern to be crowded out by her soreness and her thirst. She succumbed to unconsciousness still saying that word, like even the sound of it could bring a little relief.

The next thing she knew, a bucket of ice-cold water was poured over their heads. Nevada came awake, still exhausted, not even sure she had slept, except that there was so little heat left in the air that the water soaking through her clothes seemed to freeze her solid.

"Terrorist humor… I would've thought there'd be more Jeff Dunham."

The moon had a toehold on the horizon, polishing the world silver. With her senses reeling from the shock, it took Nevada a moment to distinguish one shadow from the rest.

Their leader was almost unnaturally tall—at least six foot seven inches—his body lean, made even narrower with his hands clasped behind his back. His face was seamed and weathered with the years, but they didn't make him appear aged—they were more like scratch marks on some much-used piece of armor. A well-tended beard dominated his jawline, suitably balanced by a hawkish nose and the dark slashes of his eyebrows. It was a face given to nobility. In another life, Nevada could've imagined him as some celebrated teacher or leader. But in this life, he had empty eyes, eyes that could only be filled with hate, looking for something to destroy. Nevada had witnessed men like him before. Despite the impressive face, the only thing behind it was madness.

"You are enemies of Islam, accused of blasphemy, idolatry, adultery…"

The list went on and on—Nevada could barely hear it over her pounding headache. The Khamsin grabbed her and Candice, cutting their bonds and frog-marching them to where a stake had been driven into the sands, the speaker leading the way. They were shoved down back to back, their wrists chained around the stake with heavy manacles. Nevada tested hers. She was going nowhere fast.

The leader finally finished his recital with: "And you are guilty of the murder of my son."

"In the interest of full disclosure," Nevada said, "when I was in college, I didn't have a Halloween costume one year, so I put on a winter coat and went as an Eskimo. Was that insensitive?"

"Yes," Candice said. "It was."

"Oh, you're speaking for the Eskimos now?"

"They prefer to be called Inuit."

"What, do you have an Eskimo cousin? Does he show up at family reunions and rub his nose against yours?"

"Silence!" the Khamsin leader cried. "These are charges to make Allah weep. The punishment is severe."

"I'm sorry," Candice said, "who are you?"

"I am Nazir al-Jabbar, Khalif of Sudan."

"Wiz Khalifa?" Nevada asked, shaking her head as if to clear her ears. "Not sure I'm a fan of the new look. Maybe you should've just gone with a mohawk."

Nazir smiled warmly, as if they were a pair of yapping puppies, too adorable to be angry with. "I had a daughter much like you once."

"Clear complexion and really thick lashes that kinda give you this eyeliner-without-eyeliner look?" Nevada asked.

"Strong. Stubborn. Intelligent." Gathering his legs under him, Nazir sat cross-legged on the sand with them, his elbows resting on his knees. "A good woman. Or a woman who could be made good, by the hand of Allah." Nazir held up a finger. "But she refused that touch. She was tempted—drawn off the path by the flash and frivolity of your... culture. Its sugar. Instant gratification. Everything bared, cheap, easy to touch. And in time, she became easy to touch too. But by men. Not by God."

Candice spoke up, "Listen, your men were trying to kill us. We defended ourselves..."

"If she speaks again, silence her," Nazir told his nearest follower. He got a compliant nod in return. "I'm trying to teach you something. I want you to learn. You are shallow materialists, are you not? Obsessed with jewels and expensive clothes and fast cars?"

"I'm actually into Beanie Babies," Nevada said. "I think they're coming back in a big way."

Nazir nodded. "Imagine then, if you saw one of your prized possessions in the hands of another. Being used by someone who had no right to it. Being dirtied and stained until you couldn't even look at it. Would you not rather see it burned instead of its continued misuse?"

"People aren't possessions," Candice said.

"Yeah," Nevada agreed. "Wish I could be an optimist on this one, Wiz, but you might not wanna bother writing an acceptance speech for father of the year."

Nazir gestured to his man and a boot crashed into Candice's face, knocking her to the end of her chain's reach. Nevada wrenched against her bonds, but they held fast.

"My daughter's death erased the shame she had brought upon me, but all your deaths will do is put a stop to the sins you swim in. It is unfortunate. You could've made good wives, good mothers, but you turned away from Allah. You and your society."

All around them, the men were loading up again, all in perfect silence. Nazir's words rang out over the landscape, with his followers as quietly attentive as a funeral service.

"You think we have not noticed how your culture quests impotently for purity? You see the sexual immorality brought about by your immodest women, the greed and intolerance that defines your culture, and you wish to be made clean. All we offer is the simple truth of how that cleanliness may come about. But like children running from the taste of medicine, you resist what is proper." He looked at Nevada. "Even abandoning your own young."

Nevada grinned at him, all the wider for how worried she was on the inside. "Oh, let's not go there, Wiz. We were having a real good time listening to your parenting tips."

"Your child grows up in sin and corruption, without even the blood of the family to guide him. Your sins will be visited upon him. Sudan is just the beginning." Nazir stood and paced grandly around the women, his outline glowing as he swept in front of the moon. "In short order, all of Africa will see the righteousness of our cause. Europe, weak and divided, will be next, eagerly kowtowing to the relief we offer. And finally, your home, America. Even more divided than Europe, with no taste for blood, no will for sacrifice. There, I will pull out even the root of your evil. Perhaps in hell, reunited with your spawn, you can finally be the mother you should've been when he first grew inside you."

Nevada abruptly laughed. "Oh, buddy, *wow*—I'm really gonna fuck you up now."

"I do not think so," Nazir said, pointing to the west. Nevada saw the waning light dipping into holes in the ground, deep shadows pooled inside them. "Those are scorpion burrows. As the heat of the day breathes its last, the creatures will be awakened from their slumber. They will swarm out in search of prey and find you here, helpless. The flesh will be picked from your bones while you still draw breath. Just the latest in a string of conquests for Allah, conquests that will continue until all worship our god. We will not rest. We will not falter. All will follow or die."

"Oh," Nevada said, "you're Beyoncé fans."

"I highly doubt Beyoncé would be part of any scheme this half-baked," Candice said, then had second thoughts: "Okay, Tidal."

Nazir folded his hands together. "You think me a monster. And yet, what is the real monstrosity? It is allowing your whoring and immorality to continue. This is not an act of hatred. It is a merciful deed, ending your sins before you give further offense to God. Good day, Thea Quatermain, Candice Cushing—I must continue the work you so foolishly interfered with. Feel free to blaspheme as you are eaten alive, knowing our purity will not be sullied by you, even in death. Allahu Akbar."

The men chorused his final words, one leading a camel to Nazir. All were mounting up, horseflesh surrounding Nevada on all sides as they prepared to depart.

"Hey, daddy dearest," Nevada called. "If you're so merciful, don't I get a last request?"

Nazir spread his hands magnanimously. "Why not?"

"Well, I've always wondered what it'd be like with an Arab guy—no, I'm fucking with you. But how about some tunes? I've got an MP3 player in my back pocket. Just put my earbuds in and press shuffle."

Nazir laughed. "I hate to kill you, Easy Nevada. You are an object lesson in Western immorality. Even now, on death's door, you remain obsessed with entertaining yourself."

"Yeah, well, the whole 'eaten alive' thing sounds like it's gonna take a while."

Nazir gestured for one of his followers to carry out the request. He went to Nevada, dug into her pocket, and came out with an iPod wrapped in its earbud cord. He unwound it painstakingly.

"And put one in the girl's ear too," Nevada said. "Sharing is caring, right?"

The man pushed one bud in Nevada's ear and the other into Candice's, then pressed play on the small white tablet and rested it on Nevada's shoulder. With the cheers of a live recording, Peter Frampton started singing "Baby, I Love Your Way."

Nazir mounted his camel, casting one last look at Nevada and Candice before departing with his men. They were left with nothing but the sand and wind.

"You know, I think we really misjudged that guy," Nevada said. She turned her head to look at the burrows. Nothing had emerged yet, but the moonlight outlined them in horrifying detail. "He's a sweetie pie. Remind me to kill him for that thing about my kid."

Candice wasn't listening. "I'm going to die listening to Peter Frampton."

"You don't like Peter Frampton? What, do you not like to *feel*?"

Nevada turned her head, trying to get at the iPod with her teeth, but the effort of reaching for it nearly slid it off her shoulder. She raised her shoulder desperately, getting the MP3 player to balance again, and breathed tersely, trying not to jostle it.

"Could be worse," Candice said.

"How could it be worse?" Nevada asked, trying to relax her shoulders to settle the iPod into place. "Could it be raining?"

"Technically, yes. But scorpions don't eat people."

"You're sure?"

"I've watched David Attenborough for twenty years. As long as we don't agitate them, we'll be fine."

"What happens if we agitate them?" Nevada asked curiously.

Candice bit her lip. She could see stirrings of movement in the burrows. "They sting us to death."

"So as long as we don't move while a swarm of scorpions walk all over us, we get to die of thirst."

Candice shrugged. The Frampton over, Ginuwine's "Pony" played with its burping reverbs.

"You see what happened to my grandfather?"

"No. If he's smart, he kept his head down once the jeep exploded. Oh, I'm probably not going to get the deposit back."

"That was a rental?"

"Yes. Good news is, I can get us out of these handcuffs."

"Yeah?" Candice asked, sounding less than sure.

"Yeah. You see the cord to the headphones?"

Candice twisted her head. "Uh-huh."

"Bite it, then pull the player so it falls into my hands. I'm cupping them right behind my back."

"Obviously," Candice said, straining her neck for the cord. She couldn't reach it. "Whatever you're doing, I don't suppose you could've done it sooner."

She stuck out her tongue, managing to curl it around the cord, pulling it into her teeth as Nevada said "Nah, that Peter Frampton was a bop."

It made Candice's vertebra pop loudly, but she managed to twist enough that the MP3 player dropped into Nevada's hands.

Nevada took one last look at their death trap. The sand of the burrows was now brightly lit and alive with scurrying black carapaces. Scorpions, shining in the full moon. There were at least a hundred already.

"You know how Apple will void the warranty if you open up an iPod yourself? Well, I don't have a warranty, but I do have a set of lockpicks." She pried off the back of the MP3 player.

Candice let out a shrill laugh. "I could kiss you!"

"I have been pointing that out." Nevada sighed remorsefully. "I just downloaded a whole Kanye album onto this…"

Metal scraped against metal as she worked the torsion wrench of her set into the lock and bent it slightly, just beginning to turn the plug.

"Peter Frampton right in front of Ginuwine," Candice observed. "You make an odd playlist."

"It was on shuffle," Nevada said defensively, fitting a pick rake into the lock and teasing out the first pin's shear line. "Frampton is for cool vibes."

"Uh-huh. And Ginuwine?"

"I'll be honest with you. That one's for Poundtown."

Candice blew out a breath. "I'm going to die and the last song I listened to is going to be your sex jam."

"It isn't my first choice for how to eat you out, no." The plug rotated a little with Nevada's tension on the wrench. She eased the pick rake to the next pin, working it up slowly, carefully.

Nevada couldn't resist any longer. She looked over to the burrows. The scorpions were a carpet covering the desert floor, the moon glinting off their shiny carapaces like they were some living assembly of bone: butting against each other, climbing over one another, slowly coming awake into an orgiastic frenzy.

They were twenty feet away, sandwiched between two high dunes that laid on top of one another, and the level sand led directly to where Candice and Nevada were chained up.

Nevada redoubled her efforts.

"Nevada," Candice said gently. "How long is this going to take?"

The lock ticked quietly and rotated a little more. Nevada pressed the pick rake further "I've gotten two pins. Once I get them all, we're free."

"Okay," Candice said as the scorpions inched closer. "How many pins are there?"

"That's a very good question, Candice. Gold star."

Nevada thought she could hear the scorpions: their rustling bodies and chittering mandibles, that string music that always played when you saw a spider in a documentary. She tried to remind herself of what David Attenborough had said, but it wasn't like he was *there*, now was he?

"Nevada…" Candice keened plaintively.

The lock twisted more. "Three down."

The scorpions surged toward them, a rising tide of black water—Nevada could see them licking up the steep slopes, unable to make the climb, slipping back into the flooding mass that was coming right at them.

The scorpions were upon them. Nevada froze, feeling their cool touch covering her body, passing over her with a million scratching legs. She wanted to leap up, shake herself off for an entire week, burn herself alive so she was clean. A cool lick of sweat ran down her back and she prayed the scorpions didn't notice, didn't seek out an appetizing meal...

"How many more?" Candice asked. "Nevada, how many more pins?"

"I'm...not...moving," Nevada said carefully. She could feel one slipping into her pocket, nosing along the seam like the familiar weight of her wallet, but *alive*. It could touch her, it could feel her—

"You're not arachnophobic, are you?"

"Oh yeah," Nevada said, breathless. "I'm one of those weird people who are creeped out by giant bugs with multiple legs crawling all over me!"

"You have multiple legs," Candice said, needling irresistibly.

"Fuck you!"

Nevada's entire body wanted to shudder, and she focused all her will on not letting it. She felt a hundred, a thousand legs on her, airy and insubstantial, but they were alive, aware of her, trying to figure out what she was and if she was *food*.

"Calm down," Candice said gently. "Close your eyes. Breathe with me. Deep and easy, okay? Breathe." She took a deep breath. "Thea, *breathe*," she insisted, and took another breath. This time Nevada matched it, her back moving against Candice's as they both swelled with fresh air. Candice slowly exhaled, Nevada following along, and it felt like a connection.

"I can do it," Nevada said, her voice barely a whisper as her tools rustled in the lock. Another pin was driven into place, the key pin plied up, the driver pin slotted into place, then another, and another—and always in the back of her mind, Candice's breathing, and her own following along. Like Candice was breathing for her, letting Nevada feel only the surge of fresh air into her lungs instead of the scorpions crawling all over her, their stingers at the ready, all claws and legs...

The plug spun all the way around, clicking the lock open, and the sound must've startled one of the creatures because Nevada felt a sharp prick at her wrist. She swallowed a scream, jerked her hand away, and forced herself to slowly turn, crouch over Candice's bound hands, and work on those manacles. Her breath burned against the back of Candice's neck as she worked, first one pin, then another, and another, until the plug ticked all the way around and released.

Then she pulled Candice up, away from the swarm, brushing them both off as she hauled them bodily away. The moment they were clear she was jumping up and down, ripping at her clothes, scrubbing at her skin until she had almost annihilated the memory of their touch. Then she picked up a rock at her feet and threw it into the swarm.

"That seems uncalled for," Candice said mildly, plucking a scorpion out of her pocket and tossing it underhanded back with its friends.

"One of them stung me." Nevada held out her wrist. "Tell me if I'm gonna die. If I'm gonna die, just get a rock and do it now. I don't want to know what nightmares this is all gonna give me."

"You'll be fine," Candice said. "Scorpions can't kill a full-grown adult. No matter how immature they are."

"*Are you sure?*"

Candice gave her a look. "David Attenborough would not lie."

"Okay…" Nevada dusted herself off. "New rule on this adventure: all animals must have four legs, tops." She ran her hands through her hair. "God… let's get the hell out of here. I don't want to be here when the queen comes out."

Nevada could feel Candice's eyes on her back as she walked. "Scorpions don't have queens."

"You really wanna take that chance?"

Candice followed after her. "Where are we going?"

"No idea. But hopefully we find some shelter before the sun comes up. Then we sleep during the day, move at night."

Candice nodded. "If we follow the moon, we can at least be sure we're not going in circles."

"I was following the moon," Nevada said quickly.

"Uh-huh."

———◆———

As hot as the Sahara was during the day, it was even colder at night. They took turns in Nevada's flak jacket. Every other minute it seemed

Candice could feel Nevada slipping it over her, warm from her own body, and she breathed in Nevada's oddly comforting musk. Then she would take it off, put it around Nevada, and hug herself to keep warm for another dozen steps. And before she knew it, the jacket would be back around her, blocking the wind that cut into her with its chill.

Above them, the stars weren't beautiful anymore. They were mocking, an infinite reach as expansive as the desert they walked through. Candice felt less like she was walking and more like she was falling into a crevice—on one side, the endless sand, on the other, endless stars. And the burn in her mouth was still catching her tongue.

"What are you thinking?" Nevada asked, rubbing her arms to keep warm. Candice said nothing. She was enthralled by her breath visibly leaving her mouth. It looked like she was leaking. "C'mon, you're smart, you're always thinking. Tell me—"

"How smart can I be? I ended up here."

"Well, I'm here and I'm a genius," Nevada said.

Candice sighed, counting the seconds until she could put the jacket back on Nevada—trying to relish the relative warmth, which was impossible when Nevada was freezing. "I was remembering my Churchill."

"Oh yeah?"

Candice cleared her throat and quoted: "Only the Madhi's wives, if we may credit Slatin, 'rejoiced secretly in their hearts at the death of their husband and master,' and, since they were henceforth to be doomed to an enforced and inviolable chastity, the cause of their satisfaction is as obscure as its manifestation was unnatural." She grinned ruthlessly. "I think I figured out the satisfaction."

"Really? I was just thinking the exact same thing," Nevada teased. "So what were you going to ask me back at the crash site?"

Candice reeled mentally—Nevada had put her off-guard with her gentle questioning, making *this* ask seem much more pointed. "Is this the best time?"

"Do you have somewhere to be?" Nevada needled. "You asked what I was doing after we found the skull, then you tried to change the subject—"

"People started shooting at us," Candice said, taking off the jacket. "The subject changed on its own."

She moved to put the jacket around Nevada, who pushed her away. "I'm fine."

"You're blue."

"No need to get racial."

"It's *your* jacket," Candice insisted, trying to put it on her again.

Then Nevada pulled her into an embrace, tightening the jacket around both of them as her teeth chattered. Candice took a deep breath, cast back in time to sharing breath with Nevada when the scorpions were all over them. Without the danger, it was shockingly intimate. Candice could breathe in Nevada's scent, the smell of her hair, and feel like it was a part of her.

Nevada pulled away, taking the jacket with her and pulling it on. Trapping the newfound warmth in with her as she zipped it up. "It does look better on me."

It was nearly dawn, the rising sun starting to fill in the shadows with the day's first traces of color. The sands blazed with orange and red and yellow, almost hurting Candice's eyes with their intensity. Then she saw shadows that refused to be lightened—flickering on the horizon with some looping gait. Camels. Camels being ridden.

"There!" she pointed. "There, c'mon, c'mon!"

She ran, an influx of energy burning away her tiredness. Nevada was hard-pressed to keep pace with her as she dashed up the dunes and came back down them, more than once falling into a roll, then springing back up like she weighed nothing.

"Hey!" she called, waving her arms as the camel riders loomed closer. "Hey! Heeeey!"

Nevada ran right beside her. "Do you have some Coke? Diet Coke? Sprite? I'll even take Dr. Pepper if you have it..."

They pitched down a sloping dune and came up another whose sand was slippery, almost a powder. Nevada pulled Candice up it as the sand slid out from under them. Finally they were on the ridge of the dune, clawing their way to the top of it—and the camel riders were acacia trees, the heat distorting their gnarled branches and scraggly leaves into a deception.

The bait and switch ended Candice's hope with a crushing finality. She'd tried determination, she'd tried hope, she'd even tried having faith in Nevada. There was nothing left to try. The hopelessness of her situation snapped closed on her. She was going to die. She was going to die in a bloody desert, where she'd been born, like her whole life was a flat circle amounting to nothing.

And the maddening part was how unfinished she was. She'd never find Cleopatra's tomb. She wouldn't wipe that holier-than-thou look off Nazir's face. She wouldn't even tell Nevada... she didn't even know what she wanted to tell Nevada, just that it was stuck in her teeth like a popcorn kernel. She was going to die with a popcorn kernel in her teeth.

She looked at the trees like she could force them into being people.

"Mirage," Nevada moaned. "It's not even a good mirage. Where are the native girls with little coconut drinks? Where's the swimming pool I swim in and then it turns out to be sand?"

"Quiet," Candice said.

"What?" Nevada asked, examining the trees more closely. "Is one of them really a guy on a camel?"

"Just be quiet!" Candice hissed. Raising her hands to her mouth, she did a birdcall.

Nevada blinked. "If you're going crazy, please take me with you."

Candice pointed to the upper branches, where a blue, fork-tailed swallow replied in birdsong. "That's a barn swallow."

"What do crazy black women even do?" Nevada asked herself. "I know crazy white women listen to K-pop for some reason..."

Candice dropped her hands so hard that they slapped against her thighs. "Birds. Drink. Water. These blokes migrate all the way from South Africa to Great Britain. They stop at watering holes along the way. We follow this one, it'll lead us straight to water."

Nevada snapped her fingers. "That's not bad. Attenborough again?"

Candice shook her head. "It's how the Kushites established caravan routes."

The barn swallow took flight.

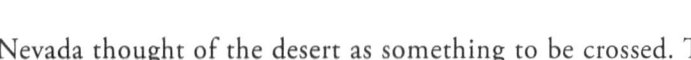

Nevada thought of the desert as something to be crossed. To Candice, it was something to be immersed in. Endured. In the desert, life was an act of resistance. Maybe it always was.

They'd been walking for hours. The barn swallow flew effortlessly, and Candice was beyond envious. She would've sold her soul to do that. But she couldn't, so she walked. Despite the heat. Despite the sun. Despite the sand burning into the soles of her feet.

It was strange. Candice had never thought of herself as particularly tough. Yet here she was, no hope, no drive, not even the numbness she'd felt after the disappointment of the acacia trees. She *longed* for that numbness—it had been better than this, feeling every jagged step she took, her throat so dry it felt scabbed over, her muscles clawing at each other in their soreness. She supposed this cast-iron core she'd uncovered should've been empowering or confidence-building or something. It felt more like she was too stupid to know when to give up and die.

She kept moving. When she started to feel lightheaded, she didn't particularly care to fight it. It was a new sensation, at least. Repetition was worse than the pain. Pain was inherently interesting. Pain was something. She was drowning in nothing. Miles of it crushing down on her, even what few thoughts she could manage going, going, squeezed out of existence—

"You really think this bird is going to water?" Nevada asked, her voice a horrible rasp. Like she had more scar tissue than lungs.

"Of course," Candice said, responding more to contradict Nevada than out of any conviction. She wasn't sure of anything. How could anything be as certain as the heat, the sand, the infinity surrounding them on all sides? "Don't you?"

Nevada coughed. "I'm fucking doing this so when that bird fucking lands, and there's no fucking water, I can fucking kill it."

Candice laughed and it sounded like she'd dropped something into a garbage disposal. "You come up with the best plans."

"Chicken tenders," Nevada muttered, continuing the conversation on some plane of existence Candice wasn't privy to. "Hot wings…"

"Chicken tikka masala," Candice said.

"Candice, you're losing it." Nevada stumbled. Candice stood next to her, not sure if she should help her up—it seemed cruel. But, painstakingly, Nevada pulled herself to her feet. "You're babbling. You're not making any sense."

Candice followed along as Nevada set off again. "It's a staple dish in Britain. I had it twice a week."

"British cooking? I just want to kill the thing, not torture it."

"If British cooking is so bad, how come you're the ones who need Gordon Ramsey to come and—where's the bird?"

They looked around. The sky was a sadistic blue belying the furnace that was under it. "I think he was going this way," Candice said, trudging up a sand dune, cataloging the interesting new pains she was feeling in her legs.

"Stupid bird... won't even let us kill it right..."

Candice wheezed a laugh. "Just as well... this seems like a pretty good time to start a vegetarian diet."

Nevada laughed like an emphysema patient sucking in air. "It might just be the heatstroke, dehydration, and extreme fatigue, but you're really funny these days."

"Don't forget starvation."

"Oh, this is nothing. You should see me before bikini season."

Candice stumbled; Nevada steadied her, a hand on her shoulder blade, and Candice was unmoored in time. She was sharing the jacket with Nevada in the night, she was being kissed on the train, she was thinking of how Nevada's touch didn't hurt when everything else *did*, and she was falling, or the world was spinning, rushing up to meet her, swallowing her into sand.

Then she was being dragged.

"Candice, look. *Look*." Nevada's hand in her hair, pulling her head up. *Probably been wanting to do that for a while.* "Please tell me that's real."

It was right on the other side of the dune they'd climbed. Forty feet of clear blue water, the water they baptized people in, the water they washed babies in. The sand couldn't even touch it—it became green grass, green shrubs, palm trees ringing the pool, protecting it, keeping it pure. An oasis. A bloody fucking oasis. Candice couldn't believe her eyes. No, she couldn't believe her ears—there should've been a choir playing. Enya. *Something*.

"It's real," she murmured.

Nevada hauled her to her feet with something like a roar. "C'mon, Cushing—get *up*—starvation my *ass*!"

Candice felt like she was flying: running down the slope and having Nevada pull her and being sucked toward the oasis like it was a magnet and she was an iron filing. "Hold on a second... hold on... I need to... think of a way..."

Nevada let go of her at the water's edge—even that soft, marshy ground felt good under her feet, felt like the water was trying to be drunk by her—and ripped off her clothes, tugged off her boots—

"To tell if... the water's safe to drink..." Candice muttered, a little before Nevada dove into it.

Candice agreed. It didn't matter. Nothing mattered. She let herself kneel down, let herself sag down, and the water embraced her. Cool and... and... and it didn't matter what else it was. It was cool and it wasn't the desert.

She felt hands on her, Nevada tugging at her clothes, freeing her from the little weight they had, and with nothing left to hold her down, she floated back into the nothing that'd been trying to claim her for as long as she could remember. At least it wasn't as damn hot as it'd been before.

Something growled. It chased Candice into wakefulness, where she realized the sound was her stomach, tightening itself into nothingness. She put a hand over her belly in aching sympathy as she took in her surroundings.

It was almost dusk, the sun laying itself down behind the horizon, shadows lengthening, the sky a hazy shade of purple. There was heat, but the roving wind took away its sting, and she'd been placed under shade that further limited it. She was on the shore of the oasis, at the very tip of the water, two date palms growing together over her, providing the pool of shade she was in. She'd been undressed, her underwear the only thing preserving her modesty, and as she moved to cover herself, her body started in with a litany of complaints, her stomach the loudest of all.

"You're up," Nevada said, and Candice turned to see that she was reaching up to pull the medjool dates from one of the palms that grew all around the water. She wore the flak jacket. Nothing else.

Candice looked away. "Where are my clothes? Where are *your clothes?*"

"I rinsed them out and hung them up to dry on that palm tree that's growing all horizontal. See it?"

Candice looked around until she found a date palm whose trunk pulled a hard right as soon as it was out of the soil, growing sideways out over the water. Her clothes and Nevada's had been hung over the trunk.

Candice got up, wincing as she did, but she'd barely taken a step before she crashed back down to the sand.

"Easy there, soldier." Nevada walked back to sit cross-legged beside her. She'd pried loose a huge piece of bark from one of the trees and then piled it high with dates, which she set down in front of Candice. "Eat up. And maybe drink some water. I hear it's good for you."

Candice could barely manage to roll her eyes before she stuffed her face. The dates were about the best thing she'd ever tasted.

Curiosity warred with hunger and they fought to a standstill. Her politeness was the real loser; she talked with her mouth full. "How long was I out?"

"Six hours at least. I took a catnap myself, once I'd eaten. Slow down. You're going to choke yourself."

Candice didn't slow down. "Why are you naked?"

Nevada shrugged. "Figured I'd spent way too long wearing pants." In acknowledgment of Candice's discomfort, she pulled the jacket closed. "Sleeping in the nude in a desert oasis. That's one for the bucket list."

Candice wanted to keep shoving dates down her throat until her stomach begged for mercy, but the slosh of the cool water was even more of a temptation. She got onto all fours and pulled herself to it, dunking her head in, scrubbing her face, and only then starting to drink. Mother's milk couldn't have tasted so good.

Candice rolled onto her back, dropping her head into the water until it was up to her ears. It felt like her brain was cooling. "So now what?"

Nevada snitched one of the dates Candice hadn't eaten. "We have food, we have water—a place like this, tourists or a caravan will have to show up sooner or later. When they do, we hitch a ride back to civilization."

"That's *it*?" Candice sat up, her body protesting less than before. With food in her belly and water lubricating her throat, she felt almost human again. "What about Nazir? What about the tomb?"

"Nazir will get his. I'm sure the Air Force has a million drone pilots just itching to get their joysticks on him." Nevada placed the dates closer to Candice. "Eat. They're free-range organic."

Candice smiled slightly as she put another in her mouth, this time savoring the taste, slowly chewing before swallowing and only then speaking. "And the tomb? We're so close!"

"We were close to getting killed. You getting killed. That'd be on me, and it's not happening."

Candice felt an almost irrational anger. It was like Nevada was giving up. Giving up on *her*. "I'm a big girl, Thea. I knew what I was getting into."

"I didn't," Nevada said. "I'm ready to die. I've been ready for a long time. But for the past *day*, I've been watching *you* die, and I can't take it. I couldn't do it at the crash, and I can't do it now."

"But what about—"

Nevada held up a hand, face flushing, knowing immediately what Candice would bring up. Who she would bring up. "Que sera, sera."

Candice shook her head. Maybe she was too tired to muster up anger, denial, all the other emotions. She could only manage a weary acceptance now. "That's it? Whatever will be, will be?"

"I don't see another option here. I have been thinking and thinking of some way out of this, some trick, some scheme, but all I can think to do is keep you safe. You shouldn't be here. I never should've brought you."

Candice guffawed. "Come off it, Nevada. It's not like you pushed me out of a plane or anything."

Something of Nevada's indomitable personality cracked her face into a smile. "I might have entertained the possibility."

"I knew it," Candice grinned.

"But then you put on a parachute, so…"

Candice flicked a date at her. Nevada caught it and popped it in her mouth. "Don't waste food." She got up, dusting herself off. "It'll be dark soon. Wanna see me start a fire?"

It didn't take long for Candice to become exhausted once more. She dressed herself against the coming cold, as did Nevada, and managed to stretch a little before her body was ready to give out again. So much for cast-iron toughness. If it was still there, Candice would be happy never to need it again in her life.

The campfire Nevada had built lapped at the darkness, its orange light shooting out over the water. The wind stirred waves as gently as a mother rocking an infant, and the fire glinted off them as they sloshed. Candice lay looking at the water, taken by how beautiful it was. She wasn't surprised when Nevada lay down behind her—spreading the jacket over both of them and wrapping Candice in her arms.

"I never thought I'd say this, but—this is a better Oasis than the Wonderwall guys."

Candice groaned. "Why is it Yanks can only appreciate Oasis for *Wonderwall*? Noel's had ten straight number one albums..."

She felt ridiculously at ease considering the circumstances. It was a perfectly ironic reversal of being stranded on a desert island. She and Nevada had washed up from a sea of sand onto an island of life-giving water. Scant supplies, little hope of rescue—all she had was Nevada. It seemed like enough, and she wanted to thank Nevada for that. At least show Nevada she didn't blame her for getting them into this. It seemed the least she could do was be honest.

"Back at the crash, I was going to ask you if you wanted to get a drink when all of this was over."

"Oh." For once, Nevada sounded genuinely taken aback. "Okay. I'd like that."

Nevada put her hand on Candice's hip, not squeezing, but clearly feeling the firmness of the flesh and the heat of Candice's body through her clothes. Candice looked out at the water. The fire was dying now, casting less light to reflect off the waves. When Nevada kissed her cheek, it was so soft that Candice felt like she was blushing. Nevada ran a finger from Candice's hair to the line of her jaw. She cupped Candice's chin, fingers brushing her lips with the same admiring touch, and kissed behind Candice's ear, below it, her tongue slipping inside—

"Thea, I haven't brushed my teeth in forty-eight hours," Candice said plaintively.

Nevada nibbled on Candice's earlobe. "I can avoid your mouth."

"I'm not wearing any make-up."

"You don't need it."

"I don't even have on deodorant!"

Nevada stopped, drumming her fingers on Candice's hip. "I don't know what you expect me to do with your armpit, but I feel like we should discuss it first."

Candice sighed and turned over onto her back so she could face Nevada. "I just don't want our first time to be right on the heels of a death march. I want to wear a nice dress and have a nice meal—put on a CD, maybe…"

Nevada grinned. "You wanna wear a dress for me?"

"It's not a romantic thing," Candice insisted, shaking her head. "I'm not the kind of girl who shags in alleys and backseats… and there is an awful lot of sand here."

Nevada took a deep breath and lay back down, resting her head on Candice's chest. "Okay. I would hate for you to think I'm wearing my usual underwear. I dress much cuter when I'm not expecting anyone to shoot at me."

Candice found herself wrapping her arms around Nevada, holding her with a degree of comfort she wouldn't have expected. On a whim, she slid her hands under Nevada's shirt, touching the bare skin of her back, and heard Nevada breathe a little heavier.

"So, what are we gonna do after we get that drink?" Nevada asked.

"Well, I can take you to my council flat, which I've been subletting to my friend Marsha, who will need lots of advance notice to get out before I come back."

"What if I slip the cheeky guv'na a quid to get lost for a few hours?" Nevada asked, showcasing what had become of Dick van Dyke's accent after he finished filming *Mary Poppins*.

"If this is gonna work, I'm gonna need you to stop doing British accents. Forever."

"I can live with that. So then I get you alone in your flat…"

"Please, you're American. Call it a hovel."

Nevada scoffed. "Oh no, my brother's boat, that's a hovel. There's no way you sleep in a hovel. I bet you fold all your clothes and put them in drawers."

Candice's brow furrowed. "Do… is there something else you do with them?"

"Well, in your case, I rip them off you and run an ice cube over your body until it melts."

"Mmm," Candice purred happily. Credit Nevada for coming up with good post-desert ideas. "And then what?"

"I want to taste you."

Candice felt a horribly nauseating giggle rising up in her. Her plan to defuse the situation was not getting along with her plan not to have sex outdoors. "I was picturing more foreplay…"

"No, right now. I wanna taste…"

Nevada's hand brushed over her hip again, delved between their bodies. It stopped at Candice's belly and Nevada looked up to meet her eyes. Candice found herself winking. She could've cringed hard enough to erase herself from the space-time continuum, but Nevada seemed to find it charming.

"You're adorable," she said, flashing a smile that made Candice feel more than that—feel beautiful.

Her hand crept slowly under Candice's waistband. Candice knew Nevada was giving her time to think it over, object to it, but she was unable to resist, which made the painstaking slither under her panties feel maddeningly tantalizing. Nevada seemed to wait until the last possible second before finally letting her fingers slide against the lips of Candice's sex, and the touch made Candice gasp—tingling at her opening, with shockwaves going deep inside her to places where she could only yearn to be touched. Nevada didn't enter her, though. Her fingers ran, almost perversely soothing, over her labia, following its little twists, the slight tremors going through it. Candice ached to spike her hips up and take those fingers inside her, where they belonged, and she shook with the determination not to do it. She held no illusions—she was thoroughly seduced. It was only stubbornness that had her clinging to the rules she'd set.

Her clitoris stung, swollen and craving to be touched, and as Nevada's fingers approached it from below, Candice let out a low moan that made her cheeks flame in embarrassment. Nevada chuckled deep in her throat and took her hand away before it could reach that tender little place, either sparing Candice further humiliation or denying her as peevishly as Candice had denied her. She brought her fingers to her mouth and Candice closed her eyes, knowing that watching would be too much—it was bad enough *hearing it*, the *relish*, when Nevada could be smacking her lips and moaning her pleasure between Candice's legs.

Nevada swallowed like she'd had a glass of lemonade at the end of a hot day, then snuggled back down against Candice's burning body. "Not bad. Night, Candice."

Candice stared up at the night sky, feeling so aglow that she might be seen from one of the stars up there in the firmament, and knew it would be a long time before she slept.

———◆———

Candice woke up to Nevada's hand covering her mouth, swallowing up any noise she might've made. "Don't move," Nevada told her in hushed tones. "Don't make a sound."

Candice's heart raced, the blood flowing hot in her veins—she felt like steam would come off her, going from the chill of the night to this sudden, blushing warmth. Then she heard footsteps in the sand.

Moonlight was bleaching the sand white and making the water pitch black. Where the surface was moved by the wind there were silvery ripples like buried bones being uncovered. Her eyes adjusting to the sublime light, Candice saw a dark figure creeping through the oasis, visible only as an absence of stars.

Nevada's other hand sank into the ground, taking up a fistful of sand. They waited—Nevada keeping her palm over Candice's mouth, Candice letting it stay there, actually finding it reassuring as the figure came closer and closer. The sand sinking under his boots, his breath coming with a wisp of condensation into the chill air.

Candice was almost in pain, having gone from the cold of night to a heated excitement, with the shock of arousal now replaced by fear.

He came closer. Candice could actually feel Nevada tensing, muscles tightening, minute shifts in her weight. This must have been what it would feel like to embrace a tiger as it readied itself to pounce.

The man was a few steps away when Nevada lunged up, throwing the handful of sand into his face. He cried out in surprise as Nevada collided with him, driving her other hand into his belly. The outcry cut off like a switch had been thrown. With a quick twist, she was behind him, pinning his arm around his back. The wrenching move drove his face into the moonlight.

"Grandpa?" Candice asked.

Nevada paused midway through breaking Usama's arm. "I don't suppose this is your other grandfather? And he's an asshole?"

"Nevada!"

She let him go. "What were you doing sneaking up on us?"

Usama held his stomach as he answered in an understandably winded voice. "I thought you might be sleeping… Didn't want to wake you… Nice punch…"

They rekindled the fire. Usama had brought three camels; he took two blankets out of one's saddlebags. Nevada and Candice gratefully huddled in them as the fire roared back to life.

"How'd you get away from the Khamsin?" Usama asked, warming his hands.

Candice started to answer, but Nevada spoke over her. "Lockpick in my iPod, then we followed a bird here. What's your story? Where have you been?"

"Nevada," Candice chided.

"I'm also sorry for punching you in the gut. That was a low blow," Nevada added.

Usama waved her off. "I deserve such a treatment for allowing you to be taken. When the horsemen attacked, I hid to wait for an opening. None came, so when they captured you, I followed at a discreet distance to free you when the chance arrived. Unfortunately, they split up. I followed one set of tracks, but it was the group going back to their camp. When I realized you weren't there, I borrowed these camels and came back the other way. But by then, the tracks had faded."

"So how'd you find us?" Candice asked.

"I thought to myself that if you hadn't escaped, you'd be dead. And if you had escaped, this is the only source of fresh water in a hundred miles, so if you weren't here…"

"We'd be dead." Nevada turned to Candice. "This is what I like about men. Coolheaded logic. That and handlebar mustaches."

Usama took a deep breath and patted his belly as if to affirm he was intact. "So! We are alive. We have camels. Where to now?"

"Nearest town with phone service," Nevada said. "And phones for sale."

Usama looked at Candice in confusion. "What happened to finding the next clue?"

"There is no next clue," Nevada interrupted. "It's too dangerous. We're folding our hand."

Usama glanced at her, then back to Candice. "And you're letting her?"

"What do you mean I'm letting her?"

"What do you mean she's letting me?"

Picking up a stick, Usama stoked the fire. "Nevada, you don't seem the kind of woman to give up when the odds are not in your favor."

"Stubborn?" Nevada asked him.

"Suicidal," Candice suggested.

Usama didn't answer either way. "So if you are giving up now, it seems to me you must be doing so on my granddaughter's behalf. A very thoughtful gesture, but I am surprised she's letting you do so."

Candice felt oddly put on the spot. "Nevada is really the being-in-danger expert here, so if she thinks it's too risky, it's probably too... I mean, she wouldn't call this off for no reason."

The fire popped and crackled, spitting sparks up into the air.

Nevada bit the inside of her cheek. "Look, Usama, you said you found their base camp?"

Usama nodded. "But there's probably more. The Khamsin keep themselves scattered, like packs of wolves. If you see one, there's probably ten more you don't see."

"That's cockroaches," Nevada said dryly. "But if you can put this camp on a map, we can call it in to the American embassy, get a drone strike going. They take out any high-value targets, that could be a fat bounty."

"Is that likely?" Candice asked.

Nevada shrugged. "It's a lotto ticket, but that's no reason not to play it. So, Usama—coordinates?"

He gave a bemused toss of his head. "It's not hard to find. You just look for the big boat in the middle of the desert."

Nevada leaned forward until she was almost kissing the fire. "What boat?"

CHAPTER 7

"I JUST WANT TO LOOK at it," Nevada said, strenuously innocent, as she took the looking glass and aimed it at the boat.

They'd set out almost the moment Usama had mentioned it, barely stopping to fill their canteens, and riding the camels hard enough to piss off any self-respecting animal lover. After half a day's ride, Usama had called a halt. They'd dismounted and he'd led them to the top of a dune overlooking the camp. There, on their bellies, they looked out at their treasure.

Nevada handed Candice the telescope. "So much for an air strike."

Candice took a look.

Under a web of camouflage netting, a dozen military surplus tents were set up, their army-green tarped over to match the desert sands. There was a corral for camels, a shooting range, stacks of supply crates and gasoline barrels, jeeps and pick-up trucks. Everything needed for a terrorist training camp.

And in the middle, slanting up the graceful slope of a dune, sat a papyriform boat. It reminded Candice immediately of the famous Khufu barge that had been discovered miraculously intact in 1954. It was over a hundred feet long and twenty feet wide, its hull long and lean, turning up at the ends into a proudly vertical bow and stern. In the middle was a deckhouse, thirty feet long, seven feet high, and undoubtedly holding much weight. It was there the boat met the summit of the dune it lay on, one half on the slight incline of the dune, the other half balanced in the air over a precarious slope, either excavated by the terrorists or laid bare by the ever-shifting sands of the desert.

It couldn't be closer. It couldn't be further away.

"Either they're waiting for us, or…" Nevada trailed off.

"Okay," Candice said, nervous to be even this close to the camp. "You've gotten a look at it."

Nevada nodded. "How many people you think are down there?"

"No," Candice said firmly.

"At least a hundred," Usama said.

"A hundred," Nevada said thoughtfully.

Candice rapped her on the head with the scope. "You said you wanted to quit, remember? 'We're folding our hand'?"

"That was before I knew we had a straight flush!"

"That's a straight flush?" Candice asked, gesturing to the army of Khamsin.

"I didn't say it was a royal flush," Nevada said defensively.

"I don't play poker," Usama said.

"What happened to this being too dangerous?" Candice insisted.

"I thought we'd have to find another ten dumb markers doing the 'Goonies are good enough' thing. But look!" Nevada jabbed her finger repeatedly over the dune. "It's right there. That's gotta be the last stop. And it's gotta be in the deckhouse, which is smaller than a mobile home. We just have to walk in, grab the shit, and walk back out. I bet there isn't even a death-trap."

"There's an army of crazed terrorists *squatting* all around it!"

"Yes, but if they weren't an issue, we could just walk right in and take it."

"But they are an issue."

"But they're the *only* issue."

"*There doesn't need to be another issue!*"

"There is another issue," Usama said.

Nevada looked at him. "Don't do this to me, Ozzie. Don't be the pineapple on my pizza."

Usama was unmoved. "Whatever you're going to do, you'll have to do it before the sandstorm gets here."

Candice and Nevada turned. The horizon looked like God had rubbed it out with a pencil eraser, smearing the vanishing point into a haze of graphite. At this distance, it resembled a fogbank. Only it seemed so—hungry.

"Sandstorm," Nevada muttered. "How long would you say until that gets here?"

Usama scrutinized the horizon, his eyes narrowing. "An hour, give or take."

"And when it gets here, the Khamsin, what do they do?"

Usama wove his hands up and down as if weighting two objects. "If they're sane, they'll go inside and wait out the storm."

"So you're saying the boat will be unguarded?"

"Nevada, *no*," Candice said unequivocally.

"You heard him!" Nevada protested. "They're all going to be in their tents. Someone could walk right in—"

"*No*."

"I've seen sandstorms peel the flesh from a man's bones," Usama pointed out.

"Eh, I could stand to lose a little weight," Nevada said.

"What if one of them goes out to take a leak and sees you?" Candice asked.

"I take the clothes off one of them. These guys are covered from head to toe. As long as I don't get too close to anyone, I might as well be your run-of-the-mill Ms. America contestant for all they know." Nevada snapped her fingers. Grabbing the scope from Candice, she scanned the camp again. "And where will I get their clothes, you ask? They must have guards on the perimeter. I grab one of them—bingo. Three o'clock."

"What happens at three o'clock?" Usama asked.

Nevada gestured around herself clockwise with a chopping hand. "Ten, eleven… forget it. Usama, watch the camels. Be ready for a fast getaway."

She started to rise, but Candice grabbed her arm. "And what happened to not being able to watch me die?"

"Who said you're coming?" Nevada countered. "Congratulations, you're now assistant camel-watcher. If, for any reason, Usama is unable to discharge the duties of his office—"

"I'm coming with you," Candice insisted.

"Like balls you are," Nevada laughed. "It's literally snatch and grab. I don't need a sidekick on this one."

"Snatch and grab are synonyms—" Candice started, before shaking her head. "Never mind. If you think I'm passing up a chance to see the inside of a solar barge, you're insane. Besides, what if there's something to decipher in there? My ancient Egyptian is a lot better than yours."

"It's a boat," Nevada said. "I think I can figure it out."

"In how much time?" Candice persisted. "There's no telling how long you'll have in there. Two heads are better than one, after all, and it's not like you need me out here."

"Maybe I do!" Nevada said stridently—maybe too stridently. She clenched her teeth and dislodged herself from where she'd been lying, skidding down to the bottom of the dune.

Candice went after her. She noticed Usama didn't follow. "Don't say you're protecting me."

Nevada kept walking for the camels. "No, I'm not getting you killed. It's way lazier."

Candice grabbed her before she could get any further. "Just because you care about me is no reason—"

"That's not what this is," Nevada insisted.

"If you care about me you have to respect me—"

"When did we establish that?"

"And if you respect me," Candice concluded, "you have to respect my decisions!"

"What about my decisions?" Nevada demanded.

"Your decisions are stupid."

Nevada crossed her arms. "Okay, you have a point there."

Candice smiled despite herself. "Do you trust me?"

Nevada pursed her lips, blowing out a long exhale. "As much as I trust anyone," she said, then paused and added, "As much as I trust myself."

"Then *trust me*. We work better as a team." Candice reached out and patted Nevada's shoulder. "Besides, with your habit of blowing up everything in sight, this might be my only chance to get a look at that thing up close."

"Keep talking. Next time I'm bringing Usama along and you're on camel duty." She called out, "Hey, gramps, really hope you're not going commando under the robes. We're gonna need 'em."

Candice bellied down to another dune, now wearing her grandfather's jellabiya. The camp was set on wide, sandy flatland, the plain broken only by the subtle incline of the dune that finally grew to hold the boat. She grinned sardonically. Maybe it was a long-dry riverbed or drained lake, some stopping point for the ship that had been erased thoroughly enough that the only thing left was the sand flowing as the water once had.

Thirty feet overhead was a sentry post, set into the last dune before the curving landscape collapsed into the flat expanse. A Khamsin stood watch, pup tent at the ready for him to sit out the sandstorm. By now it was a wall of sand as tall as a skyscraper, swallowing up the landscape it dwarfed, steadily growing larger as it prowled closer, closer.

The machine gun in the sentry's hands wasn't nearly as imposing, but it was probably more deadly. Candice was more worried by the radio clipped to his belt.

"I suppose one call on that radio and we have the entire camp after us," she said.

"Who needs a radio?" Nevada asked. "He lets off one shot, same difference."

"So what do we do?"

Nevada folded an arm under herself, propping her chin up on her fist. "Okay. You strip naked. Dance around a little. Sing a little song. While he's looking away, I walk up behind him and take him out."

Candice glanced at the sentry again. "He's looking away right now. Why don't you just take him out now?"

Nevada shoved herself up to her feet. "You're no fun."

She walked briskly but quietly, reminding Candice of a cat fast-trotting across a busy street, until she was almost on top of the sentry, then: "Excuse me, does this feel like a punch?"

Her fist came in, lined up precisely with the space between his nostrils and the point of his chin, and unmoored his brain from his skull. He went down so hard that Candice winced, and Nevada was instantly dragging him off the top of the dune, letting gravity take over so his body rolled to the valley between the summits. She skidded down after him, and Candice joined her.

"Tie him up," Nevada said, undoing his clothes. "And hey, back at the oasis, when I, you know—" Nevada demonstratively covered the man's mouth with her hand.

"Yeah?" Candice asked, taking his belt off.

"What did you *think* was going to happen?"

"I had just woken up. I don't think before I get either half an hour or a cup of coffee."

"Really? Because you were getting all… *breathy*…"

"Shut up."

———◆———

They crouched low, watching the camp fall under the shadow of the sandstorm like it was about to be eaten by some horror movie monster. Nevada wore the Khamsin's thawb, though she'd politely declined the *serwal* he had on under it.

"What are you thinking about?" Candice asked suddenly. "And feel free not to answer that if it doesn't involve clothes."

"I don't think about sex all the time. I'm not a guy." Nevada's brow crinkled. "Although I do own a lot of men's shirts. Oh my God, is that like them wearing our underwear?"

In what felt like no time at all, the wait was over. The red-orange sandstorm towered over them as high as the clouds, striking Candice as simply *impossible*. She had no frame of reference for it. It was Biblical to her, a deluge—the feeling people must've gotten when a dam broke or a tsunami came to shore. And no matter how much she told herself it was just wind and dust, a sense of unease remained. She was going to be swallowed up.

Even more worryingly, crouching down next to Nevada made her feel better. She didn't actually believe that Nevada was guaranteed to keep her safe, but God, she wanted to.

Nevada hauled her scarf up over her face. "You ever get the feeling your life is about to suck?"

"Ten minutes into *The Last Jedi*."

Nevada nodded. "Opening credits of *Aquaman*. But I was pleasantly surprised there. I wouldn't mind watching it again if you haven't seen it."

"You've already got me down for a drink," Candice retorted. "Now you're just being greedy."

"I'm a mercenary. Greed comes with the territory."

"The least of your vices, I'm sure."

"I could show you a few more if you're not too busy later." Nevada reached out and took Candice's hand.

"By Jove," Candice said sarcastically. "I'm scandalized."

"It's because of the sandstorm. Honest."

The darkness covered them.

"Bollocks," Candice said, covering her eyes with her free hand.

The sandstorm hit like a wave bowling her over at the beach, sand instantly everywhere, in her clothes, scraping against her skin, wrenching her down to the ground and nearly pulling her out of Nevada's clutches—only Nevada tightened her grip until Candice's bones creaked.

She was being mauled by a pack of wolves, banshees screeched in her ears, concertina wire wrapped around her and cut through her clothes. Candice opened her eyes, pulled her hand away, and saw through her veil that the world had turned red—what little she could see of it with the haze falling all around her like a curtain. Her jellabiya billowed and flapped wildly as the wind pulled at, clawing at her in turn.

Nevada pulled hard on her hand until they were shoulder to shoulder and shouted something, but Candice couldn't hear her over the howl of the storm. She pointed forward with her other hand, in the direction where the camp had been before the sandstorm obliterated the world. Nevada nodded and they set off, leaning against the wind just to stay on their feet.

Nevada held firmly onto Candice's hand, pulling her along. Visibility was so low that Candice couldn't tell if they were making any headway until she saw one of the military tents swimming by, lit from the inside, human shadows thrown up on the walls, black on dark.

The further they walked, the more tents they passed, all lit up like giant lanterns. Inside, the shadows didn't look like evil men—they were talking, sitting around TVs or radios, reading, playing cards. Normal. Candice wondered what made them want to hurt people, hurt the world, be more like this raging storm than anything human. Visions of some glorious past or magnificent future, perhaps, but how could anyone turn their back on a past that was already as glorious as that solar barge, or fill the present with blood in hope the future would justify it? It made no sense to her. She didn't know if it even made sense to them, or if they'd rather live in peace—if it was only threats or lies that had brought them here and made them enemies.

The tents passed, and now there was only the sandpaper of the storm raking Candice's skin. She had no way of knowing if they were going in circles or moving at all. Nevada was the only true north she had.

When the ship's prow loomed out of the obscuring sands, it could've been a Viking longboat coming to shore out of a fogbank. They staggered up the side of the dune, clinging to each other like drunks. The storm wasn't only hurling sand through the air, it also ripped it off the ground, out from under them, making Candice feel like she was in an earthquake. She saw the ramp of packed sand leading up from the ground to the deck. Each step up it was precarious, her weight making the sand tumble away underfoot, but they made it up onto the wooden deck, the planks giving a reassuring creak at their weight. The deckhouse was only a few yards away.

Excitement overcame Candice and the last few steps passed in a rush. Clutching the AR-15 she'd taken from the sentry, Nevada shouldered the door open and swept inside, aiming at... no one. The space was empty.

Candice piled in behind her, and together they closed the door, barring out the howling wind. They were inside history, wrapped up in it like a cocoon. Candice could feel millennia in the air. Then she forced herself to look with a critical eye. She was a scientist, after all—not a tourist.

The space was about the size of a two-car garage and however the Egyptians had originally furnished it, it was picked clean now. Either the Egyptians themselves had taken everything with them or—Candice winced—the Khamsin had pitched everything out into the desert, burned it, buried it. There was a dining table in the middle of the room, but it was comparatively new—medieval instead of ancient, and not made of cedar. Surrounding it were folding chairs and stools, and on the tabletop were disassembled electric power drills, and big glass jars right out of a candy shop: they held ball bearings, coins, marbles, spent shells, razor blades, nails, screws, even LEGOs. There were piles of prepaid phones, lengths of detonating wire, bright red blasting caps, and enough bricks of plastic explosive to go with all of them.

"They're making bombs," Candice said.

Nevada nodded. "This isn't a training camp; it's a beachhead. They make IEDs here, suicide vests, then move them through the desert. No border control… You find the treasure. I'll deal with this."

Candice looked around, coughing into her hand. With all the sand she'd breathed in, it felt like her throat had been strip-mined. There was nothing in the room except piles of sand blown in from outside. Candice prodded her foot into them, working her way to the back of the room.

"What's it look like?"

"It's a skull! Haven't you ever seen a horror movie?"

"I'm just trying—" Candice stepped on a rotten plank that gave way under her, dropping her foot down into the open air of the boat's overhang. She cringed and pulled her foot back.

"You okay?" Nevada called.

"Yeah." Candice toed experimentally at the planks around the hole. They creaked threateningly. "Not up to code. Wait a minute…"

If her foot could break through a plank, there was no reason someone long-dead couldn't have removed one, hidden something away, and re-secured it. She poked and prodded at the walls, but gently, careful not to demolish the place any more than she already had.

"Do you ever wear men's underwear?" Nevada asked, apropos of less than nothing.

"What? No!"

"Me neither. I guess it's just a one-way thing. Probably because they don't make thongs for men."

"They make thongs for men," Candice said.

"They do?"

"They do."

"How would you know?"

"Because I'm European."

"Oh. Right."

A plank shifted under Candice's touch. She pried at it, finding plenty of give. Once she found the right angle, it popped out, showing her a recessed space. Inside was a codex. One of the first books, and it looked it, the papyrus yellow and weathered, the binding so faded and discolored that she feared it would fall apart in her hands if she dared to touch it.

"You aren't supposed to show up for two more centuries," she breathed. "Take that, Bembridge scholars."

"You two need a moment alone or are you going to pick it up?" Nevada demanded.

Candice resisted the urge to ask if Nevada was jealous. "It's a priceless relic."

"It's luggage!"

Cringing, Candice picked the codex up. It was reassuringly solid, miraculously well-preserved. She chanced opening it, finding hieroglyphs spread out before her like a feast.

"It's a ship's log," she reported breathlessly. "I think we just set Egyptology ahead by a century!"

"Uh-huh," Nevada said. "Skip to the last page. See if they mention the Aegis."

Candice didn't argue. Moving with painstaking care, she eased the codex to the final page and found blank papyrus staring up at her. She flipped backward, the sound of the storm outside and Nevada's frantic work falling away as she lost herself in touching something that was older than the country she'd grown up in.

Finally, she came to the last entry. The ancient words flowed into her eyes. "There was a storm…" she translated, wincing a little over how rough her summary was. "It ran the ship aground… they decided to build a burial chamber for the queen… then come back and repair the ship." Candice looked up. "They never came back."

Nevada sighed. "Of course not. Does it say where they went?"

Candice flipped back another page. "Yes. They sent out scouts to find a proper burial site and they found one… in the mountain. Mountain? Fifteen miles north of here."

"That'd have to be the Tibesti Mountains," Nevada said. "But they're not fifteen miles north of here… more like fifty."

"Take it up with them," Candice replied.

"I intend to." Nevada shoved something in her pocket and picked up the AR-15. "Pack it up. We're leaving."

Candice looked around. There was a pile of gym bags, backpacks, and vests in the corner—no doubt intended to carry the explosive payloads built in this lab. She picked up one of the backpacks, carefully nestled the codex inside, and zipped it up as tightly as she could.

Nevada pulled the scarf back over her face. "Ready?"

Candice nodded.

Nevada threw open the door. The sandstorm charged inside like a rampaging beast. Candice and Nevada had to force their way out, arms linked. In the rush of discovery, Candice had forgotten how miserable the sandstorm was. The screeching winds, the grating of the sand against every body part, no matter how tightly bundled, the precarious footing, the air snatching at them, all made even worse by how they were going downhill on the slanted boat. Tasting the sand as it inevitably got in her mouth again, Candice couldn't think of anything worse.

Then the wind died down. The clouds parted. The sun came out, illuminating Nazir with an entourage of his men, not thirty feet away.

Nevada didn't hesitate an instant. She hauled her rifle upright, the stock braced against her shoulder, finger around the trigger. But the pull only resulted in the dull clicking sound of the trigger being moved. Nothing came out of the muzzle but a trickle of sand.

The Khamsin still reacted to having a rifle aimed at them, throwing themselves to the ground. It took them a good second to realize nothing had happened, and in that second Nevada spun around and ran back for the deckhouse, pulling Candice so hard she was nearly lifted off her feet. Candice's brain finally edged from shock into reaction. She ran, the howl of the storm fading from her ears, replaced by the crack of gunshots behind her. Bullets ripped into the cedar deck all around her, kicking shredded splinters into the air for what felt like hours before they made it back inside. Nevada threw the door closed. From outside, they heard Nazir yelling angrily, and the gunshots stopped.

"They won't shoot in here," Nevada said confidently, pushing the dining table against the door with a minimum of grunting. "It's full of explosives!"

Then she realized what she'd said.

"If I could critique your plan…" Candice started.

"Go easy on me, would you? I'm about to die." Nevada pressed the mag release on the AR-15 and pulled the clip out. A dollop of sand poured out of the receiver. Nevada tossed the rifle aside with a noise of disgust. "This is why you test-fire new guns, by the way. Lucky I didn't blow my damn hand off…"

"I think they may take care of that for you."

Nevada rolled her eyes to a particularly disgruntled height. "You okay?"

"Yeah, I'm—" Candice smelled something bitter. Looking about, she noticed a wisp of smoke trailing from her shoulder. She turned her head and saw a blackened hole in her backpack—a bullet that had seared its way into the codex and been stopped by the thick papyrus. "Bloody wankers!" she hissed, moving for the door when Nevada caught her by the arm. Candice's checked momentum spun them in a circle before she was hauled to a stop.

Nevada whooped with laughter despite the circumstances. "Save it for the play-offs, champ."

Candice sputtered indignantly, just aware enough of her impotent rage to be still more angered by it. "This is exactly—*exactly* what happened to the Library of Alexandria!"

"History repeats itself," Nevada said, her voice droll, her body in furious motion. "Or maybe just the eighth grade, I don't know."

Candice forced a cleansing breath on her heaving lungs and only then was cool-headed enough to notice what Nevada was doing. She'd collected a vest from the pile, brought it to the table, and was now stuffing the pockets with plastique, wiring them with electrical cord, and threading those into one of the electric drills.

"Nevada," Candice said gently, "are you making a bomb vest?"

"Yes," Nevada said. "But don't worry, it's perfectly safe. They let amateurs use these things all the time."

A strong blow rattled the door, knocking the barricading table half an inch. Nevada pushed it back into place. Looking to arm herself, Candice snatched up a mallet from the tabletop.

"It's rubber," Nevada told her. "No sparks."

"Great, I can test their reflexes before I die." Candice tossed it away.

Khamsin clambered on top of the deckhouse—Candice could hear them walking across the planks, see their shadows through the slender gaps. Some of them dropped down on the other side. They were surrounded.

Nazir spoke from the other side of the door. "You've earned a screaming death, Easy Nevada."

"Shoot, I picked up a screaming death at the store last week. I knew I should've held off until there was a sale…"

Nazir rapped his knuckles against the door. "Shall we really play this out in full? You have nothing to defend yourself with and no way to keep us out. If you're willing to be reasonable, I can offer you a quick death."

Nevada cleared her throat. "I can offer you eighty Navy Seals, the First Armored Division, and a squad of Apache helicopters, all within five klicks and just itching to wipe this place off the map."

"I doubt that very much."

"Would you believe John Wick with a pencil?"

"No."

"How about me and the suicide vest I'm wearing?"

"You're bluffing."

Nevada flung the table aside and threw the door open, suddenly in Nazir's face with a half-dozen of his men's guns pointed in hers.

"ERHH! Sorry, Nazir, wrong answer. And you didn't even use your lifeline."

Nazir didn't back down an inch. "Do you think I am not prepared to die for what I believe in?"

"Well, your boy wasn't. I'm guessing he was supposed to make sure that train went ka-boom, but he was ready to jump ship the first chance he got. Like father, like son—am I right?"

Candice couldn't move, couldn't breathe. The guns held tightly onto Nevada. She didn't move an inch. The detonator in her hand didn't waver.

"And what do you believe in?" Nazir asked. "Whatever it is, are you prepared to die for it? Because that is your only choice. Die now and you take me with you. But do you have the will?" He smiled. "You love life, despite all it has done to you. But you don't hate like I do. Not enough to make the hard choices. That is why you're going to die here, and I am going to walk away."

"Wiz, right now the only thing keeping me from pushing the button is wondering if I'll stay alive long enough to see the look on your face as it comes off your body."

Nazir took a step backwards. He kept looking at Nevada, but when he spoke next, it was to his followers. "Allah has more work for me to do. Wait ten minutes, then shoot them both."

Nevada swung the door shut. "I'm going to count that as a moral victory."

Suddenly Candice could breathe again. And as though her mind and body had been waiting for that spine-tingling paralysis to end, an entire train of thought flooded into her mind all at once. She knew at once what to do, how to escape—she felt like she could kiss God on the lips if she wanted to.

"Nevada—"

"I know, I know," Nevada said offhandedly. "You love me, you've always loved—"

Candice grabbed Nevada's head, making an effort not to break her neck, and forced her to look at the spot on the deck where her foot had crashed through the floorboards.

"Oh," Nevada said.

She rushed over and pried experimentally at one of the jagged splits. It broke off in her hand; she dropped it down the hole.

"Take off your jellabiya," Nevada said.

"Why?" Candice asked, mainly out of disgruntlement with the fact that she was already pulling her arms out of the sleeves.

Nevada lowered her voice to a whisper. "Because as soon as they figure out what we're doing, they're going to shoot through the walls and kill us." Candice threw the robe. Nevada caught it and draped it around the hole. "Besides, it doesn't go with your shoes."

She drove her fist into the broken planks, widening the hole one floorboard at a time, the fabric dampening the noise. Candice still looked around fearfully. The lurking shadows of the guards were all around the deckhouse. She wondered what it would take for them to fire. Would trying to obey Nazir's order buy them a few precious seconds?

Candice heard shouting from outside. She looked to Nevada, who threw the fabric aside, instead using her boots to kick out one side of the hole. A rifle barked, bullets chopping into the deckhouse and whizzing overhead as Candice threw herself to the ground. More shouting, even louder, and the shooting stopped. An argument, a hurried explanation—Nevada dropped through the hole, landing in a crouch. Candice followed her, landing on her hip.

"Now what?" she asked, getting up only for Nevada to tackle her back to the ground.

They rolled down the slope, the world spinning around them. Behind them, the shouting reached a crescendo, everyone on the same page as the shooting began in earnest—rifles spewing gun smoke, bullets sending up plumes of sand in explosions all around Candice. More sizzled overhead, whistling as they overshot her body.

Finally, Candice stopped, flat on her back. There was no more slope to roll down. She felt bile rising in the back of her throat and tried to fight her way to her feet but was too dizzy to make it there.

"Stay down," Nevada's voice came from close by. "We're out of range."

Shouts came from the Khamsin coming after them. Candice held her spinning head as Nevada punched numbers into a cell phone she'd picked up on the boat.

"And now," Nevada said, "the West Des Moines Historical Reenactment Society presents 'My Grandparents Using a Microwave.'"

She pressed Send.

The boat blew apart. A red-orange flame sent pieces of wood and flesh in all directions. The airburst kicked up sand down the slope before rolling over Candice like a strong tide, pushing her so hard it was like she was falling down the slope again.

The Khamsin chasing them were knocked flat and were still half-buried when the overhanging half of the boat came crashing down. It veered down the slope on its side, for a moment sailing on a wave of sand as it crushed the Khamsin under it with the merciless disinterest of a lawnmower over grass. Then it tipped, rolling end over end, the prow snapping off in the sand.

Candice felt Nevada pull at her, muttering, "Bad day, bad day, bad day!"

She ran, her heart beating so loud in her ears that it came as a shock when she heard the banging of the ship coming down the slope, louder, louder, finally so loud that the noise was physical. Candice felt the impact of the wreckage coming to a stop in the sand. It nearly rammed itself underground, like it was trying to return to the history buried under the earth. The sand shook until there was nothing for Candice to run on. She went down in a tangle of limbs, and where she landed, she could see the prow's new home and the trail of flaming debris it had left all the way across the mountainous slope. It had come to a rest only ten feet away from them.

"I think we missed the boat," Nevada said.

———◆———

They'd kicked the anthill; it was time to pull their foot out. Running as fast as their bruised bodies could carry them, Candice and Nevada made their way to the rendezvous point. For once, luck was on their side. Usama stood with the camels, all of them saddled and ready to ride.

Nevada slowed to a walk, taking deep breaths. "I think that went well."

"You managed to sink a boat," Candice replied. "In a desert."

"We didn't get shot," Nevada reasoned. "Except for you, a little bit. I think our luck's changing."

The sand exploded with human forms in desert fatigues, surrounding them on all sides, shoving guns in their faces once more. Candice didn't offer any resistance and neither did Nevada.

They were brusquely searched, Nevada relieved of her bomb vest.

"I'm sorry," Usama said. "They came at me from every side."

Their leader, balaclava-masked with an unavoidable stare, faced them. "Nevada. Mr. Singh would like a word."

Nevada lowered her raised hands. "He couldn't phone?"

"You weren't answering."

"I've been a little busy," Nevada said. Over her shoulder, the smoke from the explosion was still hanging in the air. "But if you've got him on the phone, tell him we found the Aegis."

"Where?"

"Fifteen miles north of here. It's all in the—" Nevada noticed Candice still had her hands up. "Put your hands down already. They're not going to shoot you."

"Then why are they pointing guns at me?"

Nevada gave the team leader a look. "It is pretty rude."

The leader made a quick gesture and his men lowered their weapons. Candice immediately went to stand alongside Usama.

"He okay?" Nevada asked, still eyeballing the leader.

"Everything but his pride," Candice reported. Nevada opened up her backpack, and as she got the codex out of it, Candice muttered, "Nice crowd you run with."

"Said the academic," Nevada retorted. She opened the codex to its last written page, showing the hieroglyphics to the commandos' leader. "It's all right here. Their ship ran aground, so they decided to build the tomb fifteen miles north."

The leader took hold of the page between his thumb and forefinger, rubbing it experimentally. The papyrus cracked slightly at his rough touch. Candice winced. "Can you be more precise?" he asked.

Nevada looked to Candice, who said, "Fourteen miles, two thousand three hundred and fifteen feet."

The leader took his hand away, pressing it to an earpiece under his ski mask. "You get all that?" He waited, listening, then regarded Nevada again. "He'll meet us there."

"Singh is here?" Nevada asked.

"He loves to watch you work. Come on, we'll give you a ride."

Nevada handed the codex back to Candice. "As long as it doesn't spit."

Nevada was following the commandos when Candice cried out, "Hey!" They turned. Candice thrust the codex out, showing the inky black thumbprint left behind where the leader had touched it.

"Sorry," John Gore said. "Happens all the time."

CHAPTER 8

Two jeeps were parked nearby under camouflage netting. In short order, Candice and Nevada were being jostled about in the back of one, sputtering on the sand that the wheels kicked up as the driver redlined it. Candice clutched the codex protectively. After she'd judged that no attention was being paid to her, she lay her head down on Nevada's shoulder.

Nevada accepted the gesture with a visible start. She was about to put her arm around Candice in return when Candice said, too low for anyone but them to hear, "That's the guy from the hotel."

Nevada blinked in surprise. "The hotel where you drugged me?"

Candice fumed for a moment. "Yes," she replied, motioning at John Gore. He'd taken off his balaclava, revealing his mild, unlined face. "That hotel. He took me to the train…"

"Train that got attacked by terrorists."

"That train," Candice agreed.

"Could just be a coincidence."

"Uh-huh."

"Uh-huh."

Usama leaned in near them as well. "What are we whispering about?"

"We're not whispering," Nevada told him.

"Yes, we are."

Gore glanced at them. "Stop whispering!"

Candice buried herself in reading the codex, while Nevada tried to look innocent. Usama told him, "We are not whispering."

Fifteen miles and an hour later, the flat plane of desert they traveled was broken by jagged gray rocks tearing through the sands. In the middle of the expanse, a white canopy had been set up. It shaded a minimalist place setting—three director chairs, a folding table holding a smartphone plugged into a Beats Pill+ playing Eddy Grant, and an ice bucket sitting on the sand. Akbar Akkad Singh sat in the center seat, nattily dressed in a paisley suit and a necktie that looked like a dentist office aquarium.

"That's Singh," Nevada told Candice as they marched up to the canopy, Gore and his men keeping up the rear. "My boss. So rich he pays for music."

"He doesn't look like a billionaire," Candice said. "He looks more like he works at E! News."

A few hundred yards behind the tent, a Mil Mi-26 idled. The Russian heavy-transport helicopter, its thirty-one tons sheer Soviet brutalism, seemed to have more in common with a pachyderm than anything capable of flight. Looking at it, Nevada was keenly aware that it could hold ninety-odd troops and Singh didn't go anywhere without an entourage.

Singh spread out his arms in greeting as they came within range. "Easy! I have henchmen! Crazy, right? Come, come, have something to drink." He gestured to the ice bucket. "Corona? Corona Light? Corona Premier? Corona Familiar? Corona Refresca?"

"Water?" Candice asked hopefully.

"We don't have that," Singh said.

Nevada took a bottle from the ice bucket and opened it on her belt buckle. She collapsed into one of the director chairs. Candice took the another. Usama sat on the ground while Gore and his men stood nearby. Not even in the shade, Nevada noticed.

"If there's one thing I like about you, Singh, it's your management style." Nevada tipped her bottle to him. "You're not usually so hands-on."

"Ah, but this is an auspicious occasion. The last of the skulls! Number twelve! I was beginning to have my doubts. I got so worried when you stopped checking in, I might've tasked a satellite to look for you. Excessive, maybe. Morocco hasn't gotten HBO for two days. So here we are—how's that Corona treating you?"

Nevada pulled back from drinking. "I'm pretty sure it's beer. Anything for my friends? Maybe some cold cuts? A cheese platter?"

"Where's the skull?" Singh asked bluntly.

"I gave you the coordinates."

"Where do you think we are? I have metal detectors. We've been up and down this biyatch. There's nothing here."

Nevada got up from her chair. "You wouldn't be trying to cut me out of my fee again by grabbing this thing yourself, would you?"

"*Where is it?*" Singh shouted, his sudden rage rolling out into the distance.

Nevada sighed and took a swig. "It'll turn up," she said. "Trust me, these ancient Egyptians, they've been jerking us around for the last week. Go here, now go here, turn left at the next intersection. It's all very Google Maps. Candice?"

Candice looked up from the codex. Even with the drama unfolding before her, it was an obvious struggle to tear herself away. "Yeah?"

"Tomb," Nevada said. "Supposed to be a tomb around here. Right?"

Candice nodded. "This is the spot they scouted out. So far, all their directions have been accurate. The mountain should be here."

Singh sputtered for a moment, like he'd eaten a hot pepper. "Mountain? There's supposed to be a mountain?" He let out a shrill laugh. "Who is this madwoman? Why are you listening to her?"

"She'd a PhD," Nevada said before Candice could say anything. "If she says there's a mountain, there's a mountain."

"And I say there's nothing! I say you've broken down right before the finish line, which is worth *less than nothing*!"

Nevada sipped her beer again. "You sure your guys programmed the GPS right?"

Singh slapped the bottle out of her hand, so hard that it traveled several yards before crashing against a jagged outcropping of rock. The moment it shattered, the rock exploded with inky blackness, a cloud of it spewing from its top like a geyser from an oil derrick. The darkness brought with it a shrieking cacophony so loud that Nevada clasped her hands over her ears. She stared at the liquid void jetting up into the sky for a moment before discerning that it was a swarm of long-tailed bats fluttering up into the evening sky.

And just like that, they were gone. Nevada lowered her hands from her ears and saw the others held themselves similarly. Gore and his men were standing with guns at the ready—itchy trigger fingers. The nervous silence was broken by Singh's sudden, shrill laugh.

"That was *weird*," he said.

"Where'd they all come from?" Usama asked.

"Good question," Nevada replied. "Anyone bring a pickax on this archaeological expedition?"

A few minutes later, a pickax careened into the rock. Three of the commandos steadily dismantled the pillar of stone as Nevada watched. She stooped to pick up a shard of rock that had landed in the sand and showed it to Candice.

"What would you say this is? Siltstone? Greywacke?"

Candice took it, rubbing its texture between her fingers, then licked it. "Basalt."

"Formed from lava." Nevada turned to Singh. "There's your mountain. An extinct volcano. No wonder they built the tomb here."

"Where? I don't get it."

"Underneath us." Nevada gestured to the rock. The commandos pried the cracked debris away, revealing a shaft running downward, the size of a manhole cover. "That's a lava tube. Like a cave for lava to flow through. And when all the lava was gone…" She looked around. Some of the rocks were simple borders, but the bigger ones all seemed to form a large circle. "We must be standing right on top of the crater. And this." She patted the lava tube. "This is the rim of the crater. A little decayed, covered in sand, but yeah—volcano."

"That actually makes sense," Candice said. "The Tibesti Mountains are volcanic in origin. This could be a lost part of the same mountain range."

Usama crossed his arms. "It sounds as if your treasure does not want to be found."

"Quiet, the millennials are talking," Singh said. "So you're telling me I have to dig up a fucking desert to get my skull?"

Nevada shrugged.

"Maybe not," Candice said. "The codex mentions—well, here." She knelt down and drew the familiar truncated cone of a volcano in the sand. She pointed to the crater. "This is called the caldera, right? It's the hollow left behind after the magma chamber erupts. However, what the Egyptians describe in their writing sounds a lot like a lava dome." Inside the caldera, she drew a dome. "It's basically a big bubble made of dried lava. The Egyptians most likely built the tomb inside the dome, which would obviously protect it from the sands. So in theory, all you'd really need to do is find a way inside the dome and you could walk right into the tomb." Everyone was looking at her. "I really liked volcanoes as a kid."

"So we just need a way down, huh?" Nevada kicked a small rock into the lava tube. It bounced off the sides several times before making a last tinny impact on a distant bottom. "I don't say this lightly, but—to the batcave."

A flare dropped down the lava tube, bleeding its red light all the way to the bottom. It was followed closely by a length of climbing rope.

"Age before beauty," Nevada said, holding the rope out to Usama.

Singh coughed. "Maybe it's better that he stay here. John, don't you think it's better that he stay here?"

Gore's stillness was a gesture in itself. "It could be dangerous down there."

Nevada took a deep breath. "I want the money ready to be transferred to my account."

"It will be," Singh said offhandedly.

Candice hugged Usama goodbye. "Take care of yourself," she said.

"You take care," he told her. "You're the one going in the hole."

"I'll have Nevada with me."

"I suppose that could be taken as reassuring."

Nevada broke a glow stick and stuffed it in her belt. She started down the rope, Candice behind her. The further down they got, the more the daylight was replaced by the moony green glow from the stick. It was slow-going, repetitive work. When the entrance had dwindled too far away to be seen, Candice had an impression of motionlessness. Like they weren't getting any closer to the bottom no matter how far they descended.

"If nothing else," Nevada said when they were far enough down not to be overheard from the surface, "we discovered a mountain. That's pretty cool. Do you think we get to name it?"

"I suppose so," Candice said.

"I suggest Mount Candice."

Candice stopped climbing. "As a name for the mountain?"

"That works too," Nevada said.

Candice moaned and shuffled downward. A minute later, still not at the bottom, she said, "This Singh… you trust him?"

"I don't trust anyone."

"Okay, that's nice, but I wanted a real answer."

The glow stick gave out, plunging them into darkness. The surface world was a white dot far above them. Nevada cracked another and stuffed it into her belt. They started moving again.

"He's paid me before," Nevada said.

"He's still needed you before. This is the last one, right? You don't think they're just gonna give you the money and go?"

"What can I say? I worked retail."

"What's that mean?"

"It means, be polite, be professional, but have a plan to kill everybody you meet."

"You must not get invited to many parties," Candice said.

The passage they were in narrowed and widened, twisted and straightened, before finally leveling out into a horizontal crawlspace just tall enough to force them to their hands and knees. Candice didn't try for any further conversation. She could tell that Nevada was as worried as she was, her mind darkly whirling with the plotting it was built for, and she'd be no help simply voicing the thoughts that must already be occurring to Nevada.

Candice herself was so worried that she almost missed the sudden sense of emptiness overhead. She reached up and, feeling nothing, slowly stood. Nevada stood beside her. The green light from the glow stick pushed back the darkness but showed only a stretch of stony ground. Nevada lit a flare that seemed to fill the void with light, but it still touched nothing except the wall they had come out of. Candice looked at that. It curved inward and upward—the dome.

"You smell that?" Nevada asked.

"Smell what?"

Nevada gestured to the ground. Candice saw something kicking back the light from the flare, something liquid. "Oil."

She dropped the flare into it.

Fire raced away in all directions, prompting Candice to take a step back before she saw that the fire followed a trail: it circled around to either side, outlining the dome, and then plunged inward, the flame filling trenches dug in the earth. Then it was shooting upward, over the edges of a pyramid, not stopping until it reached the capstone. The point of the pyramid glowed, wreathed in blue fire.

Candice's feelings were indescribable. She could barely think enough to actually take in the pyramid, to believe her eyes. It wasn't the epic size of the Pyramids at Giza, that was for certain—it fit neatly within the confines of this dome, which was, what, maybe the size of a rugby stadium? Bigger? Smaller? That would make it... God, she couldn't even guess. It dwarfed her, that was what mattered. It was literally transcendent.

"That is a really nice pyramid," Nevada said.

Candice looked at her, unable to believe she could understate something so thoroughly.

"What do you think a pyramid like that would cost? Ten thousand? Fifty thousand?"

Candice shook her head. "Surely more than that."

"You think it's a hundred-thousand-dollar pyramid?"

A chuckle shook Candice's body. "Piss off," she said, and took a step forward. Her body tingled, like she'd been struck numb by seeing the edifice. Candice giggled. It felt nice. "Come on. We can study it later— never thought I'd say that. But the sooner we get this skull, the sooner my grandfather's safe."

Nevada put a hand on Candice's shoulder. "I'm not coming with you on this one."

"What are you talking about?" Candice asked, feeling like she'd been struck numb again.

"Plan B," Nevada said. "You go. Get the skull. If Singh takes it, fine. If things get messy, well... I cover your ass, you cover my ass."

Candice shook her head. "No, no... we do this together. I need you. What if there's... What if something—"

"It's a tomb, Candice. Everything in there has been dead for two thousand years. You'll be fine."

"And what if there's a death-trap?"

Nevada sighed. "There isn't always a death-trap."

"What?"

"One in three times, maybe one in four... I'm not really due for one. Anyway, they built this thing in the middle of a desert, inside a volcano. I don't think they'd bother."

"You don't *think*?" Candice insisted.

Nevada grasped both her arms. "Candice, listen to me. Think what you've been through. You've been shot at, beaten up, blown up, thrown from a moving train, taken hostage—there've been lions, scorpions, a sandstorm—you've been in a plane crash and a shipwreck and a snuff film—you've been eaten out—"

"I haven't been eaten out," Candice said.

"Not yet, but we have a few minutes."

Candice rolled her eyes.

Nevada gave her a shake. "You've got this. I trust you. Go kick ass." Then she drew up close to Candice, her lips warm as they kissed her on the forehead. "You're one hell of a woman," Nevada finished. She climbed up the first rung of the pyramid.

"Hey, Easy," Candice called.

Nevada stopped. "Yeah?"

"Do you have a plan to kill me?"

Nevada sat down on the base of the pyramid. "Yeah. 'Firm shove.'"

"Firm shove?"

"I don't like to overthink things."

"That's become painfully obvious."

Nevada started climbing again. Candice walked around the pyramid, almost lost in its symmetry, its size, the sheer reality of it. Smoke whispered off the flames, stinging the air up to the apex of the dome, where it pooled like water at the bottom of a dish. Finally, she came to an opening, a corridor with flame lining the walls, cutting into the darkness within in two streaking ropes.

Candice walked inside. Her footsteps echoed on the volcanic rock, a frozen mire of dried lava. The pyramid's walls and ceiling were made of the same black stone, almost absorbing the light, until it felt like Candice was walking on nothing, through nothing.

It was too much to have been built by the crew of a single ship, Candice told herself. That must've been who the directions were meant for. A whole fleet could've followed after the solar barge, bringing the workmen and supplies to build this tomb. That could've been where the crew went—home on another ship that hadn't been wrecked.

Hopefully.

She followed the flames to a large round chamber where the fire circled the room, revealing five doors on the opposite wall, each marked with hieroglyphs. Candice considered them for a moment before going to the first door on the left. There wasn't a doorknob, obviously, but when she pushed on the door, it gave inward.

"Simple enough," Candice muttered, and gave it a shove.

The door collapsed away from her and then instantly rebounded, carried back at her by a stream of molten lava spilling out of the passageway. Candice backpedaled furiously, tripping over her own feet, falling on her ass. She kicked and scrambled away, scratching her elbows all to hell, shocked at how viscous the red-hot liquid was, how it seemed to chase her. It lunged at her and she rolled out of the way, feeling its heat scorching her skin as the lava finally stopped pursuing her. It was headed down the incline of the room, and in the center of the floor, a tile gave way, allowing the river of lava to pour down a stone drain.

She couldn't believe it. *A bloody death-trap!*

Candice backed herself up to the corridor she'd come through, putting as much distance as possible between herself and the flood of lava. She could still feel its oppressive heat filling the room, covering her skin with a suffocating sweat. The door she'd unmoored, having been carried along the lava like a raft, lay beside the drain, steam rising off of it.

"Nevada!" she called back the way she'd come. "I could use some help over here!"

No answer. Candice examined the room again. She could guess the game. After the First Dynasty, the ancient Egyptians saw foreigners as ravenous animals, so they would trap their tomb to let in only people who knew about Egyptian culture. And they would have needed to let people in for the 'opening of the mouth' ceremony, so at least one of the doors had to be real. But which one?

She looked at the writing on the doors again. It was random gibberish—nothing like 'open me and don't die.' Candice closed her eyes and pounded her head with her fists. Think, *think*. Something was pinging at her memory, scratching at the inside of her skull, trying to get out. Five. Why five doors? Why not two, three, four? It would've been less work. So why five?

"The fivefold titular," she said aloud. The pharaohs of Egypt had five names, one for each aspect of their kingship. She scanned the doors again. There. The second from the right was a serekh—the Horus name. "The great Lady of perfection, excellent in counsel," she read. That was Cleopatra.

Skirting the very edge of the room, Candice made her way around the wall. Doing so put the fiery oil at her back. It was cool compared to the blazing lava, but still uncomfortably warm, sending fresh gales of sweat pouring down her body. The incline of the room seemed as steep as a cliff now, pulling at her feet, trying to suck her down into the lava that had pooled at the center. She skipped over the first door she reached and came to the second. Staying to the right of it, she reached over and pushed. It was no good. She couldn't get enough leverage from here to move the door.

Breathing harsh and fast, Candice stepped away from the wall and positioned herself in front of the door. She was right about this, right? She had to be right. If Nevada were here—if Nevada were here, she would just be asking Candice what door they should open, so really, what difference did it make? She was cutting out the middleman, that was all.

Whatever Nevada was doing, it had better be one hell of a Plan B.

Candice pushed against the door, trying to be ready to throw herself back at a moment's notice, but the door's weight demanded she push harder. Commit more of her weight to it. Until she was totally off her backheel, pushing with all her might until the door finally gave—

It fell with a resounding *thud* to the floor of a corridor, leading deeper into the pyramid.

"Blimey O'Riley," Candice swore, falling to her knees and gulping in air.

She didn't know how long she would've stayed there if a trickle of sweat hadn't stung her eyes. She wiped her brow and got up, figuring that whatever lay ahead of her, it had to at least be cooler.

"Oh, come off it!" Candice cried a minute later.

The corridor had brought her to another slanted room. Five doors. This would have to be the Nebty name. Only she couldn't remember Cleopatra's Nebty name.

"This is it," she moaned. "This is the moment all those teachers talk about where I can't just look something up on my phone."

She closed her eyes and tried to think. Process of elimination. The Nebty name always began with the hieroglyphs of a... bird and a snake between two baskets. She looked at the doors. Only one had those. Candice forced herself to walk up to it.

"I paid too goddamn much for a college education to be wrong about this," she said, and shoved her shoulder against the door.

It gave. Another corridor, and the heat of the lava was a distant memory on her back as she walked down it to another slanted room. This one would have to be the Golden Horus name, and *that* she knew.

"The great one, sacred image of her father," Candice said as she walked to the hieroglyphs without a serekh or cartouche. But when she reached out to push the door, she found herself paralyzed, her hands shaking so hard they threw off the sweat in her palms. Three more times. She'd have to do this three more times. How could she throw herself in the path of death even one more time and trust that she wouldn't get hit?

She would've given anything to have Nevada there with her. Or Usama. Someone. Maybe in front of someone else, she'd be embarrassed to be so frightened. She knew what to do, she could remember the rest of the names, but *God*, if she was wrong...

Suddenly dizzy, she reached out to steady herself on the wall and felt the cold rock under her hand—porous volcanic rock, vomited up from deep within the Earth. In a million years, it would be sand.

"And only a fool would try to sort sand into this row or that," Candice said.

She went to the door.

"My name is Candice Cushing," she said. "I come from Sudan, from the Hadendoa and the Dinka. From Meroe and Kush and Nubia. From the blood of Amanirenas. I'm a daughter of... heroes and villains, fools and wise men, liars and truth tellers. And I'm just me."

She pushed at the door. It fell on empty space.

So did the next two.

Candice ran her tongue through her dry mouth. She couldn't feel the bump on the roof of her mouth anymore.

The tomb was... impossible. Simply impossible. Statues standing at guard, hieroglyphics lining the walls, burial goods from bronze work to exquisitely carved chairs. All of it arranged exactly as it must've when the burial was carried out, not a single artifact out of place, not a tile of faience missing. There was dust, there was decay, but otherwise, the two thousand years that had passed might as well have been minutes.

And in the center of it all, gleaming despite the layer of fine dust that covered it, a gold-plated sarcophagus. The final resting place of Cleopatra VII Thea Philopator. Only its hands weren't crossed as was tradition, weren't holding a crook and a flail. Instead, they were cupped at her belly, holding a skull.

It was made of crystal. A single piece of quartz crystal. Cut against the grain, which should've been impossible. Candice strained her eyes, but she couldn't see any tool marks, any sanding. And the design was exactly the same as the famous Mitchell-Hedges skull, which was supposed to be Mesoamerican. But there was no historical contact between South America and Egypt.

Yet there it was. An artifact over five thousand miles from where it should've been. And she had just found it in a tomb that'd been sealed for two millennia.

"What the hell are you?" she whispered.

The skull glowed white-hot.

CHAPTER 9

Nevada sidestepped the lava flow running through the first room. Candice must've gone through the other door. Her footsteps tracked down the corridor in grains of dust. "I leave her alone for five minutes and there's a volcanic eruption," Nevada muttered. "Typical. Candice! Hey! Candice Cushing!"

She found her through the next door. Candice was walking up the corridor, clutching something wrapped in Nevada's jacket.

"You got it?" Nevada asked.

"Yeah," Candice said. "It was the, ah, skull made out of pure crystal, right?"

"That's the one." Nevada took her arm. "C'mon. You can go over this place with a fine-toothed magnifying glass later. We're getting the hell out of here."

"Crystal skulls are a pre-Columbian artifact," Candice said, sounding frazzled. "Hell, they're not even supposed to be real; they're a hoax. What's one doing in the middle of the Sahara?"

"What would one be doing in Siberia, or Alaska, or half the places I've been to?" Nevada asked wearily. "Come on!"

Candice went along with her. "You've found more of these?"

"Eleven more."

"All over the world?"

"Japan, Hawaii, Indonesia—real world tour."

"And you didn't tell me?"

Nevada stopped. "You didn't ask. Now do you have any other questions, or can we go?"

Candice took a deep breath. "Do you know Cleopatra's fivefold titulary?"

"Sure. The great Lady of perfection, excellent in counsel—"

"Piss off."

Nevada was confused. "Doesn't everyone know the fivefold titulary?"

Candice grabbed her and kissed her until Nevada felt like her lips would never be the same again. "I said piss off."

Nevada kept silent.

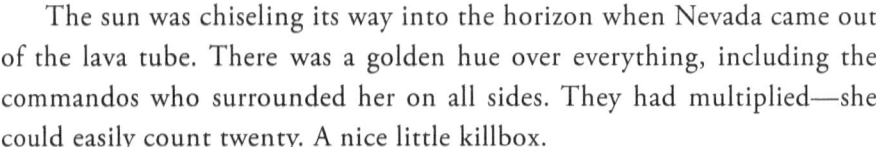

The sun was chiseling its way into the horizon when Nevada came out of the lava tube. There was a golden hue over everything, including the commandos who surrounded her on all sides. They had multiplied—she could easily count twenty. A nice little killbox.

Usama was under the canopy. The old man was actually asleep, stretched between two director chairs. It almost made Nevada laugh; she could imagine him calling it a night while Singh and all his men were pacing, smoking, taut with tension.

"The boys wanted some air," Singh said by way of explanation. "It is a long flight back to civilization. How was the tomb?"

"Dead," Nevada replied. She looked at Gore, sticking to Singh's side like a faithful hound. He had the usual soldier boy paraphernalia—thigh holster, Ka-Bar knife, grenades dangling from his chest—but he also had a pack of cigarettes rolled up in his shirt sleeve. Nevada gestured to it. "You mind?"

Gore gave her one and lit it for her. Nevada thanked him and took a drag while Singh waited patiently. She guessed he did trust her to deliver. Didn't seem to have any worry she had come up empty.

"We found the skull," she said. "It's safe. You make the payment, you get it."

Singh chuckled. "What difference does it make? Why don't you give it to me and then I pay you?"

"Singh, I respect you too much for a movie quote right now. So please— display me the cash."

Singh took a tablet from his jacket. Like anything involving vast sums of money, the whole thing had the feel of a religious ritual. He punched in the needed commands, then handed the tablet off to Nevada. She took her time verifying that the transfer had gone through; three separate call-and-response protocols from her Bitcoin account to convince her that this was really her money now, not some dummy server. The sheer tension of the situation made Nevada want to bark out a laugh; it had the feel of a Craigslist deal, only with eight-digit payouts.

Finally, she handed the tablet back to Singh. "Pull the rope up. Candice is tied to it. She has the skull on her."

Gore was already gesturing to his men, who ran to haul the rope up.

Singh hummed pleasantly. "Pleasure doing business with you."

Nevada dropped the cigarette to the ground and crushed it under her heel; as if there were anything here it was in danger of burning. "Yeah, maybe I'll use you as a reference sometime. Say, any chance we could get a ride to the airport?"

Singh barely seemed to hear her, fixating on the lava tube as more and more rope came up from it. "Sure. Take one of the jeeps. Take both of them." And then, like a man coming out of a fever, he looked at her. "I hope things work out with your boy. I really do."

Nevada said nothing.

Candice came out of the hole, helped so much by the commandos that she was almost crowd-surfing. Singh went up to her, hands held out like he was holding a bag open on Halloween. "I'll take that—"

Candice almost reflexively jerked the skull away from him, but Nevada fixed her with a look. "Give it to him, Candice. It's fine."

She held it out. Singh snatched it from her. Nevada let out a sigh at his hastiness and looked to Gore, who had stayed in place beside her. "Keys?"

He dropped them in her hand. "Good work, soldier."

"I'm not a soldier anymore. By the way, tell your boss: next time he wants to cut a side deal with the Khamsin... I don't know. Make up something very threatening for me." She cupped her hands around her mouth. "Usama! Naptime's over! We're leaving!"

He toppled out of his makeshift bed. Nevada winced. She turned to Candice to ask her if she needed to take a piss or anything before they hit the road, but Candice was in another world. Staring after the crystal skull with the same fervor Singh had holding it in his hands.

"Where'd it come from?" she asked.

Nevada raised her voice: "Candice." She started walking to her. "We are leaving!"

"Where'd what come from?" Singh replied innocently, as oblivious to Nevada as Candice seemed to be.

"Don't give me that," Candice said. "The crystal skulls were improbable enough when they were confined to South America, and now they're spread around the world? That's impossible."

Nevada grabbed Candice by the arm. "Have you never heard the expression 'take the money and run'?" she whispered through gritted teeth. "This is the run part!" She pulled Candice away, looking bemusedly at Singh. "She gets this way sometimes. Low blood sugar. I'm just gonna find her a Mars bar. She'll be good as gold."

"You're not the least bit curious?" Candice whispered to her.

"Rich guy, lots of money, top secret—I assume it's a sex thing and leave it at that."

"That's willful ignorance," Candice told her.

"No, my ignorance is more instinctual. I went to public school." Candice was still resisting being pulled away. Nevada gave her a hard tug. "I swear to God, Candice, I will *carry you* out of here!"

"You really don't want to know?" Candice insisted.

Nevada looked over at Singh. His men were gathering around him. Either preparing to get on the helicopter or…

"I really don't," Nevada replied. "He's a rich collector; now he's got a complete set. And if you could explain any of this crap, it wouldn't be worth anything."

"So that's it then? This was all just the whim of an avid nightlight collector?"

"Rich nightlight collector," Nevada said, before realizing Singh was walking closer to them.

"What'd she say?" he asked. His men were following behind him like sharks smelling fresh blood.

"Who knows?" Nevada retorted. "British slang, right? Makes me glad we declared independence."

"She said 'nightlight.'" Singh stopped walking, his gaze fixed on Candice. "Why would you call it a nightlight?"

Nevada forced a laugh. "That's actually British slang for like an ounce of marijuana—"

"He wasn't talking to you," Gore said, appearing behind Nevada. She couldn't back up if she wanted to. "Why are you talking to him?"

Before she could say anything, Singh repeated his question to Candice: "Why'd you call it a nightlight?"

"Because it glowed," Candice said.

Nevada pinched her sinuses between her fingers.

"It glowed?" Singh repeated. He took a step closer to Candice. "Do you know how many millions of dollars I've spent on these things? How many scientists I've paid to examine each square inch? Do you know how many people I would kill—" He broke out in sudden laughter, tears forming in his eyes. "Do it again. Make it glow again."

Nevada stepped between Singh and Candice, painfully aware of Gore's hand dropping to his holstered sidearm, his men pressing in on all sides. "She was seeing things. It was dark, she was scared, and it's a fucking skull. Now, we're going—"

"Go," Singh said to her, wiping his eyes. "Candice stays."

"Singh," Nevada said slowly, "you're not being real cool right now..."

Candice started to back up, but looked behind her to see Gore glowering at her, his hand squeezing black oil onto the gun it was wrapped around. She pressed close to Nevada. "I want to stay with Easy," she said.

Singh snapped his fingers. "Wait, wait, that actually works for me. Gore, you thinkin' what I'm thinking?"

Blinding pain exploded out from the back of Nevada's skull. She went down on her knees, heard Candice scream her name. The world bobbed and weaved as it tried to get away from her. She fell onto her outstretched hands and felt Candice kneeling beside her, holding her close, saying her name all soft.

"Ha, I love that!" Singh enthused. "Right in the back of the head, wow. *Thunk!* This is how you get the Christmas bonus. You and you, goatee guys, you're on old man duty. Bring him."

Nevada heard two sets of boots hoofing away from her. The world swam in and out of focus. She held the back of her head; she'd have a lump there in no time. Singh was right—it was a choice pistol-whipping. She couldn't have done it better herself.

Singh knelt down in front of her. "I actually really like you, Easy. But unfortunately, so does Candice here. So, if she doesn't want you to be in just *crazy* amounts of pain, she'll do as she's told."

Gore cleared his throat. "Sir, if we have the old man, we really don't need two hostages."

Singh pointed at him. "That is a good point. I take it you're voting for old school? You think Easy'll be more trouble than she's worth?"

"When has she not been?" Gore reasoned.

Singh backed away. "Don't get it on my suit. The humidity is bad enough for it…"

Gore clicked his tongue and a commando collected Candice, pulling her away kicking and screaming. By now, Nevada was well enough to sit up, parking herself on her ass and rubbing her aching head.

"You and I, we may be assholes, but hell if we won't cop to it," Gore said. His gun cleared its holster. "Business."

"Business," Nevada repeated. "Do I get to see it coming?"

"Least I can do."

Nevada fixed him with a look. "Don't miss."

He took aim. Nevada closed her eyes. Russell. In another life, she would've named her son Russell.

Sounds of a scuffle. Nevada twisted her neck to see Usama breaking free of the two men who had collared him. His hands were tied, but he drove an elbow into one's nose, kicked the other in the balls. As the man twisted away protectively, Usama threw his bound hands over the man's head, down to his chest, grabbing the grenades hanging there.

His eyes locked with Nevada's. "Get her out of here."

"Shoot them both, shoot them both—!" Gore was shouting, but Usama had already pulled the pins. The grenades went off, erasing all three men from existence. The pressure wave broke over the rest of them, knocking everyone to the sand.

Adrenaline wouldn't let Nevada stay down. She was suddenly on her feet, taking Candice by the hand, *running*. But Candice was pulling against her. Nevada turned her head and saw Candice stooping to grab the skull away from Singh's limp hands. Nevada was trying to think of which obscenity to refer to her with when Candice threw it into the lava tube—a series of weighty thuds as it bounced its way down the shaft.

"Fetch!" Candice cried, and then they both were running.

They didn't get far. Gunshots crackled overhead in less than half a minute. Nevada threw herself behind one of the rock formations, dragging Candice along with her. Unarmed, it wouldn't take the commandos long to close in on them. The only thing slowing them down was Singh frantically demanding someone go down and get the skull while Gore was ordering them all after the women.

Nevada reached into her boot and came up with another cell phone from the boat. "Just once, I would like Plan A to work out."

She'd programmed the number into the phone's memory back in the dome. All it took was holding down the right number on the keypad.

The explosive she'd planted above the pyramid went off, breaking apart the lava dome, letting down hundreds of tons of sand. It had to come from somewhere, and a sinkhole opened underneath the canopy, swallowing it up along with, judging by the screams, several people. All the smoke from the burning oil was released into the atmosphere, a scale model mushroom cloud rising out of the earth.

That would have to do for a distraction. Taking Candice's hand again, Nevada ran. She felt like she could run forever. Adrenaline gave her wings and between pissed off, terrified, and whatever the hell she felt when Candice squeezed her hand like the sky was falling, she had plenty of adrenaline.

But not enough.

It might've been minutes later, or hours, but the two jeeps swung in from the sides and crossed in front of them, coming to a stop. Guns pointed at them. Gore swept out of his seat with another man following behind.

There was no point in more running. No point in trying to fight. All Nevada could do was get Candice killed alongside her. Her body was rebelling against her, heart pumping hard, muscles clenching, nerves vibrating, but there was nowhere for all that energy to go. She sat down in the sand and gave her lungs the air they were begging for.

Candice still held onto her hand. "It's fine," she said, gasping for breath herself. "It'll be fine. They can't kill me, and they can't kill you, or I won't do what they want. I'll do whatever they want, I just... I won't let them..."

Nevada ran her thumb over Candice's knuckles. "Do whatever you have to do. Stay alive. Don't worry about me."

"I'm not," Candice giggled, sounding like she was suffering from oxygen deprivation. "I'm worried about me. If you don't make it—who's gonna come rescue me?"

Nevada ventured a smile. "If I do save you, does that mean I get a hood pass?"

Candice's hand was gone then. Gore wrenched her away from Nevada and shoved her into his subordinate's arms. The man started dragging her back to the jeeps while Gore stood over Nevada.

"How's this hostage thing work, anyway?" Nevada asked him. "Like, what do I put down on my taxes? Employee, contractor—unpaid internship?"

Gore's pistol appeared in his hand like a magician summoning up a playing card. "This isn't an Indiana Jones movie. You're not a hero. It's noir, and you're the dumb schmuck who gets bumped off because you got tied up with the wrong girl."

"You need me," Nevada said. "She won't do shit for you unless I'm alive and well."

"Maybe," Gore said. "Maybe she'll change her tune after I break a few of her fingers. Either way, not your problem anymore."

He raised the gun.

"Wait!" Nevada cried, throwing her hand up.

Gore lowered the muzzle a degree. "Famous last words?"

"Rhetorical question," she replied. "Why would I hide a block of plastic explosive and a prepaid cell phone somewhere you'd really rather not know about for all this time just to air out a cave full of smoke?"

Gore crouched down in front of her. "Do tell."

Nevada shrugged. "I just figured that if, say, there were a bunch of pissed off terrorists somewhere in the vicinity, it seems like the kind of thing that would get their attention."

Gore wagged the gun barrel at her. "Nice try."

"I thought so."

His finger tightened on the trigger. And as the trigger moved back, a launched RPG round rang through the air, slamming an explosion into one of the jeeps that flung it into the air and brought it back down as flaming wreckage. The airburst knocked Gore's hand to the side as he fired. The bullet splashed into the desert next to Nevada's head; she felt sand slashing against her cheek.

She lunged for Gore, pushing the gun up and out of the way as she tackled him to the ground, her body on top of his. He rolled over on top of her, bullets pumping impotently from the pistol, massively overshadowed by the gunfire erupting from the dunes and being returned from the surviving jeep. Nevada wrenched her elbow to the side, clocking Gore's temple—he brought a headbutt down on her that stunned her before he rolled away. He came up in a crouch, holding the pistol on her. Nevada came up holding the clip.

He pulled the trigger anyway and the pistol clicked on an empty chamber. She pitched the clip at his face. He staggered back with the hit and she rushed him, but his arm lashed out, catching her upside the head with the unloaded gun. Nevada was flung to the ground, her brain only keeping a toehold on her skull.

She forced herself up only to see the other jeep speeding toward her, Candice in it, the grille growing in her vision like a nuclear explosion. Nevada threw herself back down and it went right over her, clearing her back by millimeters as it pulled to a stop. Bullets spat into the sand and sparked off the chassis, voices shouting hurriedly.

"Get in!"

"Go, go, go!"

The jeep rocked on its suspension as Gore threw himself inside—the engine roared and the tires tore at the earth until they were clawing forward, pulling the jeep off of Nevada. She picked herself up to see a trio of Khamsin horsemen riding for her, AKs in hand, blazing away.

Not my best plan, Nevada thought as she turned and ran, legs pumping, arms knifing at her sides, putting all her energy into catching up with the jeep. It had taken some punishment—the windshield cracked, the driver bleeding profusely, a dead body in the backseat. Only one other commando was still alive, and he was restraining Candice as she fought like hell to get free.

Gore ripped that man's sidearm from its holster.

Nevada poured on the speed, putting everything into the next few steps. All she had to do was make the jeep, take out Gore, take out the other commando, take out the driver, and then they were home free. Bullets whistled overhead, followed by the ululations from the horsemen behind her. Their hooves sounded like thunder. Being trampled seemed like an ugly way to die.

Gore took aim. *You can make it*, Nevada told herself, pain ratcheting through her body as old injuries flared back to life.

Gore had the pistol aimed right at her when a salvo from the horsemen shot past, deflecting off the jeep's armor in a shower of sparks. A ricochet caught him in the arm—the pistol was jogged from his hand. It bounced off the sand and Nevada dove for it. Landed on her belly, fit it into her hand, and twisted her body around as she skidded in the sand. The pistol roared in her hand three times before the horsemen rode by her, hooves just missing her prone body. Then, the horses still galloping, their riders slumped and fell from the saddle.

"Thanks for the help, guys," Nevada wheezed as she picked herself up. The jeep was already receding into the distance.

She picked her way across the desert, following in its tire tracks. Her ribs were on fire. The bullet wound in her left shoulder that she'd thought had been healing so well was torn open now, weeping blood down her arm. She kept moving.

It was time enough to think. Death. Killing. She'd gotten so used to killing other people that at some point, she'd become comfortable with killing parts of herself as well. She supposed everyone did that, just by never letting them be born. She'd been Thea the soldier, Thea the college student, not Thea the investment banker or Thea the doctor. She'd even killed Thea the archaeologist, but then, she'd never really *been* her. Even back then, she'd been Easy Nevada.

Thea the mother. That she'd been. Then she had killed her, and Russell Quatermain along with her. She'd let him die so Harry Calhoun could live. And now he was who she had set out to save. Because Russell Quatermain hadn't stayed in his grave. He'd come back, all responsibilities and obligations, and Nevada couldn't kill him a second time. Not again. She wondered if that meant Easy Nevada was dying—the mercenary, the hedonist, the grave robber—going the way of the dodo so she could reanimate into Thea the mother. Like a horror movie, she wouldn't come back right; she'd have blood on her hands and a thousand bad memories in her head, so she wasn't really *Thea* either.

If she wasn't Easy Nevada and she wasn't Thea Quatermain, who the fuck was she?

As she'd expected, the helicopter took off long before she even got close. Easy money Candice was on it. The skull too. And Nevada was in the middle of the Sahara, surrounded by desert for hundreds of miles on all sides. No transportation. No one who knew she was out here. Khamsin looking for her and Singh leaving her for dead.

Nevada checked the gun. A Smith & Wesson 4506. Three rounds left in the magazine.

The sun set. No reason not to move.

"Round two, motherfuckers."

EPILOGUE

DAVID PIKE WAS IN PERFECT darkness.

He could've had his eyes closed, only there were no flashes of color, no fireworks, no sparks, no reddening blushes when he squeezed his eyelids against each other. He didn't know if he had eyes at all. There seemed no difference between trying to move his eyelids and not.

It hurt, but distantly, like it was happening to someone else. To women. To children.

"You're awake," a woman's voice said. It had the slow coolness of the islands, some of the musical harmony of the African veldt, but he couldn't place the accent.

"Yes," Pike said. His mouth felt numb. It didn't seem to fit the words he was saying. He didn't think he could hear them… was he deaf? If he was deaf, how could he hear her?

Was he dead?

That was too frightening to ask.

"Do I have eyes?"

"We managed to save one," the woman said. "But it was damaged. It needs to rest. Like you."

"Who else?" Pike's mouth felt like it was cracking with each word. His teeth stung like he'd bitten down too hard on something that wouldn't break. "Who else did you save?"

"No one else. Just you. You're a miracle."

The darkness seemed more solid than anything Pike had ever touched, but he still couldn't feel it. It was tantalizingly out of reach. "There are no miracles. No God. There's just... nothingness."

"No. Not yet. But there could be. Drink," she said, and gave him water. "Eat," she said, and gave him food. It was something soft, too soft to be chewed, but there was no telling what it was when he couldn't taste it. Maybe he was eating the darkness.

"Who are you?"

"I am the Lady Tendai. Your friend Easy Nevada has made it her life's work to find twelve crystal skulls. And you are going to help me find the thirteenth."

———————◆———————

The next book in this series will be published in 2020.

ABOUT GEORGETTE KAPLAN

It was never easy for Georgette Kaplan. She was born a poor child in Mississippi, where she still remembers sitting on the porch with her family, singing and dancing around her. After learning she was adopted, at the age of 21 she hitchhiked to St. Louis, where she worked at a gas station and in a traveling carnival. After a shooting incident at the gas station, she decided to quit and pursue her lifelong dream of a career in writing. She now lives back in Mississippi with her life partner Marie.

CONNECT WITH GEORGETTE
Tumblr: georgettekaplan.tumblr.com
E-Mail: kaplangeorgette@gmail.com

OTHER BOOKS FROM YLVA PUBLISHING

www.ylva-publishing.com

EASY NEVADA AND THE PYRAMID'S CURSE

(The Cushing-Nevada Chronicles – Book 1)

Georgette Kaplan

ISBN: 978-3-96324-070-6

Length: 203 pages (72,000 words)

Easy Nevada is a mercenary with a taste for treasure, drawn to the secrets of a dangerous pyramid. She hardly expects to meet Sudanese British archaeologist Candice Cushing exploring her heritage, or a zealot bent on its destruction. In this high-stakes adventure, the women start to wonder if they're so different after all…and if that cursed pyramid has been buried for a reason.

PRIMAL TOUCH

Amber Jacobs

ISBN: 978-3-95533-858-9

Length: 255 pages (99,000 words)

Rumors of a rare, white tiger have lured wildlife photographer Ashley Richards deep into the Indian jungle. There, she crosses paths with a ruthless poacher and Leandra, a mysterious, feral woman, who seems at one with the fierce felines she protects. In this charged, exotic, lesbian romance, Ashley faces danger, a deadly vendetta, and the clash of two worlds, which changes everything she knows.

Candice Cushing and the Lost Tomb of Cleopatra
© 2019 by Georgette Kaplan

ISBN: 978-3-96324-304-2

Also available as e-book.

Published by Ylva Publishing, legal entity of Ylva Verlag, e.Kfr.

Ylva Verlag, e.Kfr.
Owner: Astrid Ohletz
Am Kirschgarten 2
65830 Kriftel
Germany

www.ylva-publishing.com

First edition: 2019

Credits
Edited by Alissa McGown
Cover Design and Print Layout by Streetlight Graphics

www.ingramcontent.com/pod-product-compliance
Lightning Source LLC
Chambersburg PA
CBHW020838260626
47169CB00003B/1052